THE BLACK HAWK

DARRELL BROCK

The Black Hawk

Written by Darrell Brock

Published 2019 by Darrell Brock

Copyright ©2019 Darrell Brock

Library of Congress Cataloging-in-Publication

data is available

Printed 2019 in the United States of America

Cover graphics by www.customebookcovers.com

Formatting by The Fiction Works

ACKNOWLEDGMENTS

I want to thank all those people who helped me in this book writing effort. I want to especially thank those who helped edit and correct the many mistakes I made and those who encouraged me to pursue this book: my cousins Marilyn Kilgo Freeman and Phyllis Wren Vines for their help in editing and Reba Ponder Weiss for her inspiration and encouragement to keep writing. None of this would have been possible without your help. So from the bottom of my heart, thank you.

DEDICATION

*This book is dedicated to my
grandfather, Charlie Mitchell Kilgo
One of the best men God ever
created. His stories of his father,
George Washington Kilgo
(the Black Hawk) are the basis
and inspiration for this book.*

(Photo on the following page):
*George Washington Kilgo
aka The Black Hawk, circa 1870*

CHAPTER ONE

George sat up in the saddle and stretched his back. After two hours in the saddle, his back was stiff; and he still had another hour to go to reach home. He had made the almost three hour trip into Double Springs because they needed supplies, and he needed to get his wife Emme a birthday present.

He smiled as he thought of the look that would come across Emme's face when she un-wrapped the blue dress he had bought. It was pale blue with a white lace collar and sleeves. It had cost a pretty penny; but it would be worth it, if it somehow brought her out of the funk she had been in the last few months.

They had five children, four boys and one girl. Will, the oldest, was twelve, Mary Elizabeth had just turned eleven and already she was filling out her dresses in the top and hips. Samuel or 'Sam' was almost ten, John Wesley was seven, and the youngest, Tom, was four.

When Tom was born, Emme had a difficult birth; and ever since had been cursed with 'female trouble.' At first, it hadn't been too bad with just some irregular periods and

1

such. Things had become worse lately and even though she had thrown a fit and insisted it was a waste of money, George had forced her to go see Doc Paddock over in Double Springs.

The doctor gave her some medicine that seemed to help a little. He had pulled George aside while Emme was dressing, and told him that having another child would probably kill her; they should be very careful. Tom hadn't shared that news with Emme at first, but she was very smart, and figured it out for herself when George stopped sharing her bed. When Emme could convince George that it was safe to make love, it always caused Emme to have as the Bible says "a discharge of blood" for several days. Sometimes it was so bad that it made her weak, and she would have to take to her bed for a few days. George worried that one day simply making love would kill her.

Now, she was depressed and had spells of crying and being ill with everyone. George loved her with all his heart and was determined to keep her safe, even if it meant she was ill tempered; and he was left without a sex partner.

All these things were going through his mind as he rode along the road toward home. As he topped a little rise in the road, he came upon a wagon and buckboard off on the side of the road. The wagon had lost a rear wheel. George could see where the axle had gouged out the ground when the wheel ran off.

Beside the wagon were two male black men and two black women dressed in the white garb sometimes worn by slaves. Another older black man sat on the wagon seat. A hard-faced white man stood nearby holding the reins of a gray horse. A white man stood next to the buckboard where a very pretty, red haired woman sat on the seat.

"Hey friends," George called out when he was close

enough to be heard. "Looks like you had a little trouble." He said smiling broadly.

The man on the buckboard turned around and watched George closely. "Yeah." He said. "We seem to have lost a wheel nut somewhere. We walked and searched all the way back to that last curve, but couldn't find it anywhere. I guess we'll have to go all the way back into town to get another one."

"Maybe not," George said, pulling his horse to a stop and climbing down. George approached the man and extended his hand. "Name's George Kilgo," he said shaking the man's hand.

"Jim Pruitt," the man said with a firm handshake. "This is my wife, my man Connors, and that is Moses on the wagon," he said ignoring the four slaves standing nearby. "We were on our way home with this load of cotton seed and these new slaves before this wheel decided to hold things up."

George nodded. "Let me take a look. I'd hate to see you folks have to go all the way back into town." George walked around the wagon looking at each wheel. "You got a wheel wrench?" he asked standing by the other rear wheel of the wagon.

"Hell, yeah," the man Connors spoke for the first time. He reached into the back of the wagon, pulled out the metal wrench, and tossed it to George. George bent down by the left wheel, and using the wrench extracted a wheel nut holding it up for them to see. "Wagon builders most times put two nuts on one wheel so folks will have an extra one if they need it," George said matter-of-factly.

"Get your black asses over here and pick up this wagon!" Connors shouted at the two male slaves. He produced a bull whip that had been hanging over his side arm and cracked it making a fearful sound. Threatened by the whip, one slave cowered in fear holding his hand up to ward off the blows he was sure was coming. The other one glared defiantly at the man with the whip. Neither one moved to do as the other man ordered, so he drew back the whip intent on lashing the slaves to make them comply.

"Whoa, easy there with the whip, Captain!" George said loudly. "No one is going to pick up that wagon with all those bags of cotton seed on it."

Connor glared at him, embarrassed by not seeing the obvious; but stopped in mid stroke of the whip.

"You say these are new slaves." George asked.

"Yes," Jim Pruitt answered. "I just bought them day before yesterday in Mobile, and brought them here by train".

"And where were they before that?" George asked.

"Africa!" Connor answered back. "Where the hell do you think they were?"

George was really beginning to dislike the man. For the first time George really looked at him. He had long bushy sideburns that came all the way down his jowls, but stopped short of being a beard. He had squinted eyes so one could hardly see them. He had a long scar that started just above his right eye, across the eye and disappeared into the bushy sideburns. Not only was he cruel to the slaves, but he was using curse words in front of Mrs. Pruitt, another thing George didn't like.

"They could have come from another plantation, I just wonder if they have any idea what you are saying to them. If they are fresh from Africa, they probably don't understand you or the language. They may not have even seen a wagon before," George explained.

"Oh my gosh! You may be right! That would explain the blank looks and disobedience!" the wife said, speaking for the first time.

George held one arm out toward Connors, and

approached the slaves. He took the cowering one by the arm and helped him to his feet. George looked him in the eyes and slowly led him toward the wagon. George noticed for the first time that the slaves had leg irons on their ankles. They were barefooted, and George could see the raw skin where the irons had cut into their skin.

George reached over into the wagon, and grabbed one end of a sack of cotton seeds. Picking it up, he motioned for the slave to do the same. The man understood and grabbed the other end of the sack; they picked the sack up and over the back of the wagon, tossing it to the ground. George motioned for the other slave to come, and the defiant looking one shuffled over to the wagon. Together they started unloading the sacks from the wagon.

George climbed onto the wagon and started moving the sacks toward the back within easy reach of the slaves. The sacks were heavy, about a hundred pounds each; but George was a strong, healthy man of thirty-four with muscles built by a lifetime of hard work.

Soon the wagon was empty. Connors started to push the slaves toward the corner of the wagon sitting on the ground, and made motions of picking up. Both were slow in moving to do what he wanted. "Move your asses!" Connors shouted.

"Hold on a minute," George said quietly. George jumped down and walked to the front of the wagon, took the reins of the team of horses. Clucking to them, led the horses about twenty-five feet, dragging the axle along the ground to the edge of the woods and a large oak tree.

George gave a low whistle, and his horse threw up her head, and walked over to where George stood near the disabled wagon. He took a rope from his saddle and threw it over a low limb on the oak tree. He looped and tied the end under the wagon axle. The other end, he wrapped around his saddle horn. "Back, Dolly, back," he said to his horse. Dolly walked backward and stiffened her legs as she pulled against the weight of the wagon. The back corner of the wagon lifted until it was off the ground enough to make repairs. "Whoa!" George said.

George pointed to the wagon wheel that lay nearby and made lifting motions toward the two slaves. Understanding the slaves picked up the wheel and shuffled slowly to where George stood at the back of the wagon. George pulled the wheel nut from his pocket, placed the wheel into place, and using the wheel wrench tightened the nut.

"Come, Dolly," George said. Dolly walked forward a couple of steps and the wagon settled down on the replaced wheel. George reached under the wagon and removed the rope from the axle. Then taking the reins of the team, he turned the wagon around and led them back to the stack of cotton seed sacks lying on the ground.

The others had watched in amazement as George made the task of replacing the wagon wheel so easy. Connors was embarrassed that this man was taking the lead in what he saw as his job. Trying to regain control of the situation he started shouting at the slaves.

"Get over here and reload this wagon!" He shouted at the slaves. He made motions, and they slowly make their way over to begin loading the wagon. As they were loading the bags and straining with their leg irons to pick up the bags over the back of the wagon; one of the bags snagged on the corner of the wagon, ripping a bag of seed open and spilling some of the seeds on the ground.

Connors was already mad that this stranger was making him look bad; he just snapped and started cursing the slaves calling them 'black bastards.' Out came the whip; and Connors made two lashes across the back of the slaves, ripping one's shirt and back, and slashing a gash along the defiant one's face. As he raised the whip for a third lash, it suddenly was jerked from his hand. Connors whirled around to see George holding the end of the whip.

"I don't like to see people whipped," George calmly said.

"Mind your own damn business!" Connors shouted as he reached for the colt revolver hanging around his waist. George had anticipated that the man would not be happy about having the whip yanked out of his hand, and had put his hand on his own colt even before he grabbed the end of the whip. George pulled and pointed the pistol at Connors while cocking the hammer.

"I'd think real hard about the next move you make. I don't want to shoot you; but if you pull that pistol, *I will shoot you!*" George said sharply.

"And if he doesn't shoot you, I will," Pruitt said having pulled his own revolver out and pointed it at Connors. He cocked the hammer back making that distinctive clicking noise.

Connors at first looked shocked, and then mad. "You sidin' with this joker and the blacks, against me? After six years of me working for you! Connors shouted.

Pruitt sighed, "I have just been waiting for an excuse to fire you. I was blind to a lot of things over these six years, but my eyes are open now. Now, slowly unbuckle that gun belt, and let it slide to the ground. Do it now!" Pruitt said glaring at his overseer who did as he was told. "I will make you a deal. You can get on your horse, ride ahead, clear out your things from the plantation, and ride away. If I ever see you or your brother again, I will swear out a warrant for your arrest."

"What for? I ain't done nothing to get arrested for!" the overseer said.

"I'll start with the illegal rebates you been getting from

your buyer friend for every bale of cotton we sold him the last six years. Then, I'll add the hogs that you claimed to have killed and butchered; but really sold and pocketed the money. I'll add the cattle you said were stolen; but I suspect you, your brother, and friends actually took. Not to mention the slaves that you have cost me! It is because of your abuse that I had to go and buy these slaves to replace the ones your abuse and neglect have killed! Should I go on, or is that enough to get you to clear out?" Pruitt said gritting his teeth, sneering at the other man and re-aiming his Colt at the other man's face. "Or I could just shoot you here and now, and save the law the trouble of a hanging."

Connors' face lost all color as he finally realized how close he was to dying. He slowly sidled over to his horse, mounted and jerking the reins galloped off down the road toward the plantation.

Both George and Pruitt held their pistols on him until he was out of range. Pruitt looked at George and smiled. "Mr. Kilgo, it seems I owe you a debt of gratitude; first for fixing the wheel, and now for giving me a reason to fire that vile man. I have been trying to figure out a way to get rid of him without a killing ever since a little bird told me how he was stealing from me," Pruitt said while walking over and shaking George's hand again.

"Well, I am always glad to be of service to my fellowman," George said. "I'd watch out for that one though, Mr. Connors don't seem like the kind to just ride away without having his say."

"I agree, and I plan to keep a good eye out for him. I don't think he will dare to come around now that I have other witnesses to his firing and his crimes," Pruitt said.

"Now tell me, Mr. Kilgo, where do you live and what do you do for a living?"

Before George could answer him, Pruitt's wife stood up and said "Help me down, please." She leaned over, and since George was closest to her, he took her slim waist in his hands, helping her to the ground. Then, he addressed her husband and his question.

"I'm just a poor dirt farmer. I got; as they say, forty acres and a mule farm about an hour southwest of here, near Looney's Tavern on the Old Post Road," George said as Mrs. Pruitt came and stood close to the men. George could smell her sweetness from a few feet away, and his hands still tingled from the feel of her tiny waist in his hands.

Pruitt seemed not to notice either George or his wife's red faces as they both blushed from their brief contact. "What do you raise on your farm?" Pruitt asked.

"Cotton and corn, same as everybody, I guess," George said matter-of-factly.

Pruitt nodded. "Do you make a good living? I mean, do you have some slaves, or do you do all that work by yourself?"

"Naw, no slaves. I couldn't afford slaves. Just my wife and five kids. My neighbors help out when it is plantin' and pickin' time, just like I help them."

"I just assumed that you must have slaves because of the way you handled those two," Pruitt said indicating the slaves who were now squatting down watching the two men talk.

Mrs. Pruitt was now reminded of the slaves and looking over, her eyes fell on the blood oozing out of the torn shirt of one and the deep red bloody whelp on the face of the other. "Oh my gosh!" she said. She rushed over to the buckboard and grabbed a canteen of water. She pulled up the tail of her dress and tore off a strip of slip, wet it with the water and going over to the slaves started to wipe their wounds as her husband and George watched in amazement.

The two women slaves had not said a word or done

anything except watch all the happenings in amazement. Now, they locked eyes with this other lady. Mrs. Pruitt passed the wet cloth to one of the women who took over the job of tending to the men's cuts and bruises. Mrs. Pruitt walked back to the buckboard and picking up the canteen, walked over and offered it to the women and men to drink.

Pruitt gave a fake cough giving his wife a look that said, "What are you doing with our water?" Mrs. Pruitt shrugged her shoulders. After the men and women had all drank deeply from the canteen, she turned toward her husband and George; and in what could only be described as an act of defiance, she turned up the canteen and took a drink. Even the slaves were surprised that a white woman would drink after them from the same canteen.

Pruitt shook his head and turned his attention back to George. "How many bales of cotton do you harvest each year?" He asked.

"About twenty bales," George said. "I got some pretty good land near a creek bottom so I get about a half bale per acre."

Pruitt nodded. "What do you get a pound, twelve or thirteen cents?"

"Yeah, more or less," George nodded back.

"So, I'm guessing you make five or six hundred dollars a year off the cotton and maybe another hundred off the corn," Pruitt stated.

George nodded, wondering where this was going. "Why do you ask?" George questioned.

"I'm just trying to figure out how much I need to offer you," Pruitt said. "You see, I seem to have an opening for an overseer, and I thought you might make a good one."

"I don't have any experience doing that," George said shaking his head.

"That doesn't matter, Pruitt said. "I see the way you handle yourself, and how you handle the slaves." He went on, "You know how to grow upland cotton and corn, the rest is just common sense. I think you are just the man I need."

"There's just couple of problems with all that. First, I don't like slavery; and I got a wife who is not well, five kids, and forty acres that ain't gonna farm itself. I can't very well be in two places at once so I guess I'll have to pass on that job, although I thank you for the offer." George said.

"Oh, I'm so sorry your wife is sick," Mrs. Pruitt said interjecting herself into the conversation. "Is it serious?"

George blushed red and said, "It's just...ah...female trouble, every since the birth of our last one. She has good days and bad. She is a terrific mother to our kids; and works in the fields like a man, still I don't think I could leave her there by herself," George said looking down at the ground, embarrassed at having to share that information.

"I appreciate all that and your concern for your family; but I'll pay you what you make off your cotton, six hundred a year, and you can borrow enough slaves to make your crop. It is only two and a half to three hours between your place and mine. You can go home as often as you wish. That means you'll be making twice the money you are now and still be with your family, probably more, because when you are home; you won't have to be working in the fields all the time," Pruitt said making his case. Pruitt took a deep breath before going on. "As for not liking slavery...are you an abolitionist?"

"Naw," George said. "I just never really liked the idea of one man owning another. I don't know if the South could live without slaves now with cotton being so in demand."

"Well, it is in the Bible...I mean slavery," Pruitt said using a common argument for slavery.

"Yeah, and so is having a hundred wives, but nobody

except Mormons believe in that anymore. Heck, I have a hard enough time dealing with one wife," George said smiling. George pulled off his felt hat and scratched his head. He knew what Pruitt was saying was probably true, and the money was really tempting. He just didn't know if he wanted to commit to something like the big job of an overseer. "I don't even know what kind of operation you got," George said.

Pruitt smiled, he could see George was thinking about his offer. "I got five hundred acres with three hundred in cultivation. I got ...ah... how many slaves we got, Moses?" Pruitt said, addressing the old black man who had been watching all this from his seat on the wagon.

"You'se got one hundred and fifty-seven slaves, counting these four here, lessen someone died while we was in town, Master Pruitt," Moses said is a thick heavy southern dialect.

"We grew one hundred fifty-five bales of cotton last year, but I believe we can do better than that with the right man in charge," Pruitt said.

"Well, tomorrow is my wife's birthday; that is why I went into town, to get some supplies, but mainly to get her a birthday present," George said. "I can't spoil her day by telling her I am going to take a job that will take me off for days at a time."

"Of course not!" Mrs. Pruitt said. "You go home and celebrate with your family, and you men can sort this out another day." She gave both men a big smile that seemed to say, "Everything was settled."

"Now tell me, what did you buy your wife?" Mrs. Pruitt said looking at her husband. "I'm only interested because I know some men buy really interesting things for their wives." Mrs. Pruitt gave her husband a wink and a grin, which caused Pruitt to blush red. Pruitt knew his wife was talking about the black corset he had bought her the last time he made a trip to New Orleans.

"I bought her a blue dress," George said. "Would you like to see it...maybe tell me if you think it is okay?"

"I'd love to see it," Mrs. Pruitt said giving both men a big smile.

George went to his horse and pulled down the white cloth sack that was tied behind the saddle. He reached in and pulled out the brown wrapped dress, and handed it to Mrs. Pruitt. She gently unwrapped the dress and held it up so she could see it clearly.

"Oh, my! How beautiful!" she said. "I'm sure she will be really happy with this."

George smiled, happy that it had passed her test. She carefully folded up the dress, re-wrapping it in the brown paper; and handed it back to George with a big smile.

"Look, how about this?" Pruitt said, anxious to pull George back to the job offer. "You go home and have a good weekend with the family; and next week, come over to the plantation and look things over. If you like what you see, we can talk some more about the job. What do you say?"

George nodded his head. He didn't really see how he could turn down the kind of money and deal Pruitt was offering; but, he just didn't know how his Emme would take to the idea.

Mrs. Pruitt had drifted back over to where the two slave women were standing near the slave men. She started making some motions trying to converse with the women who were gesturing back.

"Mr. Pruitt, I believe these ladies need to relieve themselves, and to tell the truth I need to also. We are just going to walk down into the woods a little ways and find some bushes," Mrs. Pruitt said.

George was surprised to hear her address her husband as Mr. Pruitt. It just seemed too formal to him. He could never imagine his Emme calling him Mr. Kilgo.

Pruitt grinned and looking at George, winked and said, "Well, dear, I don't know about that, maybe Mr. Kilgo and I should come with you in case those slaves make a break for it."

Mrs. Pruitt shot her husband a look and a frown, and answered, "Don't be ridiculous. They are tied at the waist, and in a strange land where they don't speak the language; they are scared to death. I don't think they are going anywhere; and if they do, I'm sure Mr. Kilgo could run them down in a minute." She turned and led the two female slaves down the hill toward a clump of thick bushes. George noticed for the first time that the women were tied together at the waist with a rope that was knotted at their backs.

"I need to go myself," Pruitt said, stepping over behind the wagon, putting it between him and the direction the women went. He undid his pants and took a long and loud pee. Fastening up his pants, he reached over into the wagon, pulled out a bottle of whiskey, and offered it to George.

George was not a big drinker; but he didn't want to refuse the man who might be his new boss, so he took a small drink and passed the bottle back to Pruitt. The man took three long swallows and made a hissing noise. "That is good Kentucky bourbon whiskey," he exclaimed. "Cost an arm and a leg, but it is worth it."

The two male slaves stood up, and one of them made a noise to get their attention. He made a gesture that could only mean that they needed to relieve themselves also. Pruitt laughed and waved them over to that side of the wagon while he and George walked back toward the back of the wagon. The slaves must have been about to burst. They started to urinate in heavy streams just as the women emerged from the woods.

"Maybe you ladies better wait there a minute," Pruitt said, grinning at this wife. "Unless you want to steal a peek," he said, elbowing George and laughing at his own joke. Mrs. Pruitt turned red faced and she turned her head. The two slave women remained facing the wagon and watched the pool of urine forming on the other side. Mrs. Pruitt saw one cut her eyes over at the other slave with a slight smile forming on her lips until she saw Mrs. Pruitt watching her; then, she quickly dropped her eyes to the ground.

Finally, the slaves were loaded onto the wagon; was made with some difficulty because of the leg irons and the rope holding the women together. George had to help them up and over the wagon wheel they used as steps. Mr. and Mrs. Pruitt climbed back onto the buckboard.

"If you don't mind, I'll ride in the wagon with Moses until we get to the fork where I turn off. We can talk, and he can tell me about the plantation so I'll have an idea of what I am getting myself into...if I decide to take the job," George said.

"Sure thing," Pruitt answered back. George tied his horse to the back of the wagon, and they started down the road. When they had travelled a short distance, George addressed the older black man.

"Moses, if you don't mind, I would like to ask you some questions; and I'd appreciate if you shoot straight with me. I ain't never been an overseer, and I don't know if I'm cut out for being one. If you could help me make up my mind, I'd sure appreciate it," George said.

Moses looked him in the eyes. He was surprised that this white man would address him with so much respect, and that he acted like he valued his opinion. *"I's shoot straight with you, Mr. Kilgo. Jest keep you voice down so Mr. Pruitt don't* hear. They might be some stuff he don't like to hear," Moses said.

George nodded, "First tell me what kind of man Mr. Pruitt is; how does he treat his people?" Moses took a deep breath before he answered, and then cast a look at the buckboard to make sure that Mr. Pruitt and his wife couldn't hear what he was about to say. The buckboard was leading the way up ahead, and there was little chance that they could hear what was being said in the wagon.

"Master Pruitt is alright most of the time. He ain't around much anyways; he always off somewhere doing some big time politicking. His dad owns about a thousand acres down on the river near Montgomery, and he thinks he gonna be governor of the whole state some day. Little Jim, he don't know much about what going on around here. His wife know more 'bout what happening than he does," Moses said.

George nodded, "You said he is alright most of the time. When is he not alright?"

Moses looked worried, wondering if he should share everything with Mr. Kilgo. He decided that if Mr. Kilgo was going to be the new overseer, he might as well know it all. He took a deep breath before going on.

"Lately, Master Pruitt...he like the bottle a little too much. He changes when he drinking. Used to be, he would drink a little now and then, but lately...well, he likes it too much. That demon whiskey been the ruin of many a man," Moses said.

George nodded again. "What about Mrs. Pruitt?" George asked.

Moses' face lit up with a big smile. *"Missy is just about the sweetest, nicest, kindest people you will ever meet! I don't say that just because me and my Tee raised her, I say that because it true. Even from the time she was a baby, she love everyone and every living thing. She would cry if'n she found a dead* butterfly. She got the biggest and softest heart God ever put in a person. When she and Mr. Pruitt married, she wouldn't say yes until he promised that me and my wife, Tee, could come to live with them. Then, she talks her daddy into letting us go. But shoot, she could always talk her daddy into anything. Sometimes, I worry 'bout her and Master Pruitt. When he gets to drinking, he got a mean streak; like the devil coming out in him."

George took all this information in with a nod of his head. "Tell me about the plantation and anything else I need to know about how it is run," he urged.

"Things been bad the last years, since Mr. Connors come. That man is the very devil hisself or at least the devil's right hand man! He beat people just for the fun of it...because he like to! You heard Master Pruitt...Mr. Connors and his brother steal and lie about everything. He try to starve everyone to death. He kill and butcher one hog, but claim he killed two, then he sell one for hisself. Slaves ain't had no meat to eat in two, three months."

"He steal a cow and claim someone came over and drove it off. We used to have chickens all over the plantation. You could eat plenty of eggs, and if'n a slave wanted to kill and eat a chicken, it was okay long as you let another two chickens hatch. That was the rule. If a slave ate a chicken, he had to make sure two eggs got hatched. That way, we always had plenty of chickens and eggs on the plantation. But, Mr. Connors, he don't care about nothing, but keeping hisself in whiskey. Whiskey and fornication, that was all he cared about. He let his three slave bosses take the chickens and sell them, and they could eat as many as they want. Sometimes they eat one every day. Slaves starving for a little meat, and them boys roasting and eating chicken know'n everyone can smell that chicken cooking. One time, I see'd one of the slave bosses with six chickens tied by their legs and thrown across a horse as he ride off. He come back in a few hours, drunk as a dog, with no chickens, so I know he sold or traded the chickens for whiskey. Them bosses, they just as bad as Mr. Connors, beating and whippin' their own people just like Mr. Connors did. Especially, the one called Terrell. I knows he killed One Shoe Joe. They say a mule kicked him in the head, but I see'd him; and if'n a mule kicked him, it kicked him a bunch of time. Looked to me like someone beat him to death." Moses stopped to breath before going on.

"Use to be when Mr. Campbell was the overseer, slaves had plenty of meat to eat. Mr. Campbell let some boys go hunting in the woods. They bring in lots of good meat: deer, turkey, squirrels, opossums, wild hogs! Lordy, that was some good eating! Mr. Connors don't let no slaves get their hands on a gun...too many slaves like to put a bullet in Mr. Connors!"

"Mr. Kilgo, do you believe in prayer? 'Cause I been praying that the Lord would deliver us from that devil Mr. Connors, and I do believe you are the answer to my prayers. I can see you is a good man, and I think the Lord done sent you to help ease our pain," Moses said looking George right in the eyes. George shook his head.

"Moses, I been accused of being a lot of things, but the answer to someone's prayer ain't one of them." After a time, they reached the fork in the road and the buckboard came to a halt.

"Mr. Kilgo, have a good weekend with the family, and I hope to see you one day next week," Mr. Pruitt said as George got down from the wagon to mount his horse.

George came over to the buckboard and extended his hand to Mr. Pruitt. "I can't promise anything. I mean, I would be crazy to turn down the deal you are offering; but I have to consider, sleep on it and talk with my wife and kids before I commit to anything. It was nice to meet you both."

"And it was nice to meet you also, Mr. Kilgo," Mrs. Pruitt said.

George nodded. "Please call me, George."

"And, you please call me, Mary," Mrs. Pruitt said smiling.

"Oh"...George said, "I love the name Mary!"

Mrs. Pruitt gave him a funny look, and George started to chuckle. "My wife's name is Mary, and my daughter is Mary Elizabeth."

"Oh really, how strange is that! I'm Mary Louise and your wife?" Mrs. Pruitt asked.

"Mary Emiline Entrekin Kilgo. Everyone calls her Emme, and my daughter goes by Liz," George explained.

"I have heard of the Entrekins," Pruitt said. "Are they from the Montgomery area?"

"Not that I know of," George said.

"Mary Louise, Mr. Pruitt, Moses, maybe I'll see you again soon," George said tipping his felt hat, and then riding off down the fork in the road.

CHAPTER TWO

George couldn't help but smile when he topped the little rise in the road and looked down on his farm. The little frame house with smoke curling from the chimney surrounded by the fields just starting to turn green; even in the fading afternoon light, the site was so comforting to him. George bet the smoke was from Mary Emiline cooking supper. He could almost smell the food from a half mile away.

George was just thinking about trying to surprise the family when Rascal, the family dog, came running out from under the front porch and started barking wildly. George smiled. "Good boy, Rascal," George said to the big mixed breed dog. It was good to know that Rascal was doing his job by alerting them when someone was on the place.

Before George could reach the house, the kids came pouring out the door, jumping and yelling, "Daddy's home, Daddy's home!" Mary Emiline appeared in the doorway wiping her hands on her apron. She gave George a big smile; then, started trying to get the kids to let him get down off the horse before they swarmed him under.

"Did you get us something? Did you get us some candy?

Did you get Mommy a birthday present?" A storm of questions came pouring out of the kids so fast that George couldn't keep up with who was asking what.

"Now I can't tell you if I bought your Mother a present, that would spoil the surprise and I might have got something for you kids; but you will have to wait until after supper to find out," George said laughing as he picked up the two smallest ones. He gave Dolly's reins to Will. "Be sure to brush her down good and give her a little extra feed. She has had a hard ride," George said to his oldest.

Will nodded and said, "Yes sir." George couldn't help but be proud of the respectful young man Will was becoming. George set one child down, and used his free arm to grab Emme around the waist, and gave her a big hug and kiss. Emme pushed him away, but not before returning the kiss for a second.

"Behave yourself! Go get washed up for supper," she said smiling. "You smell like a horse."

George laughed, and went to the wash stand near the back door where a pitcher of water and a wash basin sat. He stripped off his shirt and washed down his face and upper body. Mary Elizabeth and his wife put the finishing touches to a supper of smoked ham, potatoes, pinto beans and corn bread. John Wesley and little Tom came over to where George was washing, and just watched for a moment, and then asked if he bought them some candy?

"I clean forgot to get any candy this trip." George said trying to keep a straight face. Little Tom's face fell and he looked like he might cry. John couldn't hide his disappointment either. George couldn't stand their faces and said, "Of course, I got some candy! I was just teasing you!" Both boys jumped up and down with glee.

While they ate, George shared all the news he had heard

from the people in town. Mostly, it was about who was sick and who was getting married and who had died since the last time anyone had been to town. George didn't mention the meeting with the Pruitts.

After supper, the two Mary's cleared the table and George pulled out the white sack he had hauled from town. He gave each kid a piece of stick candy. He gave Will a pocket knife that he had traded two dozen eggs for. Mary Elizabeth got a new blue hair ribbon and a new baby doll, Sam got a new harmonica he wanted that George had sent all the way to Decatur for. John Wesley and Tom both got little carved wooden horses.

George sat back in front of the fire and watched as the boys played with their new toys and Emme combed and brushed Liz's hair and put it up with the new blue ribbon. He marveled at how good his life was and wondered if taking the overseer job was the right thing to do.

The next morning was Saturday; George awoke early and slipped out of bed. Since George wouldn't sleep in her bed, Emme slept with John Wesley in the only bedroom they had, Mary Elizabeth sleep with Little Tom in a bed in the living room/kitchen, and Will and Sam shared a bed in the loft over the bedroom. George slept in another rope bed in the corner of the kitchen near the back door.

George wanted to cook breakfast for Emme since it was her birthday. He went to the back of the barn where a lean-to served as a chicken house. He searched until he found a dozen eggs. George went to the smoke house and cut off several slices of ham. He went back into the house and started to build up the fire in the fireplace for cooking. Mary Elizabeth woke up and started to help him. She had learned to make biscuits, and soon the smell of the frying ham and eggs and the baking biscuits filled the house.

When it was all done, they went to wake Emme and the boys. Emme smiled while pretending to be asleep. She had heard George get up and knew what he was up to. The whole family came in and told her happy birthday. The little ones jumped onto the bed with her.

After eating the breakfast that George and Mary Elizabeth had prepared, George asked Emme what she wanted to do on her birthday.

"I don't need to do anything special. We can just stay here and do nothing," she said.

"Oh no!" George said. "We are going to do something special. Let's pack a picnic lunch, and we'll go down to Raven's Bluff and swim; if the water is not too cold." All the children cheered and started to get ready for the day.

Of course, the water was freezing as it was April, but the kids all waded and splashed in the creek water. They caught crawdads and skipped rocks and had races with boats made of twigs and leaves. They all swam in their underwear including George. Emme stayed on the bank and watched until George picked her up and threatened to throw her in clothes and all. She finally stripped to her pantaloons and camisole, and splashed in the shallows with the children.

It was a sunny day and after they ate lunch, they lay on the rocks and dried out; the young children drifting off to sleep. George lay back with his head resting on Emme's lap and watched the older children playing in the creek. He wondered how to breech the story of his job offer with his wife.

Looking up at her in her damp camisole and pantaloons, he was struck by her beauty. "God she is so pretty! How did I get so lucky to find and win such a beauty!" George thought. He felt his lust for her begin to rise. "Stop it, he admonished himself, "you know what the doctor said about her having another baby." Still, he wondered if this weekend might be a safe time to make love. He longed to hold her in his arms, but didn't dare risk getting her pregnant again.

Emme idly played her fingers through George's dark hair, and wondered what was on his mind this weekend. She could tell something was troubling him by the pensive way he looked at her and the kids. She thought she would find out tonight when the kids were asleep, and she would force him to make love to her. She knew tonight would be safe for her, and that was the only time she could get George to make love, even though they both would like to do so more often.

Emme thought she was the lucky one in having landed such a man as George. All the other girls had wanted him. He was so tall and handsome, but the thing that all the girls loved about him was how humble and sweet he was. He had no idea the way he made young girls' hearts flutter when he spoke or looked in their direction. Emme had played her hand just right, at first flirting a little with him and then pretending she didn't even know who he was when he came around. She smiled to herself when she thought about those times now.

Back at the house, Emme sent Liz down to the fruit cellar to get some apples to bake a pie to go along with the birthday cake she had started that morning. While they were cooking and baking, George took Will out with the shotgun to see if they could get a rabbit for supper. Will was learning to load and shoot the double barrel; and in spite of the kick of the big gun, he loved the thrill of the hunt. George was proud of the boy, and the way he was careful with the gun and the loading.

When the women were finishing the cake and pie, Will came bursting into the door holding two brown cottontails by the hind legs. "Mom, I got two!" Will said, not able to hold back his enthusiasm. "The first one was just sitting there, and BAM! I let him have it and then the other one jumped up from the grass and took off running; and I led him just like Pa taught me, and BAM! He went flying end over end!"

Emme smiled proudly at her son. "Great! I'm sure it was a good shot. Now, get those bloody things out of my house and clean them outside. I'll need one cut up for a stew and the other one whole so we can roast it."

George came in and smiled at Emme and the little ones who were all looking in wonder at the dead rabbits. "Okay, let's go outside and I'll show you how to skin and gut a rabbit, time to break in that new pocket knife. Come on, Sam and Wes, you can learn, too," George said. He looked at little Tom who started out the door also. "Tom, why don't you stay in here and lick the spoons clean for mom and your sister?" George said. He was not sure Tom was ready to see the skinning and cleaning process just yet. George didn't want to spoil his appetite for meat.

The meal was fit for a king, and they all ate until they couldn't eat anymore. There were potatoes and corn to go with the two rabbits. The rabbit stew and dumplings would stay in the cook pot in the fireplace and they would eat it for a day or two. What they didn't consume of the roasted rabbit would be added to the stew. Nothing would go to waste.

They sang happy birthday to Emme, and finally George brought out the package he had brought from the store in Double Springs. When Emme pulled the dress from the package and held it up, she burst out crying. George and the kids were ataken back and didn't know what to do. Finally, she stopped sobbing long enough to grab George in a big hug.

"Oh my goodness, it is so beautiful! I just love it! How did you know?" she asked George.

"I saw you eyeing it the last time we were at the store back in the winter," George said.

"I know you thought we were not watching, but we were.

Liz reminded me the other day that you said the dress cost way too much, but you really liked it," George said proudly.

"Well, it is just beautiful, and will make Nelly Wilson green with envy! I can't wait to wear it to church!" Emme said holding it up to her body and twirling around.

They all laughed at her actions. Later, when the light had faded and everyone made ready for bed, Emme went to John Wesley and suggested that he and little Tom spend the night with the older boys tonight.

Will and Liz both made a big deal out of John Wesley and Tom being big enough to sleep with the big boys. They were not unaware of the reason for their mother wanting John Wesley and little Tom to share the boy's loft.

George gave Emme a look that said, "Are you sure this is okay?"

Emme just gave George a smile as she suggested that George move his cotton mattress up to the floor of the loft so that the two older boys could sleep on the floor and the two little ones in the bed.

When the children were all in bed, George and Emme moved into the bedroom to prepare for bed. George watched in awe as Emme turned her back and undressed while slipping into her white nightgown. They slipped into bed and lay quietly for several minutes.

Emme wanted to ask what was on George's mind, but she didn't want to spoil the mood so she remained quiet.

"Are you sure about this?" George asked, leaning up on one elbow so he could look at Emme.

"Yes," Emme said. "This is a good time. Besides, I am starting to think you might have a honey in town, or be using one of the ladies at Looney's, so I need to take care of you," Emme said laughing.

George laughed and smiled, "I don't think any of those

ladies, either in town or those that hang out at Looney's, can hold a candle to you once you get started. I just hope the kids are all asleep."

Emme rolled over on top of George and started kissing him. Sometime later when they had both caught their breath she said, "Whew! That was worth the wait! Now, are you going to tell me what is on your mind or do I have to start guessing?"

George gave her a funny look. "What makes you think something is on my mind?"

"George you always get that far off look in your eyes when something is bothering you so let's hear it," Emme said raising up on one elbow and playing with the hair on George's chest.

George took a deep breath before starting. "Okay, I don't know how you do it, but you obviously can read my mind. Are you sure you are not a witch or maybe a medicine woman?"

"I met someone on the road today, and he offered me a job." George began and then told Emme everything that had happened.

Emme studied him for a few seconds before speaking. "I think you have to take the job," she said. "You...we can't turn down that much money, and the offer of slaves to help make our crop. Besides, we need to add another bedroom to the house." Emme paused to see if George got what she was meaning. When he looked puzzled, she knew she would have to spell it out for him.

"Liz can't sleep with her brothers forever. In case you haven't noticed, she is beginning to fill out in the breast and hips. She is becoming a young woman, and it ain't healthy to be in the same bed with boys even if they are her brothers," Emme said.

George nodded his head. He had noticed again today while they were swimming in the creek that Liz had definitely developed some in the chest. He not only noticed, but he also saw Will looking at her as well.

"I know you are right. I just hate to leave you and the kids here on your own. I don't know anything about overseeing slaves. Besides, I don't even like the idea that one man can own another. I don't know if I could work for Mr. Pruitt. What if I get there and things are bad, and I don't like it?" George asked.

"Well..." Emme started, "If conditions are as bad as Moses said, then I think you have a Christian duty to try and improve things for those poor slaves. Besides, you won't be over there all the time. Didn't Mr. Pruitt say you could come home as often as you like? Maybe you could come home every few days and check on things here. The kids and I will make it fine. Will is very responsible, and I am sure we can handle things here. Remember, Mr. Pruitt said you could have as many slaves as you need to plant and harvest our crop. It just sounds too good to pass up to me," Emme said with a finality that made George see that he didn't have much choice.

"That's what bothers me," George said. "If something seems too good to be true, it probably is."

"Why don't you go over there for a few days and see how things are. If you don't think you would fit, you can just say thank you, but no thanks."

"Damn it, Emme, you could convince a preacher to date the devil!" George said rolling over on top of her again. "That is why you love me so much!" Emme giggled.

Sometime in the early morning hours, a thunderstorm blew through and they were awakened by loud crashes of thunder and bright flashes of lightening. The little house creaked and moaned as the wind whipped against it. After a particularly loud boom of thunder, they were joined by the two smaller boys, John Wesley and little Tom who came running into the bedroom and jumped into bed with them where they all snuggled together until morning. The house grew cold since the storm had brought a cold front along with a lot of rain, and the fire had died to ashes.

At dawn, George got up and worked on a few things around the farm that needed fixing such as repairs to the roof where some wooden shingles had been blown off during the storm. George didn't know when; but sometime during the early morning hours, Emme had gotten up and put pans under two leaks that were dripping water through the roof from the missing shingles. While he and Will were repairing the horse pen at the barn, they had to return to the house to get their coats, as a chilly wind was blowing. George guessed the temperature had dropped into the forties. When he and Will came in to eat lunch, he noticed that Emme was packing two white flour sacks with food and provisions so George guessed he was going to the Pruitt's to check things out.

George finally kissed all the kids and Emme goodbye, loaded Dolly with the things Emme had packed, and he set out toward the Pruitt Plantation. George had a lot to think about as he and Dolly made their way along the road. The air was cold and the skies were overcast. A steady wind made it seem colder than it really was.

CHAPTER THREE

When he reached the fork in the road where he had left the Pruitt's yesterday, George turned north. If he followed Mr. Pruitt's directions he would go down the Trenton Road, through Day's Gap, and off the mountain. George had never been this way before. He had heard of Day's Gap and English Mountain, but he had never been to either of them.

As George traveled along, he passed along side the Sipsey River since the road followed the river on and off for several miles. It was one of the main rivers in this area. Most of the small creeks and streams feed into it. The road was muddy and the branches and streams along the way were all running very high and full due to the large amount of rain from the thunderstorm the night before.

As he went along, he glanced over into the muddy, swollen river from time to time. He could see a lot of logs and driftwood being swept along the way by the raging current. During one glance, he spotted something strange in the current. At first, he didn't know what it was; but just as he concluded it was the end of a log sticking just above the waterline, an arm and hand reached up and made a swimming stroke into the muddy water.

George pulled Dolly to a stop and watched. He could now make out the head and shoulders of a person being swept along in the raging waters. George spurred Dolly into a gallop and raced down the road trying to keep up with the person and the river. The river twisted and turned closer to the road, and then away from it.

George tried to think what to do. He finally thought if he could get ahead of the drifting person, he could maybe throw his rope to them. The river swung away and George was able to gain some ground and get ahead of the drifter. As they raced along, George got his rope ready and when he spotted a place where the river came back to the road, he jumped off Dolly and ran to the edge of the river.

The Sipsey was not very wide normally, with some places only twenty-five to thirty feet wide. Now, however, it was at least fifty feet wide and George was not sure if he had enough rope with his twenty-five foot lasso to reach the person. George leaned over and as the water swept the person by, he threw the lasso. Just before he threw, he saw the person look at him and their eyes made contact for a few seconds.

The person reached for the rope, but it fell short. George jumped back on Dolly without even retrieving his rope. As he raced along, George pulled the rope in and rewound it. His eyes scanned the road and river ahead as he tried to find a place to make another attempt. He urged Dolly to run faster and somehow she seemed to understand. George could feel her lengthening her stride and stretching her body out. After what seemed like several minutes, George finally gained enough of a lead to try another attempt at a rescue.

Spotting a likely place ahead, he again pulled Dolly to a stop and jumping off before she stopped completely. Racing down to the river bank he got as close to the edge as he could. He hoped the river wouldn't push the person out of his reach.

God or fate was on their side as the river pushed the drifter closer to the edge of the river. Closer this time, George got the rope right to the person who made a grab at it and briefly held it in his hand. However, as soon as the tension pulled on the rope, the person couldn't hold it and it flew out of his hand.

George repeated his actions of remounting and racing to get ahead of the drifter again. As they raced along, George realized that this might be his last chance to make a rescue as the river veered away from the road up ahead. Dolly couldn't out run the river for much longer, and the person in the water had to be cold and weak.

George knew what he had to do; and as he gathered his rope in, he made preparations. George tied one end of the rope to the saddle horn. As he galloped along, he tied the other end around his waist. That completed, he looked for a spot where he could get Dolly right to the river's edge.

When he finally spotted a place where the bank seemed to be close enough, he whipped off his coat, kicked off his boots and dropped his gun belt; planning to leap off the river bank. Now, he waited for the person to drift by. He knew this was a dangerous move, and he hoped and prayed that his rope and Dolly could hold him and the person if he could grab them; that the rope and his knots held, and that the drifter would get close enough for him to reach.

Then there they were, further away than he had hoped; but there was no time to change plans now. George leaped into the river just ahead of the person who saw George and reached out for him. Their hands touched briefly, but neither could gain a hold with their water slick hands. George grabbed at the cuff of their shirt and got a little grip. With his other hand, George reached to grab the back of the person, but couldn't quite reach them. Under the water George's hand felt something, a shirt maybe, and he grabbed hold of it and pulled. As the rope came to its end and the tension started to tighten, it pulled George backwards first and he was able to reach out with his legs and lock them around the body of the person.

The rope snapped tight and put such pressure on George's chest that it took his breath away. That and the icy water made it very hard to take a breath. The water swept over his head as the drag of the water and both of their weights pulled hard against the rope.

George heard Dolly whinny as she was suddenly pulled backwards by their weight and the force of the river. For a moment, George feared they would all be swept away. Dolly finally found her footing, and without any directions started to pull against the weight. Slowly, she made headway and began to drag George and his companion out of the river. After what seemed like forever, with the water flowing over their heads, they emerged from the waters. George could feel rocks under his body and he let off the hold of his legs while pushing and dragging the other person onto the bank of the river.

Looking down, George could now see that the person was a young girl in a denim dress. George gained his footing and pulled her up until they were both out of the river. Dolly kept pulling until George said, "Whoa, Dolly!"

Leaning over, George put his ear right next to the girl's nose listening for any sign of breathing. He heard none. Shifting around, he straddled her and pushed down on her chest just above her waist with his hands. After several pushes, the girl's mouth opened and a gush of water came out. George kept pushing and more water came out. George leaned over and listened, but heard no sounds of breathing. George didn't know what else to try so he kept pushing on her chest. Finally, more water came out and she seemed to choke on the water coming up, so George rolled her over on her side and then onto her front. He then pushed on her back. After several more pushes, she spit up more water and finally let out a choked sound and took a strangled breath. George breathed a sigh of relief.

Now, he took the rope off his waist and rolled her back over onto her back and leaned down to check her breathing again, and was relieved that she was now taking shallow breaths. George looked at her face and could see her skin was ghostly white, except for the area around her mouth which was blue. He touched her face and her arm. Her skin was ice cold. George realized that he had another problem now. There was no telling how long she had been in the icy water, and she had to be close to freezing to death. As this realization hit him, George realized that he was also very cold. His hands were shaking, his fingers were feeling some numbness and his teeth were chattering. The cold air temperature, the icy cold water and the stiff wind was making the wind chill deadly. George had to get a fire going and get the wet clothes off both of them or they might freeze. He had to do it **NOW** before he lost the use of his quickly numbing fingers.

George went to Dolly and got his bed roll from behind the saddle. Unrolling it, he got the red wool blanket he used for cover. He took off the saddlebags and then the saddle. Looking around he saw what he wanted, three large rocks, one about the size of a wagon bed and two others next to it about the size of a wagon wheel. He took the sheep skin that he used under his saddle for a saddle blanket and placed it on top of the ground. George picked up the girl's freezing body and moved her next to it.

George hesitated for a second before proceeding with the next step. Holding the girl up in a seating position, he unbuttoned the buttons at the back of the dress and peeled the wet dress down. Grabbing her under the arms, he pulled her out of the cold wet dress. Next, he unbuttoned and peeled off her camisole and pantaloons leaving her naked. Then he laid her on the sheepskin and covered her with the wool blanket, placing his long oil cloth coat on top of that.

As quickly as he could, he looked around for some wood for a fire. Luckily, nearby was a large popular tree with roots that had been undermined by the river, allowing it to blow over from a strong wind. It had been down for a while and was partially rotten. George was able to break off several limbs and make a pile about four or five feet from the girl and the rocks.

Next came the important part of building the fire... starting a fire with wet wood during a strong wind. George went to his saddle bags and withdrew a small leather pouch. Inside he found five sticks of fat-wood (rich pine wood) that George and Will had split from an old pine tree stump. Rich in pine tar and rosin this wood was easy to light and would burn hotly until other wood could dry out and be added. George also took out a small bird nest that he had found in the woods. It was made of small twigs, animal fur and straw the mother bird had woven together with great care. He placed this on the ground with three of the sticks of fat-wood and poured a small amount of gun powder onto the bird nest, then shielded it from the wind by laying his body down next to it. Taking his tin of matches, he opened it and carefully struck one and ignited the gun powder with a flash. The fat-wood ignited, and George added small sticks slowly, carefully, not to cut off air to the small, growing fire. In a few minutes he added more of the limbs that he had broken from the downed tree. Trying not to rush and add the wet wood too quickly in spite of his freezing fingers and shaking body, George soon had a good fire going.

Barefooted and freezing, he went over to the downed tree and broke off three limbs about four feet long. He leaned these against the rocks on the windward side. Taking the girl's dress and under clothes he hung them over these limbs forming a little wind break. To these, he also added his wet pants, shirt, undershirt, and long john underwear. He piled several large limbs on top of the fire which was now showing healthy signs of life. Finally, naked and shaking from the cold he knelt down by the girl and crawled under the wool blanket and his coat, pulling them over his body and finally his head. He was so cold his teeth were chattering, and he was shaking violently.

He lay with his back to the naked girl, curled up in a ball trying not to touch her in case she awoke, afraid she might think she was about to be raped. By now the fire was throwing out some welcomed heat that was reflected off the rocks, and was heating the blanket and the bodies underneath.

It was a good twenty minutes before George stopped shaking enough to relax a little. Finally, exhausted from his efforts and warmed by the fire, he dozed off for a few minutes. When he awoke, he pulled his head out and looked at the fire which had burned down to a bed of hot coals in the middle with the unburned ends sticking out of the fire circle. More than anything he just wanted to stay in that warm cocoon, but he knew the fire was the only thing keeping them warm. He pulled himself out of the cover and began breaking and gathering more wood for the fire. It took him ten or fifteen minutes to gather enough to revive the fire. He felt of the clothing laying across the limbs and found it still quite damp.

Naked, he was freezing again by the time he had gathered

enough wood. He was shaking heavily as he crawled back beside the girl. With his back to her, he could feel the heat of her body even though they were not touching. Suddenly without warning, the girl turned slightly toward him and threw her leg and arm over his body and pulled George close. George could feel her warm body pressed to his. With that sensation, he drifted off to sleep again.

This time, George slept at least an hour. When he awoke again, the sky had lightened and rays of sunshine were filtering down through the trees. The air was definitely warmer and with less wind. Looking out, George could see the fire was again just a bed of coals. He could feel the girl next to him. She had rolled back onto her back and was breathing in deep regular breaths. George lay there a few minutes dreading to getting out in the cold again. Finally, he crawled out and stood up. His back was stiff from lying curled up in a ball. He felt his clothes and decided they were dry enough. He put them on and then went to the white flour sacks Emme had packed. He found a small tin, pulled it out and took out five coffee beans and a small cloth. Using the butt of his bowie knife, he crushed the beans inside the cloth.

From the sack, he pulled a tin cup, filled it with water and set it in the edge of the coals. In a few minutes, the water began to boil. George added the crushed beans to the water, and went back to the sack to find another cloth with several pieces of smoked ham wrapped inside. George took two pieces, placed them on the wide blade of the knife and propped it over the coals.

The smell of the coffee and cooking meat soon filled the air. Turning toward the girl, he spoke to her for the first time.

"Do you feel like sitting up? I have some coffee and food for you if you are able to eat and drink." When he got no response, George tried again. "I know you're awake. I saw you peeking out a few minutes ago. Are you okay?"

There was a rustling of cloth, and the girl's head poked out from under the red blanket and coat. George could see that she had sandy blond hair and a very pretty face. There were two bruises on her face, one on her right cheek and another one on the left forehead with a slight cut in the center of it. Her hair was tousled and wild looking, but otherwise she looked pretty good considering what had happened to her.

"I...think...I am okay," she said in a harsh strained voice. "My voice sounds funny," she said holding the blanket up to her neck; she sat up and looked around.

George walked to her with the tin coffee cup held with a rag around the handle.

"Be careful, it's hot," George warned. She reached out for the cup and that caused the blanket to slip off one shoulder slightly. She pulled it back up and blushed.

"Thank you," she said, taking the coffee cup.

"Don't thank me until you taste it," George said smiling.

"No...I meant, thank you for saving me," she said looking down shyly. "I thought I was going to die. I would have died if you hadn't come along. I...was just about to give up," she said choking up a little.

"Well...you are much too pretty to let drown," George said smiling.

She blushed again and brushed her hair back out of her face tucking a strand behind her ear.

"How did you end up in the river?" George asked.

"We were just riding down the road...Oh my Lord! My husband! Did... you see my husband?" She asked.

George shook his head. "You were the only one I saw."

She started to cry with her hands over her face. In a few minutes, she spoke again. "We were just driving the wagon down the road when the horses balked; and then the wagon started to tilt, and the next thing I knew I was in the river." She started to sob again. "I...we've only been married three months...now, I may be a widow at seventeen!" She started to sob again. George didn't know what to say, so he just let her cry.

After a few minutes, George walked over to her with the ham on the knife and offered it to her. She started to take it, but almost dropped the blanket when she reached for the food. She had to set the coffee cup down so she could hold the blanket with one hand and eat with the other.

"Could your husband swim?" George asked.

"I don't know." She sobbed.

"Well, I'm sure he could, most people can. Being young and strong, he probably swam out and is probably looking for you right now," George said as hopefully as he could.

"What is your name?" George asked as they both ate their ham.

"I'm Cynthia Jane Peden...ah...Bates, Mrs. Thomas Royal Bates or at least I hope I still am. People call me Cindy."

"George Kilgo," George said. "I would offer to shake your hand, but I'm afraid of what might happen," George laughed.

Cindy blushed again.

"Well, Mrs. Bates, if you feel up to it; we can go back and look for your husband."

"I think I'm alright. Ah...could you get my clothes for me?" she asked looking sheepishly toward her clothes.

"Sure," George said. "I'm real sorry about having to undress you but... it was either that or... let you freeze to death."

"I know...it's just...no one but my husband has *ever* seen me like ...that." Cindy said blushing again.

"Well, if it makes you feel better, I didn't really get a good look. I was too busy trying to save you to worry about looking," George said grinning while he was picking up her clothes. He couldn't help smiling when he handed the pantaloons to her which caused her to blush an even deeper shade of red.

George made himself busy with his back turned from where Cindy was putting on her clothes. At first, she tried to put them on sitting and under the blanket; but when she saw George looking the other way, she stood up and put them on.

George loaded everything and re-saddled Dolly. As they were about to mount to leave, George noticed Cindy was barefooted.

"I guess you lost your shoes in the river," he said looking down at her feet. Cindy nodded.

"I'm sure your feet are freezing. Here put these on," George said pulling his boots off, peeling off his socks and handing them to her. The socks were bright red and hand knitted by Emme.

"My wife knitted these. They were her first attempt at making socks and she cried because they didn't come out exactly right. They are a little misshapen, but maybe they'll keep your feet warm," George said smiling about the memory as Cindy pulled them on. They were huge on Cindy extending way up her legs, standing out against her white legs and feet.

"They are warm, and I think they were made with a lot of love so they are wonderful," Cindy said trying to smile. She wrapped up in the red blanket while George wore his oil cloth coat since the air was still cool, although the sun had peeped out and was warming things up.

"Where are you taking me?" Cindy asked when she was mounted behind with her arms around George's waist.

"Looney's Tavern, it is a stage coach stop about an hour from here and the nearest public place. If your husband is alive, he will find his way there," George said. "Why don't you tell me more about where you come from and how you came to be in the Sipsey River?"

"Well, I'm from the Whitworths and Pedens of Manchester and London, England. My uncle, Sir Joseph Whitworth is a famous manufacturer with a factory in Manchester where he makes a lot of different things. My father married his sister, Nancy. My father, Thomas S. Peden, and he were partners for several years. They won a lot of awards for the machinery they manufactured. Father wanted to expand to the Americas, so before I was born, he sold his half of the business to his brother-in-law and moved with my mother to Spartanburg, South Carolina. Later, they moved to Greenville County, South Carolina, where my three sisters, my brother and I were born. One of the things they manufactured was rifles. You may have heard of the Whitworth Rifle?" Cindy asked pausing to allow George to respond.

"No, I haven't, Missy. I guess I'm not up on the latest weapons."

"Well, it is very famous because it is so accurate at long distances. I don't know all the details; but my uncle got knighted because of all his inventions, and one of the most important was the Whitworth Rifle. My father helped develop all the inventions, but my uncle took all the credit. That is one of the reasons my father came to America, so he could start his own business, and get credit for things he built." Cindy was on a roll now telling George all the details of the family business.

"Father has a little factory in Greenville with ten employees. They make all sorts of machinery; but mostly now they make guns, gun barrels, locks, and all the parts for guns. Poppa couldn't call his guns Whitworths so he called them

Pedens. I am surprised you haven't heard of them. They are just like the Whitworths, but with a different name."

"Anyway, my husband's father had heard of them and tried to buy one. I mean, one of the real Whitworths. When he found out how expensive they were, someone told him about my father's guns, that they were just as good and cheaper. Mr. Bates and my husband went all the way to South Carolina to buy one of father's guns," Cindy paused to take a breath. She sighed and went on.

"I was just turning fifteen, and my mother was convinced that I was destined to be an old maid. I mean I had a lot of suitors, but they were just so boring and silly. The minute I laid eyes on Royal, I thought **that** is my husband; I knew I would marry him. I even told my mother that I had met the man I wanted to marry," Cindy said matter-of-factly.

"That is exactly what my wife says about me," George said laughing. "I don't know how women know that. I had no idea when I met my wife that we would be married. I knew she was the prettiest girl I had ever seen, but I didn't think I had a chance to even court her, much less marry her."

"I...don't know how I knew...I just knew it," Cindy said.

"Royal and I talked while my father and his father shared coffee. Well, I talked. Royal was too shy to say much at first. I finally asked a bunch of questions; and once I got him to talking about his life in Alabama, he just went on and on."

"I was just spell bound by all the stories he told of life on a place called Bailey Mountain. I think the Baileys and the Bates are cousins. Anyway, the reason they came to buy a new gun was because his father had a run-in with a big bear that was stealing their pigs. It seemed his father shot at the bear on two different occasions with his old musket, and the bear still came back and killed more pigs. The last time it actually ran over his father after he shot it. Anyway, my father gave Royal and his father a tour of the shop where our Peden Rifles are made; Royal asked so many questions that my father was really impressed with him. Royal begged his father to stay another day so he could see the men bore out some new barrels. I suspected and hoped that he just wanted to see me again. The next day, he was really into the process of making the guns. My father asked if he might be interested in being an apprentice. Of course, he wanted to and he spent the next two years living near my family and working in the gun factory. We spent a lot of time together, fell in love and married just three months ago. I think my father wanted Royal to stay and take over the factory so he could retire, but Royal wanted... wants to start his own gun making business..." Cindy started to softly sob. "Mr. Kilgo, I don't think I can go on living if something has happened to my Royal!" Cindy choked out.

Just then off in the distance a bell started to ring. Off in a different direction another bell could be heard. Both continued to ring for several seconds.

"You hear that?" George asked. "That is a good sign. Those are emergency bells. People ring them to let their neighbors know something important is happening...and to call out the men for an emergency... like a missing young lady. That would mean your husband would have told someone you were missing."

"Oh, I hope and pray that is the case. Please can we go faster?" Cindy asked. George agreed and pushed Dolly into a trot.

Soon they met a man in a wagon headed in the opposite direction. "Howdy, George," the man in the wagon said pulling the team to a stop.

"Martin," George said tipping his head to the man with a

black straggly beard and dressed in coarse gray pants and a black felt hat. "What's all the fuss about?" George asked.

"Some girl is missing," Martin said peering around George at the girl who was sitting behind him.

"Got a description of her?" George asked smiling.

"Yeah. She is pretty, blonde, wearing a blue denim dress... kind-of-like that one right there," Martin said looking at Cindy. Where did you find her?"

"I fished her out of the Sipsey early this morning," George said. "I couldn't stand to see such a pretty little thing drown."

"Well, there is a young fella over at Looney's about to go crazy, rounding up everybody to search for her. I suspect he will be kinda glad to see her," Martin said spitting a big mouth of tobacco juice over the side of his wagon. "I was going home to get my two boys to help search, but I guess I'll get back to plowing now. Good to see you George...Ma'am. George, be sure to tell the Misses I said hello," Martin said as he slapped the reins on the horses and drove off.

George and Cindy arrived at a two story log building surrounded by about a dozen horses tied to hitchin rails around the building. There was a hand painted sign that declared it to be Looney's Tavern and Inn. It had a front porch with a second story balcony over it. On the porch sat a couple of ladder-back straight chairs and a couple of split log benches. There was also a barrel with a checker board drawn on top. An old spittoon sat near the edge of the porch. The boards around it were stained dark brown as a testament that not everyone had hit the spittoon. There were two chimneys, one on either end of the building and smoke was curling upward from both.

Before George could pull Dolly to a stop, Cindy had thrown her body off the horse and was running into the door of the saloon. George heard a shout and scream followed by a couple of cheers. When George went into the dimly lighted room, Cindy was sitting on the bar at the back of the room swinging her feet with George's red socks flashing. A man with his head wrapped in a white bandage was standing next to her with his arms around her. As soon as she saw George, she jumped down from the bar and pushed through the crowd who had gathered around them, grabbing George by the hand, she led him over to her husband.

"Royal, this is George Kilgo, my savior. He saved me. George this is Royal Bates, my husband," she said.

"Mr. Kilgo, I don't know how to thank you!" Royal said limping forward a step to take George's hand and shake it vigorously. "I don't know how I could have gone on living if I had lost Cindy."

George just smiled and nodded his head while shaking Royal's hand.

"I am still not sure what exactly happened, but I am sure God was watching over us. We were just driving along the road when the horses stopped and balked. I slapped them with the reins, but they wouldn't move. Then the wagon started to tip and we..." he paused to look at Cindy, "we just flew off the wagon and into the river. I guess the river had washed under the road. My leg got hung under the wagon seat and twisted something awful. I was under the water for what seemed like a long time...it was so cold that it took my breath away." He looked around at those people gathered who were listening to him.

"Finally, I came up and looked around for Cindy; I could just see her head going down stream. I tried to swim, but I couldn't kick with my hurt leg, so I tried with just my arms. The current was so strong, it just carried me along. I...I think, I would have drowned...I just couldn't swim enough to get to the shore. Luckily, the horses finally kicked loose from the wagon traces, and one swam right by me. I grabbed hold of her tail and she towed me to the bank. She was so scared, she ran off. I tried to walk, but I couldn't stand to put weight on my leg." He pointed to his knee that was so swollen it looked like his pants leg would split open.

"I looked down stream to try and find Cindy," he reached out and put his arm around Cindy again and pulled her close to his side. In a choked voice he said, "I saw her disappear around a curve in the river. I...I...just knew she was lost forever. I finally was able to drag myself to the road. I just sat there until Mr. Tate came along and picked me up." Royal paused and smiled at all those around them. "I...I want to thank all of you for coming to help...I don't...I don't...know how to thank ya'll," Royal said choking up a little.

Bill Looney, the owner of the tavern who was standing behind the bar listening to Royal's story said, "Well, I know how to thank everyone. Ladies and gentlemen! In honor of your willingness to donate your time and service, and in honor of the lovely Cindy being found safe...free beer for everyone!" he shouted. A cheer went up. Bill held his hands up, "Wait! Wait! The beer is free, but these two lost everything when their wagon went into the river so Shorty is going to pass his hat..." Bill pulled a man over and took Shorty's hat off and handed it to him. "So ya'll dig deep and let's give the newly-weds something to tide them over." Bill smiled at them and went to filling metal mugs with beer from the keg sitting on the bar. Bill's wife, Senie Ellen, brought George and Royal a mug and gave them a big smile. She was short and dark skinned with a round face and black hair braided into a long tail down her back.

"George, are you still my boyfriend?" She asked as she waved them to a table over near the fireplace.

"Oh, Senie, you know you are my one true love. When are you going to run away with me?" George said laughing.

Senie giggled; then, she motioned for Cindy to follow her. Cindy gave George a look, and when he nodded, she followed as Senie led her up the stairs.

As George and Royal sat by the warmth of the fire, Royal asked what George did for a living. George was just explaining about his farm and his new job offer when Cindy came bounding down the stairs with George's red socks in her hand.

"I guess you can have these back," Cindy said. "I'm sorry they are so dirty. Senie gave me these to wear," Cindy said pulling her dress up to show them her feet which were now covered in leather moccasins. "They are so soft and warm." Cindy leaned forward and in a lower voice said, "Did you know she's an Indian?"

George laughed, "Of course, we know. See that man with the silver hair," George said indicating an older man sitting across the room at another table drinking his beer. "That is her Dad; his name is Johnny Two Feathers Penn and like Senie he is part Cherokee. He is well known around here. When the Trail of Tears was going on, he and his wife were newlyweds just like you and Royal. They hid out and lived in a cave called the Bear's Den for about two years until the officials stopped trying to round up the Indians. Senie was born there," George said smiling.

"Senie's real name is Senie Rising Dawn Penn Looney. Bill, her husband, is part Cherokee, too," George said grinning at Cindy. "Bill and his family ran off to the Big Smoky Mountains and hid out to keep from being sent out west with the rest of the Cherokees."

"I never met a real Indian before," Cindy said. "She is

really nice, and she said we could stay in one of the rooms upstairs until Royal is able to travel."

"I can't believe how nice everyone is treating us here," Royal said. "I'd love to pay everyone back...but all my tools and supplies were lost in the river."

"Maybe everything is not lost," George said.

Royal and Cindy's eyes opened wide at that statement and looked to George for an explanation.

"The Sipsey is shallow and usually pretty calm. In a couple of days when the water goes down, I bet you can find your stuff right where it went into the river. I mean...if your tools were heavy enough, they just sunk to the bottom. You said the wagon turned over so they probably got dumped out and didn't go down stream with the wagon," George said matter-of-factly.

Royal almost jumped out of his seat. "Oh my gosh, I bet you are right! Maybe all is not lost! I just don't know when I'll be able to climb down and look for them...with my leg all swollen up."

"Look," George said. "You see Shorty and Chuck over there? They do odd jobs around here for Bill; and I bet they will be glad to fish your stuff out of the river for half a dollar, or maybe just a couple of beers."

"That would be wonderful," Royal said. "You know, I had the barrels and parts to ten rifles on the wagon that Cindy's father sent with us. Once I assembled them, they would have sold for enough money for me to buy my own boring and spiraling machines so I could make my own gun barrels."

Lowering his voice, Royal continued, "Cindy's father thinks all this talk of electing a radical abolitionist president will cause a big increase in gun sales. Mr. Peden believes the issue of slavery will eventually lead to a war; and he plans to be ready to win some government contracts for rifles, if that happens." Royal paused to look around and make sure he was not being heard at other tables. Lowering his voice even more, he asked what George thought about all the talk about the abolition of slavery and such.

"Well, none of the folks around here have any slaves so I don't think most people care too much about who gets elected," George said.

Royal looked shocked. "That is all people in South Carolina can talk about; and on the train on the way over here, everyone was talking about it," Royal shook his head.

"Now, Mr. Kilgo, you were just about to tell me about your farm and your new job," Royal said taking a sip of his beer.

"And what about your family?" Cindy asked reaching over and taking a sip of her husband's beer. She threw her hand to her mouth and made a face before swallowing the sip. "Oh, my Lord, that stuff tastes nasty! How can you stand that?" she moaned, as George and Royal laughed at her reaction to her first sip of beer.

"I guess it is a taste you have to get used to," George said smiling and trying not to laugh out loud.

"I have a wife, five kids and a forty acre farm an hour or so south west of here. As I was telling Royal, I have been offered a job as overseer for a pretty large plantation near here. In fact, I was on my way there to check things out when I saw you bobbing along in the river."

"You mean you would be overseeing slaves?" Cindy asked.

George nodded.

"But don't you think slavery is...ah...awful?" She said ignoring the look her husband was giving her.

"Mr. Kilgo whatever your thoughts on slavery are, you don't have to explain them to us," Royal added quickly.

"Royal, it's okay. I don't mind saying I don't like it much, and I have a lot of bad feelings about being involved with it. My wife says it's my Christian duty to try and make their lives a little better. I don't know about that; but I am going to give it a look, and see what I think about the job," George said.

"Do you have boys or girls?" Cindy asked.

"Four boys and a girl," George said. "My girl, Liz, is getting too big to sleep with the boys. That is one of the reasons I am considering being an overseer; we need to add a bedroom," George said finishing his beer. "I need to get going."

"Wait," Royal said. "I want to do something to reward you for saving my Cindy."

"No need for that," George said looking right at Cindy. "I've already seen my reward." Cindy's eyes got big and her mouth flew open at that statement.

George laughed and quickly said, "Just seeing you two back together is enough reward for me." George gave Cindy a sly grin which caused her to blush.

"I insist," Royal said. "What kind of rifle do you have?"

"I've got an old converted musket, just like most folks around here," George said.

"Could I see it?" Royal asked.

"Sure," George said. "I'll go out and get it since you can't walk very well." George returned in a moment with the old musket.

"Looks like an 1853 Enfield," Royal said holding the gun up and looking it over. "Standard cap lock conversion...Who did the conversion from flintlock?" Royal asked.

"Some guy came through here a few years ago. I don't remember his name. He stayed here for a couple of weeks and did just about everybody's gun," George said.

"What is the range and accuracy?" Royal asked.

George laughed, "If I hit what I am aiming at 100 yards, I feel really lucky."

"Well, that settles it," Royal said. "I'll make you a new rifle."

"I appreciate the offer, but it is really not necessary," George said.

"It will be my pleasure; actually it will be good for my business. When you start winning all the shooting contests around here, everyone will want to buy a gun from me," Royal said grinning. "I promise you will love the Peden gun that I'll make you. It is extremely accurate at 500 yards, and a good marksman can hit at a thousand yards."

George looked skeptical. "I find it hard to believe you can hit something at 500 yards much less a thousand yards."

Royal smiled, "Just wait. When I get my tools, I'll get to work and I'll be seeing you in a month or so."

George shook Royal's hand again. Cindy just about knocked George down when she jumped up, threw her arms around him and kissed George on the cheek.

"Thank you for saving me! I'll always remember how you risked your life for me," Cindy said looking deep into George's eyes.

George smiled, "Someone needs to warn you, so I better do it. The stagecoach comes through every other Saturday... that means this Saturday. The Harrison sisters will be arriving on Friday to...ah...tend to the needs of anyone who is...ah... feeling *needy* and anyone feeling *needy* on the stage come Saturday..." he paused to see if they were following what he was saying. "You may want to keep your door closed, if you are still here on Friday and Saturday," George said grinning.

CHAPTER FOUR

After about two and a half hours of steady travel, George came to a fork in the road. A sign tacked to a tree said Days Gap-Decatur and pointed to the right fork. George rode down that fork for a few minutes when he suddenly came to an overlook that had high hills on both sides while the road dropped steeply downhill ahead of him. As they started down, George was taken by how steep it was. He could feel Dolly leaning backwards as they descended downward. The hill seemed to go downward for at least half a mile.

At the foot of the hill, the land leveled off and there were no more hills to the sides of the road. The only hills in sight were those behind him. He turned to look back and was taken by the steepness of the hills he had just come down.

After another mile or so, George came to a road to the right and then another one a half mile further along. George turned down this second road as Mr. Pruitt had told him to do. He went through a stand of tall pine trees where soft pine nettles covered the roadway. He saw a clearing ahead, and then he just seemed to pop out into the open.

There spread before him were large open fields in every

direction. Ahead, George could see a large house with smoke curling from the four chimneys. It was surrounded by many other smaller buildings. There were people working in the fields and around the house and buildings. George could see the fields were filled with slaves. Some were plowing while others were bent over chopping with hoes at the earth.

George counted six mules plowing in one field followed by a small army of slaves chopping the ground. Behind them were six more mules dragging some scratchers across the newly plowed ground. In still another field, there were more mules; and the process of plowing and chopping was being repeated. Further off in the distance were woods and they too were filled with slaves. George couldn't make out what they were doing, but there were wagons and more mules there also.

As George rode toward the house, slaves along the way stopped to look at him. Beyond the house, he could see what looked like a hundred small slave cabins. These were surrounded by more slaves tending fires and wash pots, carrying wood and other items to and fro.

George pulled Dolly to a stop in front of the house at a metal hitching post. Before he could dismount, Mary Pruitt, Moses and a large plump black lady appeared on the porch.

Wiping her hands on her apron, and dressed in a pale green dress trimmed in white lace, George was again impressed with how pretty Mrs. Pruitt looked.

"Hello George, it is so nice to see you again. I was hoping you would be coming by," she said smiling at him.

"Well, the Misses insisted that I come and look things over, and try to make up my mind about the job," George said returning the smile and tipping his hat to Mrs. Pruitt.

"Hello, Moses," George said addressing the black man. "Is this the beautiful Miss Tee I heard about?" George said looking at the large black woman.

"Mmmhunn," the woman said grinning. *"Yep, I sees he is jest like you said Mrs. Pruitt, a tall drink of water with a silver tongue already trying to turn my head by calling me beautiful!"* she chuckled.

George, grinning back, walked to the porch and up the steps extending his hand to shake Moses' hand. Moses paused not used to a white man wanting to shake his hand.

"We are so thankful you are going to give us a chance," Mrs. Pruitt said.

"Well, I can't promise anything other than to give things a look and see what I think," George said.

"Please come in. Mr. Pruitt is out in the field somewhere. Would you like something to eat and drink while we send for him?" she asked.

"To tell the truth, I haven't eaten anything much today. I had some ham early this morning and some jerky on the way, so anything you have will be okay," George said entering the hallway of the house.

Moses called out to some slave children who were playing nearby. *"Joshua, you'se run and find Mr. Pruitt and tell him Mr. Kilgo is here."*

Mrs. Pruitt led George into the house and down a long hallway that seemed to run the width of the house with rooms opening off to each side. A wide stair case on one side of the hall led up stairs. He could see the rooms were all filled with nice furniture.

George was taken again by how pretty Mrs. Pruitt was. Her red hair was combed out down her back and hung almost down to her tiny waist. It also framed her face and features perfectly.

She seemed to feel George's stare and blushed when she turned around. She had led George into the dining room where eight chairs were arranged around a large table. Miss

Tee brought two cups of coffee and George a plate with biscuits and ham covered with white gravy. It smelled and tasted wonderful. Before she could leave, George asked her with a mouthful of food, "Miss Tee will you marry me? A woman that can cook like this will make a perfect wife number two," he said grinning. Miss Tee broke into a wide smile.

"Mrs. Pruitt, you'se watch out fer' dis one, he be trying to turn a girls' head with'n sweet talk and his good looks. Mmmm hum he's a dangerous one!" Tee said smiling and shaking her head as she left them.

Mrs. Pruitt asked about his wife and children, and as George was telling her about his Mary's reaction to the dress, Jim Pruitt came into the room.

"George, it's great to see you again. I'm glad you decided to come look us over. I know you will want the job when you see everything," Pruitt said shaking George's hand.

"Well, if it is alright, I thought I would stay a couple of days and just observe things; then make up my mind," George said.

"Sure that would be great. I'll have Moses take your things up to a guest room while I show you around the plantation," Pruitt said.

Ah...if it's ok with you, I'd like to stay wherever the overseer stayed. I think it would let me get a better feel for things," George said looking questioningly at Pruitt.

Pruitt gave George a thoughtful look and nodded his head. "Of course, you are a very wise man and always thinking ahead."

George finished the ham and gravy, and pushed the plate back toward the center of the table.

"That was delicious. I can't remember when I tasted

anything so good...that really hit the spot," George said smiling and patting his stomach.

"If you're ready, we can go and I'll show you around," Pruitt said.

"Well, I will leave you men to see to things," Mary said rising and smiling at the men. "Mr. Kilgo, I look forward to seeing you at supper. I'll have Tee make some of her chicken-n-dumplings; you won't believe how good they taste."

Mary walked away leaving both men standing and watching her go. They both shared a look with each other as if to say, "She is really something."

Pruitt led George outside and they mounted their horses to begin the tour of the plantation.

Mr. Pruitt talked excitedly as he pointed out the various buildings and parts of the plantation. He was obviously proud of the operation and all its working parts. There were two barns and a blacksmith shop, a smokehouse, a chicken house, tool shed, and several other buildings as well as many slave cabins. There were several groups of women and children working in and around the buildings, and a few older men doing different chores. Some were washing clothes in big wash pots, others seemed to be making candles, and cooking in large pots.

George nodded and touched his hat brim as they rode by them, while Mr. Pruitt seemed to ignore them as he talked on about how many acres they had plowed and planted and how many more they had to do.

"We got eighteen mules and ten horses...six riding or team horses and two large draft horses that we use for the heavy pulling. We use six mules to plow, six to pull the scratchers and six to pull the lay-off plows. The slaves with the white sacks follow along and drop the cotton seeds. The others follow behind and cover the seeds," Pruitt said pointing to the field where the most activity was taking place.

"What are all those slaves behind the plows doing?" George asked.

"They are breaking up the dirt clods with hoes," Pruitt said.

George nodded.

"We're doing about eight acres a day, depending on how the slaves and mules hold out. We should get all the cotton planted in about a month, if the weather holds and we don't get too much rain," Pruitt said as they rode away from the fields.

George was watching the slaves plowing and working when he spotted two slaves with whips yelling at the slaves about various things. Twice he saw them whip and shove some slaves around about something. They were too far away to hear what the slaves had done wrong, but George could hear the crack of the whip clearly. He guessed those two with the whips were some of the slave bosses Moses had talked about. As he looked closer, George could see they also had belts with large knives in sheaths hanging from their waists.

Mr. Pruitt led George away from the fields toward a line of trees at the back of the plantation. They rode across several fields that had yet to be plowed. When they neared the tree line, George could see that this land was in the process of being cleared of trees, tree stumps and brush. Several slaves were working here, chopping and sawing down trees and clearing bushes.

"This is the new ground we're clearing. I would eventually like to get all five hundred acres in cultivation. It is just such a slow process to cut the trees, and clear the stumps and roots to get it ready to plant," Pruitt said. "Right now we have most of the slaves planting, but when that's done we will get back to clearing."

They rode on deeper into the woods. In a few minutes, they came to a large swamp. It was several acres in size extending as far as they could see. It was mostly covered in shallow water with a few dead trees sticking up here and there. Swamp grass surrounded the edges and in some places in the middle, while large oak trees stood around the edges marking the boundary of the swamp.

"This is a big headache I will have to deal with in the future. It goes back pretty far, maybe ten to fifteen acres and catches most of the run-off of the rain. It's going to stop us from cultivating back here," Pruitt said. "We hunt back here around the swamp. There are lots of deer, wild boars, a few bears and God knows what else back here."

"That's pretty much it. Three hundred acres we plant and two hundred more to clear. I really would like to get more bales out of the land we are planting now and gradually add more land in the future. If this talk of freeing the slaves continues, cotton prices will go sky high and a lot of money can be made," Pruitt said.

George nodded. They started back to the front fields, to where the slaves were plowing the land. As they arrived, one of the slave bosses came to them. *"Master Pruitt,"* he began, *"they's gonna be a near full moon tonight, we could plow for a few more hours if'n you want,"* he said.

"George, this is Terrell. He is our head slave boss," Mr. Pruitt said indicating the slave.

George looked him over with the memory of what Moses had said about him still in his mind. Still George dismounted from his horse and extended his hand to Terrell. He looked shocked then, took George's hand.

"Good to meet you," George said. "I'm George Kilgo."

The slave didn't speak to George at all, just turned his attention back to Mr. Pruitt.

George felt the hair on the back of his neck stand up as he looked the man over. He was taller than most slaves, with wide shoulders and big hands. He had a mouthful of rotten teeth, and George could smell his bad breath from several feet away. He had two ugly scars on his face: one across one eye brow that extended down his cheek and another one on his chin that disappeared down his neck. George would later learn that these were from a knife fight. George would also learn that Terrell killed the other man in that fight by slashing his throat.

Mr. Pruitt looked over at the men plowing and at the mules they were using. Both the men and the mules were soaking wet with sweat. The backs of the mules were foaming in white lather where the harnesses touched their skin.

"I don't think so," he said. "Looks to me like both the men and the mules are about worn out. I guess we can pick up tomorrow."

"*Don't you worry about the men,*" Terrell said. "*They's be working when I tells them to or I'll strip the hide off their backs, but you'se the boss.*"

George felt an instant dislike for the slave. Another slave carrying a whip and wearing a knife belt approached the men.

"George, this is Big Sammy," Mr. Pruitt said. "He is slave boss number two."

George extended his hand to shake the slave's hand. He just looked at the hand for several seconds before extending his hand. "*Sorry, ain't too many white men ever offered to shake my hand,*" he said looking George right in the eyes.

Big Sammy was shorter than Terrell, but very thick in the chest. He had a mouth full of white teeth and a big smile.

George couldn't help but compare the way the two slave bosses reacted to meeting him.

"Let everyone go at dark and make sure they give the mules and horses extra feed. We need to keep them strong for the plowing ahead," Mr. Pruitt said.

He and George rode back to the house leaving the bosses to tend to the slaves. George could hear Terrell cursing someone and the crack of the whip as they rode away. George wanted to turn his head and see what was happening, but he resisted the urge.

When they got back to the house, Mrs. Pruitt and Moses were sitting in two rockers, waiting for them on the porch.

"I thought we would show you to the overseer's cabin, and see if there was anything you would need," Mary explained.

"I'm going to have a little whiskey," Mr. Pruitt said. "George, I'll see you at supper unless you would like to join me for a little of that good bourbon whiskey," he said brushing the dust from his clothes.

"Thanks, but I'm pretty tired. I'll just go clean up a little before supper," George said looking at Mrs. Pruitt and Moses.

Together, Moses, Mrs. Pruitt and George who was leading Dolly, walked between the rows of slave cabins to a wood sided cabin near the rear of the complex.

Most of the slave cabins looked to be about twenty-five feet wide and twenty feet long. These held two families with the space inside divided between the two families. Made of logs, each cabin had a fireplace on one end made of sticks, rocks and mud. There were windows either on the ends or sides of the cabin facing each other. There were no window panes just a square hole with a board covering that could be raised and propped open with a stick.

The roofs were steep with wooden shingles. There were no ceilings, just open space to the round pole rafters of the roof. The cracks between the logs were filled with red clay. The doors were rough boards or split logs nailed together to form a closure. There were no wooden floors in the cabins, just packed dirt or swept earthen floors. The slaves slept on the floors on a pile of straw covered with rags. Two families, with however many kids, all were crammed into these cabins. Here and there were smaller cabins that housed just one or two slaves, but these were fewer as it was just as easy to build a larger cabin as a small one.

When they arrived at the wooden sided cabin, George noticed it was about the size of one of the larger slave cabins, and likely was a log cabin that was later covered with wooden siding. This proved to be true when George went inside.

When they arrived at the overseer's cabin, Mrs. Pruitt pushed the door open and went inside first followed by Moses and then George. They were all immediately overcome by a horrible smell. Mrs. Pruitt threw her hand over her mouth and shouted, *"Oh my dear Lord!"* and turned to rush out the open door, gagging as she went by George and Moses. George immediately recognized the smell of an unemptied chamber pot. George and Moses held their breath and looked for the offending chamber pot, but didn't find one. George walked around looking and sniffing and finally realized the smell was coming from several places inside of the one room cabin. It was coming from the straw mattress on the bed, from several corners of the room and from the fireplace. Looking closely, George could see where it looked like someone had peed on the bed, in the corners of the room and on the fireplace hearth. In the middle of the room on the wooden floor George found a slightly dried pile of human excrement.

When they could stand the smell no longer, George and Moses went outside to join Mrs. Pruitt who was standing holding her handkerchief over her mouth and trying to keep from throwing up.

Sucking in a breath of fresh air, George said, "I would guess Mr. Connors left a few signs of his displeasure at being fired."

"I'm so sorry!" Mrs. Pruitt said. "I should have had Moses check on things down here before you arrived." She gave George a pleading look.

"Don't worry about it," George said. "Is there an empty slave cabin, maybe one of the smaller ones?"

"Yessir, they is," Moses said, *"but wouldn't you rather come to the big house and sleep in one of dem bedrooms? Those slave cabins don't got no floor, and are cold and damp. You could catch your death cold from just one night."*

"Well, I need to know what it is like for the slaves if I am going to be their overseer. One night won't kill me. I've sleep on the ground before so it will be okay," George said looking at both of them.

They made their way to a small cabin a few yards away and Moses pushed open the door and peeked inside. It was dark and smelled musty, but otherwise it was okay.

"This will do fine for tonight and I'll clean up the overseer's cabin tomorrow," George said.

"You forget, Mr. Kilgo, you have slaves to do that kind of work now. I'll send someone to get you a bucket of clean water, a wash bowl, and a chair from my house. Moses will send someone to get the bed frame from the overseer's cabin and a fresh mattress from my house. They will scrub the frame down good before bringing it to you here," Mrs. Pruitt said. "Please don't think bad of us. I should have been better prepared for your visit, but I wasn't. I am so sorry."

George couldn't help but smile at her and her pained look.

He smiled at her and laughed. "If this is the worst thing that happens to me, I'll consider myself lucky."

After they left, George unsaddled Dolly and tied her to a long lead with his lasso. Carrying his gear inside, he stripped to the waist. When the water and bowl arrived, he washed out his red socks and using one washed off from the waist up. He hung the socks up to dry on the chair they brought him.

He spread his pad and blanket on the mattress that Mrs. Pruitt had sent from the house. George slipped his boots off and lay on the half of the blanket he had spread out, and covered up with the other half. He thought about building a fire, but decided he would worry about that when he returned from supper. George was bone tired and feeling some soreness from places he must have strained pulling Cindy from the river. He unintentionally drifted off to sleep.

A while later something woke George. Almost on instinct, he reached for his colt revolver that he had hung on the head of the bed frame. He listened carefully trying to figure out what had awoken him and where he was. He realized it was totally dark now and he couldn't remember where he had put his match tin to light the lantern.

Finally, after a moment, he heard a quiet tapping at the door of the cabin. After his eyes adjusted to the dark, he could see enough to make out the door. Holding his colt in his hand, he made his way carefully to the door and peeped out the crack to see who was there.

George smiled and then opened the door wider. There stood a small slave boy. His eyes opened wide when he saw George holding the big colt revolver. He couldn't seem to speak until George said, "It's alright son. What do you need?"

Finally, the boy found his voice and said, "*Mr. Moses says supper's ready at the big house.*" Then he stood there shyly, kind of hiding behind the door frame.

"Thank you son, wait here a minute," George went to his saddle bags and pulled out a piece of jerky. Returning to the door, he offered it to the boy. He just looked at George and the meat until George said, "Its okay, you can take it." The boy took it and ran off into the darkness.

George dressed and made his way to the owner's house. As he passed between the other slave cabins, he could see and hear the families inside the cabins making supper, eating, and preparing for bed. He could smell cooking and wondered what the slaves were eating for supper.

Knocking and being lead into the house by Mrs. Pruitt, he noticed that she had changed to a different dress, and it looked like she had brushed her hair.

"I still wish you would consider using one of the bedrooms upstairs. We have plenty of room, and I know it would be much better than that damp cabin," she said smiling at George.

"Thank you for the offer, but I need to learn more about how the slaves live if I am going to know if I want to take this job," George said returning her smile.

They went into the dining room where Mr. Pruitt sat at the end of the table which was set with plates and silverware. He also had a bottle of whiskey and a half full glass.

"George, come in, come in!" he shouted loudly. George could see and hear the effects of the whiskey already.

"I'm sorry if I held supper up. I fell asleep. I guess I was pretty tired. It's been a long day," George said.

"Aw...don't worry about that," Mr. Pruitt said still too loudly. "Moses, we are ready to eat," he shouted toward the door near the end of the dining room.

Moses and Tee appeared with several bowls and platters of food. Mrs. Pruitt sat on one side of the table and George sat opposite her. Tee had indeed made her chicken-n-dumplings.

It smelled great, and after the first bite George confirmed it was wonderful.

"Tee, this is great. You will have to share the recipe with me so I can give it to my wife," George said.

"I don't knows about that," Tee said. *"I jest start puttin stuff in it and tastin it and addin more until it taste right. Does you want coffee to drink?"*

George nodded. Mr. Pruitt told her to bring another glass so George could have some whiskey, too.

All during the meal, Mr. Pruitt talked and dominated the conversation. He talked about his father and his political plans, and how he had to take frequent trips to visit with important people. He dropped one name after another of people that George didn't know.

Through it all, Mrs. Pruitt and George listened politely. It seemed to George that Mrs. Pruitt was embarrassed by her husband as she stayed slightly red-cheeked.

Mr. Pruitt finally asked George what he thought of the plantation and its operation so far.

George said he found it very interesting, but he had never been exposed to slaves before and didn't know much about how everything worked. But, he did say he was looking forward to learning more about the entire workings of the plantation including how the slaves lived and worked.

Mr. Pruitt nodded. "Take as much time as you need. I have to go into town tomorrow and will be gone most of the day. I'm sure Terrell and Big Sammy will be glad to let you follow them around and see how they operate."

"Actually...I would kind of like to just...ah...watch things on my own. I think I can get a better idea of how things really are without them around," George said. "I'm sure the slaves behave differently when they know their bosses are around."

Mr. Pruitt gave George a long look; then, he gave a loud

laugh. "Mr. Kilgo, I knew you were a special man the moment I saw you ride up the other day. You do as you wish!"

"I propose a toast then," Mr. Pruitt said holding up his glass toward George, "to a great partnership in the future!" George sipped a little of the whiskey.

Mary Pruitt noticed a red, raw whelp on the back of George's hand. "Oh, my! How did you get that mark on your hand?" she asked.

George started slowly, and then related all the events of the morning. Mary Pruitt listened carefully, spell bound by George's story. She was especially interested in Bill Looney, his wife and all the characters at Looney's tavern.

When George finished, Mr. Pruitt spoke again and talked about the political issues and the talk of a radical Republican abolitionist being elected President.

"How do the small planters feel about such a person being elected?" he asked. George felt really uncomfortable discussing this with Mr. Pruitt. He cleared his throat and said, "I don't think the small planter really cares too much who gets elected. Most I know are too busy trying to plow and plant to pay much attention to politics."

Mr. Pruitt nodded his head again. He looked really sleepy now and his eyes were hooded and droopy.

"The small planters will let the plantation owners do all the work and they just ride the train and reap the benefits of the cotton prices we fight for," Mr. Pruitt said. George felt the hair on the back of his neck stand up and his face turn red.

Mrs. Pruitt, who had been silent for a while, now spoke up as she could sense things were not going in the right direction.

"Mr. Pruitt, I'm sure Mr. Kilgo doesn't want to talk politics all night. It is getting late, and we all have an early morning tomorrow," she said looking at both the men.

Mr. Pruitt could see he might have been on the verge of saying something he shouldn't.

"As usual, my wife is right and I am really tired myself," he said standing up. He swayed unsteadily. "Mr. Kilgo, I bid you goodnight and I will see you when I return tomorrow." He shook George's hand and made his way toward the door.

George and Mary Pruitt watched him stagger slightly as he went out the door. Mary seemed embarrassed by her husband's actions, and she looked down as she rose and gave George a tortured look.

George gave her a smile and said, "Thank you so much for the supper and the company. I really enjoyed both."

"I...expect you to join me...us... for supper each evening, please. I need someone to talk to when Mr. Pruitt is gone, and it's nice to have something beside politics to talk about," Mary said flashing a brilliant smile.

"I look forward to it," George said. "Good night. Please tell Tee how much I enjoyed her chicken-n-dumplings."

George walked back to the cabin where he was staying. All along, he could hear the sounds of people preparing for bed. Here and there, a baby could be heard crying. George also heard coughing and some angry shouting. The lanterns were out in some cabins and in others they were still lit.

Outside one cabin sat three older men smoking. All three had white beards. Two had bushy gray hair and one wore a tattered straw hat. George spoke as he walked by. "Good evening, gentlemen," he said touching the brim of his black felt hat.

"Good evening, sir," they replied.

"Nice night, a little cool for April, but still nice weather," George said stopping briefly. "Is that home grown tobacco you're smoking?"

"No, sir, we ain't had no real to'baccy in a couple of years,"

one of the men said. *"This here is rabbit to'baccy. It don't taste too bad, and if'in it's all you got... You is that young fella Moses says might be the new overseer, ain't cha?"*

"Yes, sir, I'm giving it some thought. I don't know much about slavery, and I don't know about running a plantation, so I don't know about all this. I'm just a small time farmer," George said.

"Mmmm hum...Moses says you is a good man. He says you stuck your gun in that fool Connors' face when he was trying to whip a slave." The old man nodded to the other men. *"That makes you alright with'n us. Only thing better was if'n you pulled the trigger!"* That brought a chuckle from the rest of the men.

"Well, do you men have any advice for me...I mean about how to run a plantation?" George asked.

The men paused and looked at each other for a minute; one of them cleared his throat and started to talk.

"Slaves is folks same as other folks. You treat them good and they treats you good, too." When he finished saying his piece he looked at the next old slave indicating it was his turn to speak.

"We're just about starvin to death...and being worked to death! Any th'ang you do to help that situation will be better than that fool Connors," he said.

The final old man pulled his pipe to his mouth, took a puff and seemed to be thinking about what to say. Finally, he said, *"They is two ways to make a hoss run, son. One way is for the driver to whip'm. That hoss he'll run, but after a while the place where you is whipping him will get raw n' he will get ill and mean...then it'll scar over and he don't feel the whip no more so he'll slow down and stop."* The old man paused and scratched his chin. *"The other way to get a hoss to run is to hold a carrot in front of him. He'll run jest as hard as the one gett'n whipped. But after a while iff'n he don't get a nibble of that carrot, he'll quit running same as the one that got whipped.*" The old man squinted one eye and looked at George real hard. "*Which kind of driver is you gonna be?*"

George looked at the man for a few seconds; then, gave a slight nod of his head. He looked at the other men in turn. "I don't know if I want to be a driver at all," George said taking his hat off and running his hand through his hair. "I guess I got some hard thinking to do," he said. "Thanks for the advice." George nodded his head to the men. "Ya'll have a good evening now," George said walking on. When he reached a dark area near his cabin, he stopped to take a leak at the corner of the cabin.

When George arrived inside the slave cabin he was staying in, the bed looked awfully good. It seemed like a life time ago when he left his house this morning. He lay down and was asleep in just a few minutes.

CHAPTER FIVE

During the night, something awoke George. He lay still trying to figure out where he was and what awoke him. He felt a movement on his blanket near his feet. George's first thought was a snake! These old wooden cabins must be attractive to copperheads that live and thrive in these parts; or a rattler, there were plenty of those around too.

George froze, trying to be as still as possible until he could figure out what it was that was moving on his blanket near his feet. Raising his head he looked down toward his feet. In the dim light, he could see four beady eyes looking back at him. Rats!

When his eyes adjusted to the dim light, George could see movement in other parts of the cabin. George hated rats. He held his breath for a second; and then, kicked the blanket upward as hard as he could. He heard two thuds and one squeal. Jumping up, George reached for his match tin and lit a match. In the dim light, George could see more rats scurrying around fleeing the light.

George lit the lantern and turned it up as bright as possible. Holding the lantern up high so he could see, George looked around. He saw several rats sitting on the rafters and running around the dirt floor. Rising, he went to his equipment and took his rope and threw it over a pole rafter. He took his saddlebags and suspended them from the rafter. He didn't want the rats to get to his food and coffee in the saddle bags.

George went to the pile of wood near the fireplace. Looking carefully, he found what he wanted; a stick about two feet long and an inch around. He put his felt hat back on to cover and protect his head and face, laid back down on the bed and pulled the blanket up to his chin. Slowly, he drifted off to a shallow sleep. When he felt the rats on his bed again, he used the stick to make a sweeping strike along the blanket. He repeated this action several times during the night. Sometimes, he felt the stick strike something and then heard the thuds as the rats flew across the room.

It was a long night. About thirty minutes before daylight, George woke for the last time that night. It was like he had a clock in his head and it woke him every morning at the same time. He got up, lit the lantern and looked around the cabin. In the dim light he could see at least three dead rats lying on the floor of the cabin.

Putting on his clothes, he realized he needed to use the outhouse in the worst way. Since he didn't have a chamber pot in the cabin, he knew he would have to make the trip to the outhouse he had spotted yesterday. As he left, he picked up the three dead rats by their tails, planning to throw them away in the sewage. As George neared the outhouse, he met a man coming out of the building. The slave spotted the rats George was carrying.

"*Good mornin, sir,*" he said. George nodded and said good morning back.

"*I see you got some rats, is they fresh kill't?*" he asked.

"Yeah, I killed them last night," George said.

71

"If'n you don't mind me askin, what you'se plan to do with dem?" he asked.

"I'm going to throw them in the trench at the outhouse," George said.

The man hesitated, and then asked, *"Could I have dem? They make a might good stew if'n you don't mind the idea of eatin rats. I...mean they is better than no meat at all. My misses chops them up and puts them in stew and the kids don't even know what they is eatin."* George's stomach almost turned at the thought of eating rats!

"Here, you take them," George said handing them to the man.

"Thanks yea," the man said taking the rats with a smile.

Near the back of the slave cabin complex was a long, narrow, low topped building. George could smell it from a long way off. Carrying his lantern, he took a deep breath and entered. Inside, the smell was almost over powering. The space inside was about five feet wide. Along the back wall were boards that extended down but not to the bottom of the building. The bottom two feet of the building was open to a trench filled with excrement, corn cobs and leaves. There was a board nailed to the ends of the building extending from one end to the other about a foot and a half off the ground. You turned around and hung your bottom over the board while sitting on it with your upper thighs. In this way, you were suspended over the trench. There was a pile of corn cobs and corn shucks in a corner. Someone had added several green cow cumber leaves to the material to be used to wipe with. George was not used to such an open and public outhouse. Luckily, there was no one inside, and George was able to take care of business without interruption. Just as he was leaving, two more men came in. George spoke to the surprised men as he was leaving.

Outside in the fresh air, he took a few steps to look at the back of the outhouse. The trench that caught the waste was connected to a ditch that drained away from the outhouse. It was supposed to take the waste away from the area, but George could see that it didn't slope correctly, and the waste just sat in pools that were covered with flies which rose in loud buzzing as George approached. Dawn was lighting the sky now, and about fifty feet away was another similar building. George could see several women making their way into this building that appeared to be the women's outhouse.

George went back to his cabin and took a piece of the ham Emme had packed in the white bag from his saddle bags. This was heavily salted and smoked ham. It would stay safe to eat for a couple of more days. Smoked ham, jerky and salt pork, which were soaked in thick salt brine and dried, were important foods people carried with them when they traveled and hunting for fresh meat was not possible. George put the meat on the knife blade, and repeated the cooking and coffee making that he had done with Cindy beside the Sipsey River. He also pulled out one of four biscuits Emme had put in the cloth bag. They were rock hard now; but George dipped one in the hot coffee, and it softened so he could eat it. Together the ham, biscuit, and hot coffee filled him and ended the hunger in his stomach.

George had an idea he wanted to pursue today. In order to get a feel for what life was like for the slaves, he would try to do as many of the slave jobs as possible. Thinking this was a good idea, he pondered where to begin.

He was walking to the barn where Dolly had spent the night, when he passed one of the slave cabins where the smell of cooking food was coming out the door. George realized he didn't have the slightest idea what the slaves ate...besides rats. Taking a deep breath, George knocked on the door. After a few moments, the door opened a crack and a woman peered out.

"Ah...I'm George Kilgo, and this may sound strange; but I wondered if I could see what your cabin looks like and maybe see what you are fixing for your family to eat...I really don't know much about...ah...how you live. I'm sorry; if you don't want me to come in, that's okay," George said.

"*No sir! Mr. Kilgo, I's know who you is. You can come in and look around if'n you wants. The little ones still asleep, but the rest is gettin ready,*" the lady said. "*I is Tilly Mae, and that is my husband, Joseph. Joseph, this is Mr. Kilgo.*" A tall thin black man came over and kind of nodded and bowing his head toward George who reached out to shake the man's hand. Like most of the slaves, he hesitated not used to a white man wanting to shake a slave's hand.

George gave him a smile, "I just want to learn something about how you live and what you eat," George said. "I'm sorry, but the only slaves I ever saw before yesterday, were a wagon load I passed on the road. I need to find out some things...if I...ah...well, I just need to know."

"*I understands, you come on in and look things over all you wants,*" Joseph said. "*That's Willy and his wife, Bell, over there. They share this cabin with'n us.*

George nodded tipping his hat toward the others at the other end of the cabin.

"I noticed you were cooking; I could smell it outside. If I could ask, what are you cooking, Miss Tilly?" George asked.

"*I cookin corn fritters,*" Tilly said, "*same as every mornin. You is welcome to some if'n you is hungry,*" Tilly said, turning back to her frying pan where she was flipping some dough cakes over. There were several in the skillet and they were slightly brown on one side. They made a sizzling sound and smelled slightly of bacon.

George looked around. The cabin was much like the one George stayed in with a dirt floor and a fireplace on one end; only this cabin was twice as large, maybe twenty-five feet long. Willy and Bell were sitting at a crude wooden table and eating something from wooden plates with their fingers. George thought it looked like the same thing Tilly was cooking. There were several children sleeping on straw beds on the dirt floor. George counted six on one end of the cabin and five on the other. George quickly added the numbers in his head. There were fifteen people living in this cabin.

"How do you make those corn...ah...critters?" George said.

Tilly giggled and said, *"Not critters...fritters. They is just corn meal, a little milk or water and some bacon grease. Sometimes if'n we have meat, we put's little pieces in them; but we ain't had no meat in a while."*

George looked at the dough cake as Tilly took one out and laid it on a wooden plate. It smelled pretty good.

*"You can have one if'n you want*s," Tilly said looking at George.

"No thank you, I already ate something," George said. "What are those little black specks?"

Tilly looked sheepish and frowned. *"Those is weevils. I trys to pick them out, but they is just too many to get them all. They gets in the cornmeal and...they don't hurt you none. If'n they did, every slave would be dead."*

George nodded. "You eat corn fritters every morning, what about for lunch and supper?"

Tilly looked puzzled. *"We don't eat no lunch. Bosses don't let slaves stop working to eat no lunch. Fe'r supper we has corn mush."* Tilly pointed to a large pot hanging on a hook over the edge of the fire. *"You know what that is?"* George just shook his head.

75

"It jest corn meal and water cooked in a pot like stew. We's put meat and butter in it when we has some," Tilly said.

George shook his head. "Is that all you have to eat?" George asked.

"Well yeah, right now. Use to we had more meat; some pork, sometimes some chicken. Once in a while someone catch or kill a possum and sometimes use to eat some squirrels. Mmm...I sure like to have some squirrel dumplins. We use to get some flour each month, but we ain't had no flour is several months," Tilly explained.

George shook his head. He didn't see how they could work as hard as they did with so little to eat. "Well, thank you for letting me look around," George said. "Could you break me off just a little corner of one of the fritters? I would like to see what it tastes like."

Tilly broke off a corner of one of the fritters and handed it to George who looked at all the black spots in it before putting it in his mouth. It didn't have much taste, only a faint taste of corn bread and bacon. George smiled.

"You're a good cook, Tilly, that tastes good," George said walking toward the door. "Ya'll have a good day now."

It was day light out now and there were people stirring around everywhere. Men and women were headed toward the barns and sheds where others were coming out with tools and heading toward the fields.

Suddenly, George heard a loud stream of cursing and the crack of a whip followed by someone begging not to be whipped again. George clinched his jaw, and walked on to get Dolly to saddle for the day.

George and Dolly made their way to the very back of the plantation where the new ground was. George decided to start here and work his way toward the front of the plantation.

George slipped his rope over Dolly's head and just let the rope lay on the ground. Dolly would not wander far.

George picked up an axe and joined the others in cutting bushes and small trees. It was really cool, but in a few minutes, George was soaking wet with sweat. He pulled his shirt off and joined many of the other men naked above the waist. As they worked, the slaves sang and chanted. One slave would sing out something, and then the rest would sing or chant something back.

I be so glad when the sun goes down, Uh hu!
I wants to lay down, Oh Yea!
I ain't lazy but I wants to lay down, Uh hu!
I wants to lay down, Uh hu!
But the boss man won't let me, Oh no!
No the boss man won't let me, Oh no!
I can't see the end of the day, Oh no!

It was a rhythmic, hypnotic song with the workers using their tools to the beat. It seemed to George, the singing just let the mind go and drift. It caused the work to go more quickly.

All the slaves looked on in wonder to see a white man; and one that might become their overseer, working just like the others. After about forty-five minutes, George put the axe down and took a turn on one side of the crosscut saw the slaves were using to fell the large trees. He only lasted about fifteen minutes when he had to take a break. The man whose place he took grinned at George as he took the saw back from George.

George shifted to the group who were digging around a large tree stump. Digging was not much easier than pulling the saw. Women as well as men were all using picks, hoes and shovels digging and chopping the roots of the stump. After an hour or so, George was ready to move on to another job and another area of the plantation.

George joined the men and the mules who were plowing the fields preparing to plant the cotton. George walked up to one of the men who was plowing and asked if he could take a turn on the plow. The man looked surprised and reluctantly gave up his plow. These large, deep turning plows broke the ground at about ten inches deep. The mule did the hard work, and the man following just guided the plow and tried to keep a straight line. This was something George was used to as he worked his own farm. He plowed for close to an hour; then shifted to the group of slaves with hoes that were breaking up the large clumps of earth behind the plows. Twice, the slave bosses came over to see why a slave was just standing around.

"Why you standing around?" Terrell shouted pulling his whip.

"I'm taking his place and giving him a little break," George said calmly.

Terrell glared at him and the slave. He didn't like it, but he didn't want to go against the man who might be his boss soon. He spun his horse around and rode away.

From there, George went to the teams pulling the large scratcher gangs that followed the plows breaking up and leveling the ground even more. Then to another group that followed with hoes breaking up any leftover dirt clods.

Roll Jordan roll
I want to get to heaven when I die
To hear Jordan roll
My brother you ought to been there
Yes, my Lord
A sittin' in the Kingdom
To see Roll Jordan Roll
My Mother you ought to been there
Yes, my Lord
Yes, my Lord

When the water wagon came around with barrels of water, the slaves were allowed to take a drink from the buckets that were carried by the younger slaves. George was about to pass out from thirst when the bucket and dipper finally made it to him. The slave watched in awe as a white man drank from the same bucket and dipper as they did.

Next, he went to the group of mules pulling the lay-off plows. These plows were designed with a piece that slid along the ground and had a small plow blade that laid a shallow trench about four or five inches deep. This was the trench where the cotton seed would be dropped by a group of slaves who followed the lay-off plows.

George took a turn at each job. He dropped, and then worked with those slaves covering up the seeds. When he started to cover seeds, he spied a very pregnant woman and took her place. It was the heat of the day and she looked distressed. George sent her over to the water wagon to sit in the shade. Big Sammy saw her sitting and quickly came riding over cursing.

George saw him coming and stepped toward him speaking before Big Sammy could say anything to the girl. "I'm taking her place and giving her a rest," George said. Big Sammy glared at George and started to say something, but thought better of it and rode away talking to himself.

George was surprised when he took a break and looked at his watch. It was two o'clock in the afternoon. The sun was hot now, and his stomach was growling wanting some food; but if the slaves didn't get to eat, he was not going to eat either. He was tired and knew the day wouldn't end until dark which was still at least four or five hours away.

George shifted now to the area around the main house. Here in the various sheds and buildings were slaves doing other jobs to keep the plantation running. One was the blacksmith and his helper; others included a carpenter, a miller, and several older slaves who could no longer work in the fields. They were charged with feeding the chickens, horses, mules and cleaning out the barn and livestock pens. George tried his hand at these jobs, working beside the slaves in charge of each job. Here George also found out what was really happening on the plantation.

These slaves and Moses were able to see more because they were not working in the fields all day. George learned that Terrell and Big Sammy were withholding milk, food and meat to extort sex from various women. Those who gave in, got a chicken or milk or flour. The slaves they beat were most often those who wouldn't give in to their demands. George also learned that One Shoe Joe wasn't the only slave that had died from "getting kicked by a mule." Mr. Connors and the slave bosses worked together to bully the slaves and steal from Mr. Pruitt. They stole cattle, hogs, chickens and lots of cotton, sneaking it off the plantation at night and selling it to the cotton buyers at a reduced price.

George learned that the third slave boss, a man named Homer never hurt anyone; and he always tried to keep peace between the slaves, Mr. Connors and the slave bosses. If a slave bucked up and tried to do something against any of those three bosses, he and his family would suffer. One slave tried to stand up to Terrell, and a knife fight resulted. The slave was killed, but not before he cut Terrell on the face. George filed all this information away, and would have to work out a way to deal with the slave bosses, if he took the job.

George also met Nanny Haddy who was the doctor and medicine woman. She took care of the health needs of the slaves as well as acting as midwife to deliver all the babies. She was old and bent, but had a twinkle in her eye that said she understood a lot about life. She had jars and baskets of herbs and roots in her cabin. She mixed salves and potions that served as the only medicine the slaves received. George pulled up his pants legs and showed her the bites all over his legs and ankles.

"Those is flea bites," Haddy said. *"Most cabin's got fleas. The rats carry's th'm from place to place."* Haddy gave George some salve to put on the bites, and the itching went away.

George went back to his cabin with all this new knowledge. George was used to hard work and farm labor yet he was very tired after the day's work he had put in today. He sat at the table and used a scrap of paper to write down some things that he wanted to discuss with Mr. and Mrs. Pruitt. After an hour or so, George had made up his mind, and went to see Moses about some questions he had.

When darkness finally came, the slaves came in from the fields and set about doing the chores related to their families. After working in the fields all day, the women still had to cook supper for their families, and do the wash if they had any to do. (They didn't wash their clothes very often...didn't have many to wash.)

George built a fire in the fireplace and brought in a large cast iron wash pot from outside. He sat this in the edge of the fire and poured a couple buckets of water into the wash pot. The plantation got water from three hand-dug wells. Two were located in the slave quarters and one was located just behind the main house. George had to make several trips to the well to draw the water to bathe.

When the water was heated, George stripped and went to the back door of the cabin. The door faced the back of another cabin so there was not too much chance of being seen. George stood naked on the rock that served as a door step and took a bar of home-made soap that Emme had packed for him. George soaped himself from head to toe as he was covered in sweat and dirt from the day's work. When he was finished soaping, he dumped a bucket of water over his head. He felt much better although still tired and now sore from the hard work. George took a clean shirt out of his white sack and put it on before he made his way to the main house for supper.

CHAPTER SIX

"Well, George how did your day go? Did you learn anything about how our little plantation is run?" Mr. Pruitt asked when he had joined George and Mary in the dining room. Again, Mary Pruitt looked like she had combed her hair and dressed up a little for supper.

"Yes sir, I learned a lot about how things work around here. I still don't know how to handle slaves or how to run a plantation, but I know more about how it is being run," George answered. "And...I have made a decision about the job."

"Great!" Pruitt said. There was an awkward pause. George looked back and forth from Mr. Pruitt to Mrs. Pruitt.

"I would like to take the job...but there are... several things that have to...but I don't...ah...things that have to be done differently, if I am going to become the overseer," George finally got out.

The Pruitts nodded their heads and waited for George to explain. George took a deep breath and continued. "I want to take the job and run the plantation as best I can...but I don't really know how to do it. I only know...there are two ways to make a horse run." George told them the story just as the old slave had told him the day before. "I know that I can only be the driver of this horse...ah...plantation, if I use the carrot and not the whip," George said finally.

There was another awkward pause.

"And what carrots would you use to get the...slaves to work"? Mr. Pruitt asked.

"There are several...things that I would like to try," George said. "I was wondering if we could eat first."

"Of course!" Mrs. Pruitt said. "Moses, could we please eat now?"

"Yes'um, we s'ure can," Moses said from the doorway outside to the kitchen. Moses and Tee came in with a plate and a bowl, and set them in front of those seated at the table. The Pruitts looked down at the food.

"Moses, what the hell is this?" Mr. Pruitt asked staring down at the food.

"Ah...I asked Moses and Tee to fix us the same thing the slaves have to eat so you...; we could see what they have to... deal with," George said.

Mrs. Pruitt frowned looking down at the food. "What is this?" she asked.

"Those are corn fritters and this is corn mush," George said pointing to the platter and the bowl. "This is what the slaves eat almost every day, the fritters for breakfast and the mush for supper. Sometimes, if they have it, they put some meat in the mush or they make a stew of the meat, but most don't have any meat."

"What are those black things?" Mrs. Pruitt asked.

"Those are weevils...you know the little bugs that get in the meal. That is the only meat most of the slaves get unless they add some rat meat which some of the slaves have started to do," George said.

Mrs. Pruitt made a face, then a gagging noise, threw her

hand to her mouth and rushed from the room. Mr. Pruitt squinted his eyes and frowned.

"I know there is meat in the smokehouse. Why are they not getting meat to eat?" Mr. Pruitt asked.

"Mr. Connors and Terrell control who gets the meat. The only ones who get any meat are the ones who have sex with Connors, Terrell, or Big Sammy," George said. "That is one of the things that I want to change."

Mrs. Pruitt came back in looking quite pale.

"Moses, please come and take this food away," she said.

"You sure you don't want to taste a little?" George asked. "It is really not bad, just a little corn meal, milk and bacon grease." George reached over and broke off a piece of a corn fritter and put it into his mouth. He was careful not to get a piece with too many black specs. Mrs. Pruitt put her hand to her mouth and tried not to gag again.

"I certainly *do not* want to taste it," she said. Moses and Tee came in with the real food, and removed the corn fritters and mush.

"Ah...one of the reasons I wanted you to see what the slaves eat is that I want to use better food as one of the carrots to get the slaves to work," George said.

As they started to eat George asked, "Mr. Pruitt do you know how many slaves you had die last year?"

Mr. Pruitt looked up from his food, "I believe fifteen or maybe sixteen."

"Moses keeps up with it in his Bible," George said. Moses came in with an old worn Bible.

"I didn't know you could read and write," Mr. Pruitt stated.

"*Yes sir,*" Moses said. "*Missy Pruitt taught me when she was learnin' to read and write.*"

"According to Moses, you lost seventeen slaves last year.

They died for various reasons, six women died in child birth, and in five of those cases you lost the baby as well. Most just died of natural causes, but they died at such young ages; twenty-five, twenty-eight, only two died in their thirties. At least three, maybe more, died of being beaten by Connors or the slave bosses," George said. Before George could go on Mr. Pruitt interrupted him.

"Yeah, but we had a bunch of babies also so I know we came out to the good by several. Moses how many babies did we have last year?"

Moses shuffled over and opened the Bible to another section, and looked at several pages before announcing that they had twenty-nine babies born last year.

"Of the twenty-nine; seven died before they's was a year old, so's we got's that many left."

Mr. Pruitt smiled, "So we gained seven or eight new slaves. I guess we did pretty well then."

George just looked at him for a moment before speaking.

"Ah...I'm not sure about that, seems to me you lost a lot," George said.

"Pray tell why do you think that, Mr. Kilgo?"

"Well, how much does a slave cost if you have to buy one?" George asked.

"I believe I paid about six hundred apiece for these last four. They were prime age men and baby-ready women," Mr. Pruitt stated.

George nodded his head. "We can look up the ages of the ones that died, but I would guess that they were pretty much full grown, working age slaves."

Pruitt nodded.

"That is, workers...ah field hands you lost right?" George asked. Again Pruitt nodded.

"And how many years will it be before you get any work out of the new babies that were born?"

Mr. Pruitt wrinkled his brow and scratched his chin as he absorbed the truth of what George was saying.

"I'm guessing you won't be getting much work out of the seven new born slaves for ten to twelve years; and you've got to feed, clothe, and house them all the while," George said. He remained silent to see how Mr. Pruitt was taking that statement.

Mrs. Pruitt who had remained silent all this time now spoke up. "I see what you are saying, Mr. Kilgo. We lost workers and we gained babies, but what could we do about that?" she asked.

George paused, "I am real new to this; but it seems to me that if you could keep the worker slaves alive a little longer, you would be much better off."

Mr. Pruitt nodded his head slightly. "Just what are you proposing, Mr. Kilgo?"

George took a deep breath as he knew this was an important...make or break moment. "I believe we need to improve the way the slaves live; feed them better, make their housing better and maybe...give them a little rest and maybe even some free time off...If we do those things, they will live longer and we...you will get more and better work out of them," George said.

Mr. Pruitt looked at his wife and then back at George. Some unseen message may have passed from the wife to the husband because he asked,

"Exactly how would you do all that, and how much would it cost me?"

George rubbed his chin. "I haven't worked out all the details yet; but I think you got to buy some hogs to butcher right away, maybe kill six or seven, and smoke and salt the meat so you can start giving the slaves more meat to eat right away. Someone has got to be in charge of giving it out besides the slave bosses." Mr. Pruitt nodded his agreement.

"If you buy four hogs to breed, they will have eight to ten pigs at a time; pretty soon, you will have enough to keep everyone in meat...now that Mr. Connors ain't stealing and selling them. Also, I believe we can find a few trusted slaves to hunt for some extra meat," George went on.

"We need to make sure that for every chicken killed and eaten; at least two chicks get raised" he continued. "That should give everyone plenty of eggs to eat and still leave plenty of chickens to eat."

"What about cattle? I know we are down to just four milk cows. Should we buy more cows?" Mrs. Pruitt asked.

"Mrs. Pruitt, I think the best thing would be to buy some goats. Goats have babies about every hundred and fifty days, and they have two and sometimes three babies at a time. Plus they can help clean up the brush in the new ground. Their meat and milk is just as good as a cow's," George said.

Mr. Pruitt was leaning forward now staring intently at George. "What else do you propose, Mr. Kilgo?"

George was breathing easier now that it seemed that the Pruitts didn't hate what he was saying.

"We need to buy some flour, salt, sugar, and some other staples to improve the slave's diet right away, before you lose more of them. Remember, at six hundred dollars apiece for new slaves, you can spend more on the ones you got and still come out pretty good."

"I have several other things that I think might work. I would like to see us put floors in the slave cabins. I think it would maybe make them live longer and work harder... another carrot to dangle in front of the workers."

"I guess we could open the saw pit again, but it sure takes

a long time to saw boards and cure the lumber," Mr. Pruitt said.

"What if we loaded up the logs you are cutting off the new ground and hauled them to Turner's sawmill? It is just about an hour from here, and he will saw them on thirds. You give him three logs and he keeps one. He will let you trade him green lumber for cured lumber, so we could start to floor the cabins right away."

"How will you haul those big logs?" Mrs. Pruitt asked.

"We just take the bed off a couple of wagons, and they will haul several pretty big logs. It is not that hard to do," George explained.

"Mr. Kilgo, you are making a whole lot of sense. I knew you were an extraordinary man from the first time I saw you," Mr. Pruitt said.

"Thank you, but you may not think so when you hear what else I would like to do."

"By all means, go on if you have more!" Mr. Pruitt said.

"Well, we have to do something about the rats...and the fleas they carry. Rats are nasty critters and carry all kinds of disease. Every cabin is filled with fleas; and every slave is covered in bites, just look at my legs from just one night in a cabin." George pulled his pants leg above his boot to show them all the flea bites on his legs.

"Oh, I am sorry! Mr. Kilgo, I had no idea!" Mrs. Pruitt exclaimed.

"It's alright. I got some salve from Nanny Haddy, and they don't itch now," George paused. "What I am about to propose may sound crazy, but please hear me out before you make up your mind."

Mr. and Mrs. Pruitt both nodded.

"What if we paid the slaves a half penny for every rat they killed and turn in? We would get rid of the rats, and then we could poison the fleas with lime or borax."

"Mr. Kilgo, I don't understand how giving the slaves any amount of money would get them to kill the rats! Where are they going to spend money? We can't let slaves go into town to buy stuff. Besides the store keepers wouldn't sell them anything," Mr. Pruitt said shaking his head.

"I realize that. What if you...we...set up a slave store here on the plantation? You could just put some extra sugar, flour, meal, maybe even some candy, some cheap clothing, stuff like that, stuff you would probably give them anyways," George explained. "You are paying them for every rat they kill and they turn around and give your money back to you for stuff you were going to give them anyway. You might even put some shoes in your slave store. I haven't seen but six or seven slaves with any shoes on the whole time I have been here. We could maybe give a nickel or dime for the slave who worked the hardest that week or picked the most cotton that week, reward their hard work; just another carrot."

Mr. Pruitt looked hard at George and his frown slowly turned into a smile. "Mr. Kilgo, you are a genius! Why didn't someone think of that before! Pay them to do what you want them to do and then get the money back for stuff you were going to give them anyway!"

"I have some other...carrots I been thinking about... nothing makes a man work like giving him something he can see and call his own. I know you make them plant vegetables for everyone to eat, but what if you gave each family a little plot; just a row, to grow their own vegetables? You could sell the seeds in the store; and then what they grow, they would get to eat or keep or trade with each other or at the store," George said.

"When would they work these vegetable gardens? I mean

we have to work dawn to dark to get the land plowed and planted now. I doubt if they would have any time to plant their own food," Mr. Pruitt said.

"Ah...that is just it...I have carefully watched them work the last day or so. They work really hard, and when the slave bosses are standing over them with a whip, they work fast; but as soon as the bosses turn their backs...they don't work so fast. Don't get me wrong, the work they do is really hard work and they need to take a rest every once in a while; but I think I could get them to work faster all the time...if say... I told them...if you get this field plowed before dark you can have the rest of the day free...to work in your garden or to rest or just do whatever you want to do."

"You really think you could get the cotton planted on time; faster than normal by giving the slaves free time?" Mr. Pruitt looked hesitant for the first time.

"Yes sir, I do. Not only that, but I got a few ideas about how to make a few more bales of cotton than last year," George said smiling.

"What if I don't agree to all this...stuff? I mean some people would think this is all crazy and will never work. What if I say no?"

"Well, then I'll say thank you for the job offer, and I'll head on back home to my farm," George said.

Mr. Pruitt just sat there nodding his head thinking. He looked at George studying his face and then he looked at his wife. Finally, he stood up and said, "Mr. Kilgo, you have some crazy ideas, but I think they just might work. If you can get this all to work and improve the number of bales of cotton we produce; I will not only pay you what we said, but I will give you a bonus also!" He extended his hand to George. "You, sir, have got a deal. You do as you wish within reason. I give you a free hand."

George stood up and shook his hand.

"There are just a couple of things..." George said. "The slave bosses...I can't use them. They beat and abuse the slaves. I don't think they will take too kindly to going back to being field workers. I been thinking long and hard, but I can't come up with a solution. Ah...they may have to be sold. I mean sent off to be sold. If they are sold to someone around here, you and I both may wake up some night to find them standing over us with a bowie knife...especially Terrell and Big Sammy. Homer, he is okay. The slaves like him. He doesn't beat anyone and I might use him but the other two...do you think you could sell them and maybe replace them with field hands?"

"I agree. I will be glad to take them into town and put them on a train to Mobile. I know my slave broker can get a good price for them," Mr. Pruitt said.

"Moses! Come in here and tell me what you think about what Mr. Kilgo has proposed," Mr. Pruitt yelled toward the door. "Don't pretend you didn't hear us. I know you hear everything and you are always listening," Mr. Pruitt said grinning at his wife and Mr. Kilgo.

Moses came scuffling through the door and over to the table. He looked embarrassed to have been caught listening.

"I's thinks Mr. Kilgo makes a lot of sense. Slaves works harder for a carrot than for a whip. Ah...a man needs to think he's worth someth'n and if'n he is helpin' his wife and family, he feels like someth'n," Moses said scratching his head.

"Moses what would you say to helping run the store?" Mr. Kilgo asked, "If that is alright with Mr. Pruitt?"

"I think that is a wonderful idea," Mrs. Pruitt said, "I could help and make sure everything is working smoothly." Mr. Pruitt nodded in agreement.

"Ah...Moses, I think it would be better if the slaves don't

know that the store is selling them things that they might have gotten anyway. It might...not...help things, and it might take away their reason to work hard," George said looking closely at the old black man.

"I's understands Mr. Kilgo, I understands. I can keep a secret and so can Tee."

"Well, it is all settled then. I'll go into town tomorrow and make arrangements to buy the hogs and staples we will need. I can take Terrell and Big Sammy with me; and while we are there, I'll send a telegraph to my broker, shackle them and put them on a train to Mobile," Mr. Pruitt said.

"I will get things organized here and Moses if you would, could you help me select some new slave bosses? It has to be someone the slaves like and respect, someone that can get them to see the reasons for working hard. I think we need a boss for the field workers and a boss for the ones working the new ground. What do you think Moses?" George asked.

Moses nodded.

"What do you think about Homer for the field hands boss?" George asked.

Again, Moses nodded. "I's think that he's fine. Folks likes him 'cause he try to keeps them from getting beat with the whip. Nathan Whitehouse be liked by most everyone, too. He's might make's a good boss for the slaves working the new ground."

George left the dining room feeling pretty good about how everything went. He was still nervous because he realized a lot could go wrong.

As George was walking among the slave cabins on his way back to his cabin, he heard a strangled cry from one of the cabins. He walked closer to the cabin and peeked through a crack into the dimly lit cabin. Inside, he saw Big Sammy standing on one side of a table holding the hands of a small, light skinned slave girl. She was stretched across the table on her stomach. Terrell stood behind her. As George watched, the girl cried out again, "No! Don't!"

Big Sammy slapped her across the face. *"I's done told you'se to keep's your mouth sh'et! I ain'st gonna tell you'se again."*

Terrell dropped his pants and knife belt to the ground around his feet and jerked the girl's dress up over her waist. It was clear to George what was about to happen. George drew his colt and kicked as hard as he could against the door. It flew open to startled looks from all three people inside the cabin. "Let the girl go!" George said in a firm voice.

"It's okay Captain, she likes it. Mr. Connors been break'n her in fer a week or two, and now we's going to take over," Terrell said looking at George's big colt revolver.

"I said...let...her...go...and pull up your pants!" George said again swinging the gun over to Big Sammy first; and when he released the girl's hands, back to Terrell.

"Su're thing boss, we's don't mean no harm," Big Sammy said while backing up a step. The girl bolted out the door like a scared rabbit as soon as she was loose.

Terrell said, *"Ya'sir boss."* He slowly squatted down like he was going to pull his pants up. George could barely see the butt of the bowie knife sticking out from behind Terrell's leg on the floor with his pants. George kept his eye on the butt of the knife as Terrell reached down. As soon as George saw Terrell's hand grip the handle of the knife; he took a quick step forward and swung the Colt in a backhanded motion, smashing it into the side of Terrell's head knocking him sideways. He stumbled over the pants around his ankles, and the force of the blow. The knife went flying across the room. Terrell fell head first into the rocks of the fireplace. He let out a loud groan; rolled over on his side, and then lay still.

George whirled back around and pointed the revolver into Big Sammy's surprised face. The hand Sammy had moved toward the bowie knife on his belt froze in mid air.

"Don't!" George said sharply.

"*Don't shoot, boss! Don't shoot!*" Big Sammy called out.

"Unbuckle the knife belt, lay it on the table, and move over to the other wall. DO IT NOW!" George said.

"*Ye'sir, I's doing it. Jes' don't shoot me!*" Sammy said.

George took a step over; and using his foot, lightly kicked Terrell to make sure he was out. Blood was seeping from a cut on the side of Terrell's head. Convinced that Terrell was not a threat, George walked over to the door. Sticking his head out, he shouted for someone to come. When a man appeared and peeked in the door, George told him to go to the big house and get Mr. Pruitt; and to have him bring the shackles.

In a few moments, both Pruitts came to the door. Looking over the situation Mr. Pruitt asked what happened. "I caught them with a light skinned young girl stretched out over the table. They were about to rape her," George said.

"Oh, my Gosh! That sounds like Hannah! Where is she?" Mrs. Pruitt asked.

"She took off as soon as they let her go," George said. Mrs. Pruitt left to look for the young slave girl.

"Well, it looks like we will have to deal with these two sooner than we thought," Mr. Pruitt said. He looked over at Terrell who still lay without moving in a pool of blood next to the fireplace. "Did you kill him?"

"No, just gave him a swat to the side of his head," George said.

Pruitt threw the shackles to Big Sammy. "Put them on Terrell and make sure they are on right and tight," Mr. Pruitt said glaring at Big Sammy. "Then you put them on yourself."

"Do you have a place to put them overnight?" George asked.

"Yeah, we can lock them in the cellar of the big house," Pruitt said. They locked the two slave bosses in the cellar. Big Sammy had to help Terrell walk as he was still feeling the effects of getting hit in the head with the big colt revolver.

When they returned to the house, Mrs. Pruitt informed them that Hannah wanted to say something to Mr. Kilgo. The slave girl was shy and embarrassed; she hung her head and George could barely hear her say, *"Thank you for saving me. I's don't like what they's were doing...going to do...to me. They's mean and rough, and they's hurt me. Mr. Connors, he hurt me something awful."*

Mrs. Pruitt explained that Hannah was also being harassed because she was light skinned, and that she would be living with Moses and Tee from now on. It seems her parents had died a couple of years before, and she was living with her uncle and aunt. Her aunt was nice, but her uncle didn't like her because she was so light skinned. He called her a whore and her mother a whore.

George spend the next day getting things organized while Mr. Pruitt took the two slave bosses into town to be sent to Mobile to be sold. He took two wagons with him, and loaded them down with the goods George had requested. Mr. Pruitt made arrangements for the hogs and goats to be delivered to the plantation later in the day.

The whole place was in a buzz at the news of the new overseer; all the changes that Moses had passed along to the slaves, and the disappearance of the two slave bosses. Everywhere George went, he was met with greetings and nods from the slaves. George thought he could see a difference in the way the slaves worked. They were almost joyful in the way they went about their chores.

Later in the day, the hogs arrived and they set to work butchering some of them. That night, the smell of cooking and smoking meat filled the air. For the first time since he had arrived, George heard the sound of laughter from some of the cabins.

CHAPTER SEVEN

George went home that weekend and told Emme all that had happened. She was convinced that it was God's way of showing George that he was doing the right thing in taking the job.

When George arrived back at the plantation after spending two days at home, he was surprised to find that the overseer's cabin had been white washed inside and out. There was new furniture in place, and the whole place had been scrubbed and was sparkling clean.

George set about making some changes to the way things were done on the plantation.

"Homer, would you do me a favor and step off the width of these rows?" George asked when they were behind the lay-off plows.

"Yassir, Mr. Kilgo." Homer stepped off the distance between the rows. The first row was five steps from the second, the second was four from the third; and the third was six from the fourth while the fourth was six and a half from the fifth.

"They is all a little bit different, Mr. Kilgo," Homer said when he was finished stepping them off.

"Which is the best distance?" George asked.

Homer scratched his head, *"I's don't rightly know."*

"Well, I believe the four is about right. It seems to me that we are losing a lot of space because the men on the plows are all spacing the rows differently. Maybe it's the mules, but if we get them all at four, then we gain a couple of feet every few rows. That might mean an extra bale or two of cotton," George said.

Homer nodded as he understood what George was saying.

"Just have a couple of the young boys get some sticks; and then they can measure and mark each row for the plows to follow, and we will gain those extra rows. Also, what is this unplowed space at the end of the rows?" George asked.

"Those is where the mules turn around," Homer said.

George nodded. "Well, when the men are finished with each field, have them go to the back of the field and lay off a few rows from the back to the front of the field. That should gain us another five or six rows and maybe another few bales of cotton."

Homer nodded his head, *"You'se is right Mr. Kilgo. I never thought of that before."*

"Another thing I thought of...how many acres do we have cleared in the new ground?" George asked.

"I guess they is about three or four acres with the trees cut, but they is still a bunch of stumps n' roots in there," Homer said giving George a questioning look.

"How many acres do we plant in corn?"

"We plants about seven acres of corn," Homer said.

"What if we move three or four acres of corn to the new ground? Indians have been planting corn around tree stumps using hoes without plowing for a couple hundred years. That would give us some more acres to plant in cotton," George said.

"Homer, if I show Mr. Pruitt that I can produce more cotton bales than he got last year, then I can keep my job. If I keep my job, then I can make life easier for the slaves...if I get replaced...well, you might get another man like Connors as overseer. Do you understand what I am saying?" George asked.

"Yassir, Mr. Kilgo, I's understand," Homer said nodding his head.

"Do you think you can make the other slaves understand?" George asked.

"I'll make sure da understand...ah Mr. Kilgo...I's sure is glad you is the overseer now."

"Thank you, Homer. There is a whole lot I don't understand yet, but I will try my best. I just need your help and the other bosses too" George said.

Things seemed to move quickly after that first meeting with his field slave boss. The pace of work in the fields seemed to pick up, and the workers on the new ground seemed to be working harder, too.

George supervised the cutting and loading of the first wagon loads of trees to take to the saw mill. The lumber was put to use right away, and the first floors went into the slave cabins. Borax and lime were spread to kill the fleas before the floors were put in place. George was pleased that there were a couple of good carpenters among the slaves.

The rat buying went well. The first day the slaves brought a hundred and twenty-two rats to the big house cellar which was now functioning as the plantation store. Moses took the rats, and recorded the numbers each slave turned in. The idea was that they wouldn't really give out any money; just credit the slaves a half-cent for every dead rat they turned in; but George soon changed his mind.

The second day of the rat buy, an older slave brought in a dozen or so rats. When Moses explained that he didn't really get any money, just credit at the store, he was obviously unhappy. George, who happened to be there, could see he was disappointed.

"Mr. Bones, I can see you are not happy. You realize it is the same thing as giving you the money; when we give you credit, you can buy whatever you want," George said.

Bones nodded his head. *"Yessah, Mr. Kilgo. I's under-stand. Its jest...sometimes a man jest wanna feel de weight of a nickel or dime in his pocket. It reminds him...he's worth some-thin, I jest wanna walk around with money in my pocket. I ain't never had no money ta speak of before,"* Mr. Bones said grinning.

George nodded. He thought Bones had a point. "You're right," George reached into his pocket, pulled out a nickel and a couple of pennies and gave them to Mr. Bones. Bones grinned and pushed them deep into his pocket and left smiling. George went to Mr. Pruitt and explained that they needed to pay out the rats in cash. Mr. Pruitt agreed knowing he would get the money back in a few days.

One day, George asked Tee to make a bunch of biscuits; and at noon Tee and others brought the biscuits and jam into the fields, and all work stopped for thirty minutes while the slaves ate lunch. From then on, every day, work stopped for a lunch break with the understanding that everyone would work harder in the afternoon to make up for the lost time.

George was pleased with the way things were changing on the plantation. Emme believed George was showing signs of being more relaxed when he came home on Saturday or Sunday.

The middle of the next week, a stranger showed up on horseback. He rode up and dismounted where George and Homer were watching the plowing and planting. Holding out his hand to George, he introduced himself.

"You must be Kilgo, the new overseer," he said. "Names Keller, I am the owner of Keller Plantation, located a couple of miles down the road."

"I ran into Mr. Pruitt in Double Springs a few days ago," he explained. "He was telling me about all the changes you are making around here. Some of the things he told me made some sense, but others just seemed plain crazy to me. I wanted to come by and talk to you about them. Pruitt seemed a little vague on some of the details," Mr. Keller said.

"What do you want to know?" George said. "I'll be glad to explain as best I can."

"Well, why don't you start with the difference between the whip and the carrot? I want to make sure I understand. I have over two hundred fifty slaves. Also, I want to know why you are feeding yours so well and treating them so well."

George spent the next thirty minutes explaining how he believed he could get more work out of the slaves by feeding them better, and how keeping them healthy and alive was important. He ended with the rat buy and the plantation store.

Mr. Keller listened carefully and asked questions along the way. When George was finished, Keller gave George a strange look and didn't say anything for a few moments. Finally, he pulled off his straw hat and wiped his brow. He narrowed his eyes and said, "Kilgo, I don't know if you are a genius or a lunatic. Giving slaves money seems crazy to me. The rest of the stuff seems to make sense. I lose a lot of slaves every year so keeping them alive longer seems smart. I just got to think on all this a while."

George smiled. "Just remember, you will get back any money you give them because they don't have anywhere to spend it except at your store."

Keller nodded, "I may need you to come over to my place and explain all this to my overseers."

"I'll be glad to when I can," George said.

The two men shook hands and Mr. Keller started to ride off, when George thought of something.

"Mr. Keller!" George called out after Keller, who turned his horse back and rode the few feet back to George.

"Mr. Keller, do you have any slaves who might speak African?" George asked. "I got four new slaves who don't speak English, and I would like to be able to at least speak to them a little."

"I got a couple. I'll be glad to loan you one. You can get one when you come to talk to my overseers," Mr. Keller said. George thanked him and made plans to go the very next day to Keller's place.

George was up early and after letting the slave bosses know that he would be gone most of the day, he rode off toward the Keller Plantation.

The Keller place was a few minutes away, and George was amazed at the size of the place. The fields went on forever; rows seeming to disappear into the distance. There were slaves everywhere. They were repeating the processes of the Pruitt Plantation, but there were more of them plowing and planting.

George asked a slave where to find Mr. Keller. He was directed to a back field where Mr. Keller and a couple of men who George believed to be the overseers, were standing talking.

"Ah... Mr. Kilgo, it is good to see you again," Mr. Keller said when he saw George. "I guess you are pretty eager to talk to my men."

"Well...I am eager to get someone to talk to my new slaves. I would really like to ask your men some questions about how they run things here." George said.

Keller nodded. George spent the next half hour asking questions: What happened if a slave got sick and couldn't work? What happens to those women who get pregnant and can't work? What happens to families when someone dies? Do they take off for the burial of the dead? Do the slaves have church? Do they get married? George had a lot of questions. Only when George had answers to his questions did he finally begin to answer some of their questions.

"I only began this overseer job a week or so ago, I don't know anything about how to run a plantation," George said. "I just had this idea that the slaves would work harder if they got rewarded for their work."

George went into the "carrot versus whip" story then, an explanation of the plantation store, and finished with the advantage of keeping the slaves alive longer. When he was finished, the overseers were all looking at each other and scratching their heads.

Finally one of them spoke, "Well, that is just the craziest thing I ever heard. Slaves don't have enough sense to understand the idea of rewards. They only understand that if they don't work, they feel the whip," the man said. The rest of the overseers seemed to agree. They all looked to George to see how he was going to take that.

George pulled his hat off, and wiping his forehead with his sleeve said, "Well, I guess I will just have to find out if it'll work or not. My slaves seem to know the meaning of rewards, and they seem to work harder than they did when they were getting the whip."

Mr. Keller spoke up and said, "First, we are going to try the store part, and we'll see about the rest, when I have had some time to think about it." The overseers all mumbled and groaned that they didn't think it would work.

When they all left George and Keller alone, Mr. Keller laughed and said, "Mr. Kilgo, what you are talking and teaching is not something that Southern men want to think about. I see the slaves and they bleed just like we do, and they laugh and feel just like we do. Now, I don't know if my men are ready to believe that, but I think maybe it is time to see if they can learn some things about slaves being more like us than they want to admit. Times are changing, and if cotton prices go up like they say they are then, we better be learning how to get the most out of the land. Now let's go find you a slave that speaks African."

The two men rode over to another field, and Mr. Keller called out for someone name Wana. A small thin black girl put down her hoe, turned and came over to where the men sat on their horses.

"Wana, this here is Mr. Kilgo. He is from the Pruitt Plantation, and he needs someone who speaks African to go over to his place and speak to some new arrivals," Mr. Keller said.

The young woman flashed a big smile to the men and said, "Well, I will do my best; but Mr. Keller, you realize that there are about two dozen different languages spoken in Africa, and chances are they still won't understand me."

George was amazed at the way the young woman spoke. Her English was perfect and with only a hint of an accent. George got down from his horse and walked toward the young women extending his hand.

"It is nice to meet you...ah...Wana is it?" George said.

She looked at George's hand, and then shook it. "Wana is what everyone calls me," she said.

"Well, what is your real name?" George asked.

The girl smiled and said, "My real name is TaWanaju-damooca. Now do you see why they call me Wana?" she said with a giggle.

"I guess I'll have to call you Wana, too," George said returning her smile. "If I could ask, where did you learn to speak such perfect English?"

"My parents died when I was very young, and I was raised by Christian Missionaries. I learned to speak English, French, and a little German," she said. "I can also speak two different African dialects so maybe I can help you.

George shook his head, "How...I mean how...why are you a slave?"

"I was going to another village for a visit with my married sister when we were taken by slavers. I tried to tell them who I was; but they wouldn't listen, and here I am," Wana said with a far-away look in her eyes.

George just shook his head and looked at Mr. Keller.

"Don't look at me! I didn't know what to make of her when she came up on the auction block. I had to out bid several other buyers when she started speaking that perfect English. No one knew what to make of her or what to do with her...my wife insisted that we buy her," Mr. Keller gave a sigh and shrugged his shoulders. "Now...well, my wife thinks...that I like Wana...ah...maybe a little too much," Mr. Keller gave Wana a look that George recognized; it was the same look he gave his Emme sometimes. Wana gave Mr. Keller the same look back; George began to understand.

"Maybe it would be better if Wana stayed with you over at the Pruitt place for a while...that is, if she can help you,"

Mr. Keller said. "Just for a few weeks...to let the wife cool off a little. I'm sorry Wana, but you understand don't you?"

Wana looked very sad, but she nodded her head. "Can I go to my cabin and get some things?" Mr. Keller nodded yes.

"Tell me about these slaves you want me to talk to," Wana said as they left Mr. Keller. George pulled Wana up behind him on Dolly and they rode off toward the Pruitt Plantation.

"There are two men and two women, but I don't think they speak the same languages," George explained.

"What do they look like?" Wana asked.

"One of the men has these funny bead-like marks on his forehead. They are all the way across his face. He is tall and skinny, with long legs and arms," George said.

"That sounds like he might be a Maasai," Wana said.

"Do you know that language?" George asked.

"Yes, they speak Maa, which is like Dinka that my tribe speaks, so I should be able to speak with him," Wana said.

"What about this...ah... Maasai? Is that a tribe or what?" George asked.

"It is a tribe. They are cattle herders and hunters. They are very fearsome warriors, and are much feared by everyone. My tribe used to be enemies with them, but they always defeated us in battle. Our warriors say it takes three of our warriors to kill one Maasai warrior. They use spears and big shields that protect them. They throw war clubs called orinkas that are very deadly. They can kill people with one from a hundred meters away. Our chief made peace with them, and formed an alliance with them because we could not defeat them," Wana said.

George nodded, "What else do you know about them?"

"They are wanderers who wonder around following the grass for their cows. They live off the cattle. They drink the cow's milk mixed with the cow's blood. It makes them very strong. Their enemies are the lions that kill their cattle. When a boy becomes a man about fifteen or so, he must decide if he wants to be a warrior. If he wants to be a warrior, they pull the skin on their foreheads out and push a thorn through the skin. That is what makes the beads on the skin. After the skin heals around the thorn, it is pulled out and it leaves the bead behind."

"Wow! That sounds painful," George said.

"Yes, it is very painful...it is a test to see if the boy is ready to be a warrior. If he can stand the pain, he is ready to become a warrior. If he passes that test, then he must kill a lion. He chooses two trusted friends, and they go into the grass lands to find a lion."

"What is this lion like? Are they like a bobcat or cougar?" George asked.

Wana looked shocked. "No they are very big and dangerous. They are almost as big as a cow, and have teeth and claws this long," Wana held her fingers about four inches apart. "They kill and eat many people every year."

"Well, they must be good shots if they can kill such an animal," George said.

"No!" Wana said looking shocked again. "They don't have guns. They must kill them with just a spear. They get the lion to charge them; and when it leaps on them, they squat and hold the spear with the end stuck in the ground. If it works right, the lion lands on the spear. Sometimes it doesn't work right and the lion is only wounded. Then their friends must try to kill the lion before it kills them. Many young Maasai have been killed trying to kill their lion."

George just shook his head, "And these lions are as big as cows?"

"The males are almost as big as a bull, and they are the ones that attack most often. The big males try to protect their family, and they charge the men," Wana said. George listened intently as Wana talked on and on, all the way back to the plantation. George wondered how it was fair that such a smart woman could be held a slave.

When they reached the Pruitt's Plantation, George took her to the new ground, where he knew the new slaves were working. As they neared the workers, Wana said, "Can I just watch them for a few minutes before we say anything?"

George nodded his consent. They dismounted Dolly, and just stood several yards away watching the slaves work. George could see that the Maasai was a head taller than the others. George had thought he was skinny; but he now could tell that he was very strong, all muscle and sinew. The ax he was swinging made a different sound than the others when it hit the log he was chopping. He was naked from the waist up, and his body was covered with lines of beads and marks similar to those on his forehead. George also noticed five large scars on his back. They were several inches long and went from his back around to his side.

Wana watched him from the back for a few minutes. Finally, she walked around to the front so she could see him better. Suddenly, she froze in place. Her mouth opened and her eyes bugged out and opened wide, with the whites showing all around. She turned to George and gave him a look.

"Mr. George, he is indeed a Maasai warrior, but...a very special one. See the lines of beads on his chest...the right side. Those lines mean he is royalty. This man is the first prince of the Maasai tribe. That means he would be the king when his father dies," Wana said. "Those other lines on the other side of his chest mean he has killed not one, but three lions. From the look of the scars on his back one almost killed him, too. Mr. George this man has been trained from birth to be king.

He has been trained to fight and kill; he could be very dangerous."

Wana spoke to the man in a strange language. His head went up and he stopped the ax in mid stroke. He turned to face George and Wana. Wana bent over slightly and lowered her head and eyes. The man looked down at her and a small smile came to his lips. He spoke back to Wana in this funny sing, song language. Wana looked up and smiled at him, and spoke back. George couldn't make out any of what she was saying, but one time he thought he heard her say her name.

"He says his name is Matoomba, and he asks your name. He says you are a very good man...that you stop people from hurting others...he also says he wants to go home," Wana explained to George.

George pulled off his hat and ran his fingers through his hair. "Tell him...tell him that this is his home now. Tell him... that the many days he spent on the ocean...in the boat...means that he can never go home...and...tell him, I am sorry." George watched his face as Wana told him all these things. He looked from Wana to George and back several times as he tried to understand what these things meant. Then he spoke more to Wana in a rapid manner for several minutes...the words seemed to just pour out of his mouth. Finally, after several minutes of talking, he stopped and waited for Wana to translate what he had said to George.

"He says that if this is now his path; he will follow it as best he can, but he begs you to let him hunt. He says he will be your protector, if you will let him fight for you," Wana explained. "He says the men that took him killed six men to take him and his sister. He says he can't understand this. Why he is made to work so others can do nothing."

George looked closely at the man. He was struck at how black he was. Wana was black, and many of the slaves were dark, but this man was the darkest of all. He had a high fore-head with very close cropped hair and very sharp features. His eyes were dark brown almost black in color, which made the whites seem even whiter.

"Tell him...I will have to see if I can work things out so he can go hunting...and if I have the need...I will be glad to have him protect me." George finished speaking and reached out his hand to the man who looked at it, then extended his hand also. George took his hand and the two men looked each other in the eyes. George tried to say the man's name as they shook hands. Wana giggled at George's attempt. She then corrected him by saying Ma-toom-ba very slowly. George repeated the name again and did much better this time. Matoomba gave him a smile and nodded his head.

One of the female slaves, who had been with them the first day, had been close by, watching and listening. Now she stepped forward and spoke to Wana who gave a little squeal and moved to the girl. They hugged and talked rapidly in that strange language for a couple of minutes.

"Mr. George, this is Ceenahtomoma, she is Matoomba's half sister," Wana said. George stepped forward and offered her his hand which she timidly took.

"Does that mean she is a princess and future queen?" George asked.

"No, the princess would be Matoomba's wife. Only the men are able to rule," Wana said.

"Well, what happens if there are no male children? Would a woman rule then?"

Wana laughed. "The king has many wives and many chil-dren; there is always a male to take over."

George tried to say the girl's name, but stumbled badly. Wana tried to break it down for him, but he couldn't seem to get it right.

Finally, the girl giggled and said something to Wana. "She said to just call her Cee. Also, she is very sad and lonely for her home and family." George just nodded.

The girl spoke to Wana and pointed to another girl and man who were standing by now; all the slaves were watching and listening to Wana and the slaves.

Wana stepped over to these two slaves and spoke with them. After a few minutes she said, "These two speak a different language, but a few words are the same as Dinka, so they can understand a little."

It was late in the day now, about an hour before sun down. George looked at the slaves who were all looking at him and the new slaves now. Finally, George said, "Well, I guess we can quit for the day."

Wana looked at George and asked, "Can I please stay with Matoomba and his sister?"

"I think that is a great idea." Turning to the other slaves, "Ya'll go now and rest a little before supper," George said. They all smiled and some said, "Thank you, Master George."

George couldn't wait to tell Mr. and Mrs. Pruitt about the break through with the new slaves and inform them they had a very special slave in their mist. Mrs. Pruitt was excited about the idea of meeting these people. She listened intently as George told what he had learned. She wanted to invite them to supper right away.

"Ah...I don't think they are ready for that yet. I don't know if Matoomba can be trusted yet. I will need to learn a little more about him first. I think you would like to meet Wana though. She seems to be an exceptional young woman," George said.

"I agree," Mr. Pruitt said. "I am not ready to have slaves at my dinner table just yet." Mr. Pruitt gave his wife a look. "Maybe you can meet her somewhere else."

Mr. Pruitt was about half drunk by now. It was an almost nightly occurrence. If he was home, he started drinking right after dark and continued until supper ended and he staggered off to bed.

George and Mrs. Pruitt had to put him to bed tonight. He was not able to walk without help. When he was in bed, there was an awkward moment when George and Mrs. Pruitt were very close together. It passed quickly as they both pulled back.

George made his excuses and walked back toward the overseer cabin. As he walked, he could hear the sounds of the camp. There were more people out and about now. The slaves had a little more energy now that they were eating better. They had taken to spending some time after dark sitting around fires talking, laughing and joking around.

Someone was playing a homemade fiddle and another one was playing a homemade banjo. Some slaves were jumping and dancing around. George walked around the edge of the area, just watching and listening.

He could see Wana, Matoomba, Cee and the others sitting together and talking. George looked across the clearing and could see there were other slaves looking at the group, and it seemed they were talking about them. George walked around closer while still staying in the shadows until he could hear what the other slaves were saying.

"*That fool don't be looking like no prince like I've ever seen,*" the biggest one said.

"*And how many princes have you'se ever seen?*" another one said laughing.

"*Hell, I's ain't never seen no princes; buts I see'd a lot of stupid Africans, and this one looks like a stupid African to me,*" the big one said. "*And that little whore, she sayin' he done killed a lion, I's bet he ain't never even see'd a lion, much'n less killed one. And he's got them' stupid looking bumps on his face!"*

"He is purd'er than you!" the other one said. *"Jest look at how that little one be'a droolin' all over him. I's bets you be'a wish that was you!"*

"She's don't know what she be'a missing!" the big one said laughing.

George was about to move on when the talk took on a meaner tone.

"I's don't give a damn what they be'a say'n, that skinny boy ain't no prince and he's ain't never see'd no lion much'n less killed no lion. He's jest thinks he be better than us. I bets that little gal, she's jest trying to get'n him in her bed and she be make'n all dat stuff up," the big one said speaking very loudly.

"Shush...not so loud, you'se want them 'a hear'in you.

"I's don't cares if'n they's hear me. What's he gon'na do? I's whup his skinny black African ass."

Matoomba, his sister and Wana rose and started to walk across the area toward their cabin. The big slave, who was talking loud, rose and walked toward them, blocking their path.

"Hey! African boy! You'se think'n you'se be better'n all the rest of us! You'se thinks you'se gon'na come in here'n strut'n around like some's kind of king?" He asked in a loud voice. Everyone stopped talking and watched, sensing something was about to happen.

"You know he doesn't understand what you are saying," Wana said turning to try to get by them.

"Oh, he's may not know's them words, but he's knows what I' is saying," the big slave said. He put his hand out and pushed against Matoomba's chest.

Matoomba looked down at the hand on his chest. George thought he could see a smile on the edges of Matoomba's lips.

"I wouldn't do that if I were you," Wana said.

"Get's the hell out of my's way, you'se little whore," the bigger slave said, feeling embolden by having his two buddies beside him. He pushed Wana with his other hand, while pushing Matoomba again in the chest.

George started to move in and break things up, before they got out of hand. As he was stepping forward out of the shadows, things happened so fast he could hardly follow them.

Matoomba reached up with his left hand and grabbed the man's arm that was on his chest and pulled it down and away; twisting the arm so hard it pulled the man's whole body down and forward. At the same time, he brought his right hand upward and struck the man with the web of his hand, the part between the thumb and fore finger. Matoomba struck the man right in the Adam's apple of his throat. George thought he could hear a crunch.

It was like a snake strike, it was so fast George and those watching could hardly see it. The man's eyes bugged out and he grabbed his throat and started making gagging noises while falling to his knees.

His buddy came in swinging a round house right aimed at Matoomba's head. Matoomba stepped toward the man and raised his left arm blocking and causing the man's punch to go past Matoomba and across his back. Matoomba grabbed the arm and rotated his body into the man. Bending over quickly, he threw the man over his hip and body. The man's feet left the ground and went straight up in the air. He flew up in the air, over Matoomba and slammed into the ground with a loud thud. Before anyone could grasp what had happened, Matoomba spun around and used his heel to smash into the pit of the man's stomach. There was a loud groan and a whish of air that rushed out of the man. His eyes rolled back in his head until only the whites were showing.

The third man, seeing what had happened to his friends, decided to play the bull and rushed Matoomba with his head down and his arms out, planning to tackle him. Matoomba waited until he was right on him; drew both hands up above his head and slammed them down into the back of the man's head. The first thing to hit the ground was the man's chin. He slid forward with his arms limp at his sides, instantly unconscious.

It all happened in less than five seconds. Before anyone could react to the scene, the first man had started to regain his feet. He was still holding his throat and making gagging noises as he tried to get air into his constricted windpipe. The man drew Matoomba's attention now, and he stepped to the only attacker still conscious. He had just taken hold of the arm the man held out to ward off Matoomba when George stepped into the opening and called out Matoomba's name. When he looked at George, George shook his head and said, "No!" Matoomba dropped the man's arm and nodded toward George; then, turned and walked away leaving everyone stunned at what they had seen.

As they walked away, Wana said, "I told you not to do it."

George stayed around and helped the dazed slaves back to consciousness. He called for some water and splashed a little on the two who were unconscious. When they could sit up, and the one with a constricted windpipe stopped gagging, George addressed them.

"I don't think you want to be messing around with that African. If I hadn't been here, he might have killed you. He has been trained to kill since he was very small, and is very dangerous, so you better stay clear of him. Do you understand?" George asked. The men all nodded.

George looked around at the faces of the other slaves standing around. They all heard what George said and several nodded their heads also. Everyone marveled at what they had just seen. Three large men had been knocked out in just seconds by a tall, skinny, African.

CHAPTER EIGHT

The next day about noon, George went to the new ground where Matoomba and the Africans were working. "Good morning," he called out to Wana. "Ya'll come with me. Tell Matoomba I am taking him to the blacksmith to make some spears so he can hunt."

Wana relayed this to Matoomba who broke into a wide smile. As they started to walk with George, Matoomba stopped and went over to a stack of brush. He reached into the brush and pulled out two wooden spears about six and a half feet long. They were about an inch around and sharpened on one end. He also pulled out two pieces of wood about three feet long and about eight inches around. As the group looked questioningly to Wana, she interpreted as Matoomba spoke.

"He says they are for spears and orinkas."

George could see that Matoomba had already been working on crudely carving the wood into weapons. George felt relieved that he had made friends with this man.

Cee called out to them and spoke to Wana. "Cee is afraid

to stay here by herself. She has never been separated from her brother. She wants to know if she can come, too."

"Of course," George said, "tell her to come."

George took them to the blacksmith whom George had spoken to earlier. He was a short thick man with well muscled arms from all the hammering and work with heavy metal. His name was Luke, and he quickly showed Matoomba around the blacksmith shop. In a matter of minutes, Matoomba had selected some metal, heated it and was hammering on it with a hammer. Luke watched and showed him some things, but overall he didn't need much instruction. Wana interpreted instructions between Luke and Matoomba. "This is not the first time he has done this," Luke said while watching him work.

George took Cee and led her a few yards away to where some women were washing clothes in a large black wash pot. He instructed the women to show her what to do and to treat her nice because she didn't understand the language. In a few minutes, she was more relaxed although she still kept an eye on her brother working a few yards away.

When George returned later, near the end of the day, Matoomba had fashioned two spear heads about ten inches long. They were hammered to razor sharp edges with very sharp points. Each had a tang about eight or ten inches long. Matoomba was shaping the wooden spears with a draw knife and a coarse type of sand paper.

George got busy on other things and didn't check in on Matoomba for a couple of days. One day, a young slave boy came to George and said, "Luke would like you to come by the blacksmith shop today, when you can."

When George arrived at the shop, it was empty. He heard voices out back so he went out there. When Luke spotted him, he came rushing over.

"You'se have got to see this!" he excitedly said.

Matoomba was standing there with Wana and holding two spears. Nearby, on the ground lay two clubs that George took to be orinkas. Luke motioned to Matoomba, to throw the spears. Matoomba took a spear and stepped back a couple of steps and launched the spear upward in a high arch, fifteen to twenty feet in the air. The spear flew straight and true, turned downward and ended by sticking into a tree stump about sixty yards away.

"You ever see'd anything like that?" Luke exclaimed. *"Damn'est thing I ever see'd! "Do it again!"* Luke said. *"Back more,"* he said as he guided Matoomba back another ten spaces or so. Again, Matoomba threw the spear, and again it flew up and then stuck into the tree stump.

"Toby set's up the bucket," Luke called out to his young helper who was standing by the tree stump. The young man picked up a metal bucket, set it up on the stump, and then walked a few feet away. Luke pointed to the clubs laying on the ground and made throwing motions to Matoomba.

Matoomba picked up one of the clubs and walked forward to their original position about fifty or sixty yards away from the target. He took two hopping steps forward and released the orinka in an over head, throwing motion. The club was about two and a half feet long and had a smooth handle with a large knot-like head on one end. The club flipped end over end for a few turns and then settled into a straight line, with the large knot leading the way. It also sailed upward first and then downward to the target. The club crashed into the bucket with a loud clang, sending the bucket winding across the yard.

Luke shook his head, *"Ain't that the damn craziest thing you ever see'd!"* Luke picked up the other club and handed it to George. *"Here you try it. I can't get it half way there."*

George turned the club over and ran his hand over it. It was smooth and surprisingly heavy, with the head very heavy. George held the handle of the club and made a couple of practice motions before trying to throw it toward the bucket Toby had reset. George's throw only traveled about half way to the target. It was truly amazing that Matoomba could throw the club so far.

They walked to the thrown club and picked it up. Matoomba again held the club, drew back and from this shorter distance unleashed a mighty throw. The bucket flew up into the air and went flying off the stump. When Toby picked it up, it had two huge dents in it where the orinkas had struck the bucket.

"Wow!" George said running his hand over the smashed bucket.

"Now do you see why our warriors couldn't defeat the Maasai," Wana said, walking toward the men. George could only nod and imagine what damage a thrown club or spear would do to a man.

CHAPTER NINE

When George went home a week or two later, on a Saturday, he noticed a different horse in the corral. Out near the barn he saw a buckboard. When he dismounted and approached the porch, Emme and Cindy Bates greeted him.

"Well, hello again," George said smiling at them.

"Oh! Mr. Kilgo, it is so good to see you again. I loved meeting your family, your sweet wife and kids," Cindy said smiling. "Royal insisted that we bring the gun to you as soon as it was finished. He has been hobbling around, working on it day and night for the last few weeks."

Emme smiled and added, "It has been wonderful having another woman to talk and laugh with. I'm so glad ya'll come to visit." Just then, Royal came around the side of the house with all the boys and Liz tagging after him. They were all laughing about something Royal had said.

"Mr. Kilgo, it is good to see you. I hope you don't mind that we dropped in on you like this. I just had to bring the new gun to you as soon as it was finished," Royal said coming over to shake George's hand. "We didn't mean to be here over night. We just planned to drop the gun off and then spend the night at Looney's; but since you were not here, Emme insisted we stay over and give it to you in person. I must say, I love your kids. They make me want to have a bunch of my own."

George smiled and rubbed the head of his youngest. "Yeah, they make me feel the same way...not about having a bunch more, but...I love to be here with them," George said.

"Lunch is ready so let's all eat; and then, you men can try out the new gun," Emme said.

They ate a wonderful meal; then, Royal went over to the corner and pulled out a long package wrapped in white cloth. He handed it to George who unwrapped it to reveal the gun underneath. It was long and heavy.

"Wow, it sure is heavy," George said hefting the gun. "What caliber?"

"It is a fifty caliber. Large enough to drop just about anything you want to shoot," Royal explained.

It had a shine to the black barrel and the wood of the stock was shiny light brown with darker stripes in the wood. There were shiny brass pieces on the butt and around the barrel in different places. George pulled it to his shoulder and pointed it toward the wall. "It is really nice. I can't wait to shoot it. You really didn't have to do this, but I am thrilled to see it."

"Wait till you shoot it," Royal said. "You won't believe how accurate it is."

George passed the gun around to the boys who ooohed and ahhhed over it. He had to help the small ones hold it, it was so heavy. While the women cleared the table, the men and boys went around to the back of the house to try out the gun.

Royal had set up targets of firewood standing on end at different distances. The first one was about a hundred yards away. The next about twice that distance, and another one was so far away George could barely see it. Royal gave George a leather pouch filled with strange silver looking cartridges. He took one out and handed it to George.

"These are the latest bullets and loads which are a type of thin metal that wraps the powder. You load it just like the others, but it has the powder already measured, and the metal makes the bullet fly straighter and faster," Royal explained.

George loaded the cartridge into the barrel and tamped it down with the rod. He placed a cap on the nipple of the gun and cocked the hammer. "Which one...?" He asked.

"Try the nearest one first; then, we will go for the longer ones," Royal said. George held the heavy rifle up to his shoulder and looked down the barrel. "Do I allow any up or down?" he asked.

"No, it should be dead on at this distance...really at all three of these distances."

George took a deep breath and let it half out, lined the sights up on the fire wood and slowly squeezed the trigger. Everyone jerked at the sound of the roar of the gun. It was shockingly loud. The stick of firewood splintered on one end and flipped over.

"Good shot!" Royal exclaimed, "You got a good eye and steady hand."

"It is going to take some getting used to...the weight of it... holding it steady," George said.

George handed it to Will who was anxious to hold it. He put it to his shoulder and struggled to get it steady while looking down the barrel and aiming it at the next target. He could only hold it steady for a short period of time.

"Do you want to load it?" George asked Will, who nodded and smiled. Will carefully took the cartridge, placed it into the barrel of the gun and tamped it down. He selected a cap and placed it on the nipple and handed the gun to his father.

The little ones held their hands over their ears as George raised the big gun and took aim at the next target. Again, the stick of wood flipped over, as George hit the target. He pulled the gun down and held it out looking at it in amazement. He had never been able to hit anything the size of a stick of firewood at two hundred yards, yet this gun made it seem easy.

Royal smiled and said, "I told you. This gun is dead on accurate."

They reloaded it and George aimed at the dimly visible stick of wood. It was so far away, he could barely make it out. He squeezed off the shot and for a second thought he had missed. The stick of wood spun around and fell over.

They stepped the distance off as they walked down to look at the damage to the wood. George was amazed that he could hit something at these distances. The fifty caliber bullet had ripped open and splintered the wood. The nearest two were both hit near dead center at the top, right where George was aiming. The one that was so far away, George had missed a little to the right of center, yet it was still a hit.

They re-set the targets and repeated the shots again, three times. Each time, George was dead on target. Royal and Will took a turn. Both of them hit the nearest target easily. Royal hit all three, but Will missed the longest target.

George was concerned about using all the cartridges up, but Royal insisted they let the younger boys, Sam and John Wesley, take a turn. Neither of them could hold the big gun steady enough to hit the target, but they were thrilled to get to shoot it. Little Tom begged to try and with George holding the gun steady he got off a shot. They all laughed when he fell backward on his butt from the kick of the gun.

They were about to call the practice over when Liz came out and wanted to take a turn. After a little instruction, she loaded and fired the gun. She too was able to hit the target at the hundred yard marker. Finally, they were finished with the target practice.

George was amazed at the accuracy of the weapon. Royal explained that the heavy octagon barrel had been bored with more spirals, causing the bullet to spin at high speeds, allowing it to travel through the air with greater accuracy. George thanked Royal again for the gun. Royal gave George several sheets of the metal/paper for making the special cartridges, a measuring tool, several pounds of lead, and a bullet mold for making the fifty caliber bullets the gun fired. Royal and Cindy left them with the promise to visit again soon.

When George and Emme were in bed that night, Emme asked George why he didn't tell her about stripping Cindy the day he saved her. George blushed and said, "I didn't really think you would appreciate being told that. Besides I didn't really take a good look at her."

Emme rose up on one elbow and looked at George in the dim light. "George you are a terrible liar. You want me to believe that you stripped naked a seventeen year old, and you never even looked at her...not even a little?"

"Well...maybe I took a little look. I mean how many times do you get a chance to see something like that? I can say this, she hasn't got anything on you in that department," George said.

"Now you are just trying to talk me into letting you have your way with me," Emme said giggling.

"Is it working?" George asked.

"Why don't you try me and see," Emme said.

Before George left to go back to the Pruitt's place he gave Will the old musket and told him to be really careful with it, to keep it loaded and hanging over the fireplace, but to not put a cap on it until he needed to use it.

A couple of weeks after they made the spears, which George had to insist remain in the blacksmith shop, he was ready to take Matoomba and a couple of other trusted slaves hunting.

Mr. Pruitt gathered his hunting dogs; and they gave shotguns to two slaves, and an old musket to another. Mounted on mules, Matoomba and Wana, who had been teaching Matoomba to ride, joined the group. They rode into the woods, behind the swamp and turned the dogs loose. In a few minutes, the dogs struck a trail and set out on the chase. About ten minutes after that, the dogs started barking excitingly, indicating that they had something cornered.

When the hunters arrived at the scene, they found three large wild hogs standing on a slight rise with their backs to a downed tree's roots. There was a large boar hog that must have weighed six or seven hundred pounds. He was a large brute with long tusks that extended five or six inches out both sides of his mouth. A large sow that was only slightly smaller than the male also had large tusks. The third hog, also with large tusks was probably their offspring and weighted maybe three hundred pounds. They all had huge heads and coarse black hair that was now standing up on their backs.

The dogs were worrying them and dashing in and out, snapping and barking at the hogs. As the hunting party watched one dog got too close and the big boar whirled around, scooped the dog up on its tusk and threw him several feet into the air. It landed with a whine and stumbled to its feet, showing a large gash in its side.

The men shifted about on their horses, trying to decide what to do. Matoomba spoke to Wana and she said, "Matoomba wants to take them." George looked at the others and said, "Okay, just tell him to be careful. They are dangerous and tough to kill." Wana spoke to him and he nodded.

Matoomba got down from the mule and started to move toward the hogs. He was holding the two spears and wearing the bowie knife that George had given him before they started out. The two orinkas were tied together and hanging over the saddle of the mule, unneeded for this task.

Matoomba moved forward until the hogs got real nervous and started to stir around, threatening to run again. Matoomba stopped and moved back and forth, shifting the hogs around. When the smallest one turned sideways to him, he pulled back the spear and let it fly. It hit the hog in the side just behind the front leg. It was thrown with such force; it went all the way through the hog and a little was sticking out the other side.

The hog let out a blood curdling squeal and seemed to jump straight up. It turned its head down and bit at the shaft of the spear sticking out of it. It whirled around in circles two or three times, ran about twenty steps to the left, away from the hunters and crashed to the ground.

The sow saw its offspring in pain gave a loud grunt and suddenly charged Matoomba. For a large animal, it moved with remarkable speed. George raised his new rifle and was about to fire when he saw Matoomba raise the second spear up over his head with two hands. George held his fire and just watched, fearing what might happen to Matoomba.

The huge sow charged with its head down ready to scoop Matoomba up on the large tusks. Just as it came to within a couple of steps of him, Matoomba jumped into the air and plunged the spear down with both hands. The spear went into the hog just behind the large head. About three feet of the spear disappeared into the hog which now threw its head up and gave a squeal that caused George's hair to stand on end. The force of the sow's charge and the thrust his spear, threw Matoomba up into the air. He rolled over the hog's back; hit the ground, rolled over and to his feet as he pulled the big bowie knife, almost in the same motion. It was like he knew what was coming next...the huge male boar!

With its mate and offspring gone, the boar charged at the man who had attacked them. This was six hundred plus pounds of mad hog. He lowered his head meaning to destroy the enemy. It also moved with amazing speed for such a large animal. He took a dozen or so steps toward Matoomba when George fired his rifle. The big fifty caliber bullet flew fast and true, striking the hog somewhere near the front shoulder, the big bullet crumbled it to the ground.

All of this took place in a matter of seconds, in a din of barking dogs and snarling hogs. Matoomba stood dazed for a few seconds staring at the huge hog lying about ten feet from him. It was breathing its last breaths while the other two were still. Suddenly, Matoomba started to jump and shout and dance around.

The whole group watched amazed at the whole scene; but mainly at the skill with which Matoomba had taken out the two hogs. George got down off Dolly and walked through the barking dogs to where the large boar lay. He smiled at Matoomba and reached for the bowie knife. Taking it from Matoomba's hand, he cut off the ears of the big boar, the sow and the younger hog and presented them to Matoomba who began to chant in that strange sing, song language, and dance around again. When George looked up at the others, they were all smiling. You couldn't help but get swept up in the joy Matoomba was expressing.

The hunters slit the throats of the hogs to bleed them, and rode back to the plantation for the wagons and more men to help load and haul the huge beast back to the plantation to be butchered. George had them leave the spears in the hogs so the others could see Matoomba's handiwork.

In the coming days, everywhere George went on the plantation, he saw young slave boys practicing throwing spears made of cattails, reeds and sticks of all kind. Matoomba had become a hero.

CHAPTER TEN

On a weekend trip home, as they were riding in the wagon back from church, Emme said, "George, I've been thinking."

George winched and made a face. Usually when Emme was thinking, it meant there was something she wanted George to do.

"George, I know you have been working hard to improve the lives of the slaves, but I wonder...what have you done about their souls?" Emme asked. George just gave her a look that said, 'What do you mean?'

"George, do they have church and a chance to save their souls?" Emme asked.

George paused, "There are people who would say that they don't have souls."

"And they would be wrong," Emme said. "They are children of God just like we are. You have to find a way to give them the chance to be saved."

George frowned, "What if Mr. Pruitt doesn't agree?"

"Then you will have to find a way to change his mind. I

am sure Mary Pruitt will agree that they need to have church. I am sure you will find a way to make it happen; it is your Christian duty," Emme said. George just shook his head. Damn it! Emme could sure make things complicated.

George went back to the Pruitt Plantation. He spent the ride over trying to figure how to convince Mr. Pruitt to let the slaves have church. When he arrived at the plantation, he sought out a couple of friendly slaves and asked how they felt about going to church. They gave each other a look. When one started to say something, the other cut him off and said they thought that would be fine; but they doubted Mr. Pruitt would agree. George nodded and went on his way.

Later, just before supper, George asked Moses what he thought about trying to find a way to get Mr. Pruitt to let the slaves have time to attend a church.

Moses gave George a long look. *"Ah...I's don't know what to say."*

"Well, I's know what to say," Tee said coming around the corner of the kitchen where they were talking. *"Go on, tell him what you been doin' for all these years."*

Moses gave her a hard look, sighed and turned to George. *"I's been preaching some, when the others want me to,"* Moses said. George looked surprised.

"I's...we...sometimes go somewhere's off in the woods, and I's just talk a little about what God wants for his people, and how bein' a slave is just a part of the suffering we's has to do to get to heaven," Moses said. George looked at Moses and Tee.

"How long...and why haven't I heard about this before?" George asked.

"Well, most folks don't want no slaves getting no religion... afraid if'n we get together, we'll get all stirred up and might rebel and go around killin' our master and all, like some slaves

did before," Moses said. *"We's don't do it but about once a month, and we has to do it late at night to keep from being found out. Most folks too tired to come anyways, jus' some of the women and a few of the men. If'n we gets caught, we would gets a beatin' so most folks afraid to come."*

George nodded. He had made up his mind he would take it up with Mr. and Mrs. Pruitt tonight at supper.

When they had finished eating and Mr. Pruitt was on his third or fourth whiskey, George asked, "Mr. Pruitt have you ever considered letting the slaves have a church service once in a while?"

Mr. Pruitt looked shocked, "No, I haven't. Why would I do something crazy like that? I know you are new to being around slaves so...you probably haven't heard about the slave uprisings in the past. We have found it better to limit their gatherings and learning. It keeps them from developing crazy ideas that could lead to rebellion."

"Well, that is just my point," George said. "You said it yourself that slavery is in the Bible so that could maybe help. Also, it seems to me like it would help if they understood that God teaches; thou shall not kill or steal. The preacher would have a lot to do with how the slaves react. If he was worried about saving their souls and teaching them to do right, it could really help with the way they act."

Mrs. Pruitt chimed in, "I think it is a wonderful idea. It is our Christian duty to save them from their sins," she said.

Mr. Pruitt rolled his eyes, "How often would this preacher be preaching to them and how much time will it take away from their work? Can we afford to lose the time? Who would we get to do the preaching?"

George looked at Mrs. Pruitt. "I believe we might find someone from here to do the preaching, and I think about once a month would be enough to start with. I think we could just take off a half day on a Sunday...maybe from lunch on. We are doing great with the planting and such; I'm sure we can take off a little time once a month."

"Moses, could you come in here," George called out. When Moses appeared, George winked at him and asked him if he knew anyone who might be willing to do a little preaching...maybe one day a month...someone who would emphasize goodness and mercy, and not be too radical in their preaching?

"Ya'sir, Mr. Kilgo, I would be glad to do the preachin' if'n you'se would have me," Moses said.

"Well, it is settled then," Mrs. Pruitt said smiling at Moses and George. Mr. Pruitt just nodded his consent.

They set the next week as the day for the first service. Some of the men took some time to build a brush harbor in an open space in the middle of the cabin area, where they normally did the washing. Everyone seemed excited to be having the chance to attend.

The morning passed quickly that Sunday and before George knew it, it was twelve o'clock. The service was set to begin at one and last until Moses and everyone gave out. George didn't go home that weekend; he stayed in case there were any problems. Some of the men said they were not going and would just use the time to go fishing or rest. George suggested that he might need some work done if they were not going to the services, so they quickly changed their minds.

George planned to attend for a few minutes. Inside the frame of poles and limbs covered with branches, the slaves brought out split log benches and chairs from their cabins. There was seating for a good number of people.

Mr. Pruitt was out of town and since George was not usually around on Sundays, he didn't know if Mrs. Pruitt went to church or not. He figured she might go to the Methodist Church that was about three miles down the road. He was surprised when she sent word that she would like him to escort her to the service at the brush harbor.

When George arrived at the main house, he found Mary Pruitt decked out in a white and blue lace dress with a blue hat. George was reminded again of how pretty she was.

She must have felt his eyes on her because she turned bright red. "I appreciate your willingness to escort me to the service. I thought it would be good for the slaves to see me there. Since my husband seems to like to travel so much, I needed an escort."

"Wow! I must say you look lovely. I am honored to be seen with you," George said. Mary Pruitt laughed.

"Why, Mr. Kilgo, I do believe you are trying to turn my head," she said.

They walked the short distance to the newly build 'church,' nodding along the way to the slaves who were also making their way there. People were sitting under the shade of the harbor or on the ground around it. They made two seats available for George and Mrs. Pruitt on the front row.

Moses started out by thanking Mr. and Mrs. Pruitt for letting them have the service, and Mr. Kilgo for letting them have the afternoon off. He said he would try to keep the service to three or four hours so they could still have some time to rest. This was met by groans from the men in the audience, but Moses smiled which told them he wasn't serious.

Two ladies came up front and began to hum and then to sing. The congregation rose and started to clap, sway and sing. George and Mrs. Pruitt stood and clapped with them. George didn't sing, but Mrs. Pruitt did. They sang one song after another, swaying and singing until they were wet with sweat.

Women were fanning with cow cumber leaves and other fans. The women all seemed to George to be dressed a little nicer than their usual work clothes. One or two had homemade hats on, some with feathers and ribbons on them.

Mary leaned over to George and said loudly enough to be heard over the singing, "I think we will need to put some more cloth, and maybe some lace and ribbons in the plantation store if we are going to have church...women want to dress up a little for church." George nodded.

They sang for an hour or so; then, Moses preached for about an hour and a half. George couldn't believe the way the congregation took part, amen-ing, and uh-uhing and yes'sir-ing, whatever Moses said. George was used to the Methodist church that he and his family attended. It was very reserved compared to this. Finally, Moses had an altar call for those who wanted to be saved from hell, and about fifteen people came forward.

Moses then led the whole congregation to the creek and baptized those new souls, to hallelujahs and amen's from all. Soon a lot more people were in the creek and playing in the water. Even Mrs. Pruitt couldn't resist. She slipped her shoes off and put her feet in the creek.

Finally, she and George made their way back to the main house where Tee had set out lemonade and sugar cookies. They sat and talked until supper time. It was a great day, and Emme was delighted when George told her about it.

One day, George and Matoomba were hunting in the woods, behind the swamp, when George spotted a large buck and took a shot at him. He hit a limb which changed the path of the bullet so it only wounded the deer. They spent the better part of an hour looking for the deer before finally splitting up.

George got off Dolly, walking and trying to follow the

blood trail. It was a hot day, and he sat on a stump to rest and cool off. George propped his rifle against the stump, but it fell over. When he bent over to retrieve the rifle, George saw a movement behind him. When he turned his head, he saw Terrell charging at him with an ax raised high above his head, intent on splitting George's skull. George thrush himself away just as Terrell's ax came down into the stump. George had pushed himself away from his rifle so now he reached for his colt. Terrell tried to pull the ax out of the stump for a second swing. George had just got his pistol out of the holster when he heard a swishing noise followed by a loud thud. Terrell suddenly launched to the side and fell to the ground.

George regained his feet and looked down where Terrell lay on the ground. Beside him lay Matoomba's orinka. The side of Terrell's head was caved in, blood was leaking from his nose and his ears. Matoomba came walking out of the woods about twenty-five feet away.

Th'is the one called Terrell who hurt many slaves?" Matoomba asked.

"Yes," George said picking up his rifle. He nudged Terrell with his foot, but it was clear he wouldn't ever be getting up. "I don't know how he got here; he must have escaped or been sold to someone in the area and came back to get revenge. (George found out Terrell and Big Sammy never made it to Mobile to be sold. The man charged with taking them there had instead sold them to a slave owner at the next railroad stop a few miles up the road from Double Springs. He sent the money to Pruitt and traded in the slaves train ticket for the difference in the money for the Mobile trip.)

"Matoomba is glad he protect you."

"Thank you. If not for that rifle falling over, I would have never seen him. That old stump, this rifle and you, my friend, saved my life."

"Matoomba... thinks a spirit.... may live in this gun."

"You may be right. Old stump gun, you are my lucky charm," George said looking at the gun. From then on, George called the rifle, "Ole Stumpy".

The weeks flew by and before George realized it was mid May. He was at the swamp working and supervising the digging of four ditches that he planned to use to drain the swamp. His plan was to use the swamp where fewer trees existed as new crop land. If he could figure out how to drain it, there would be new rich cotton land before the next planting season.

George looked up and saw Homer with all the slaves from the planting group walking toward him. He wondered what was going on. When Homer was close, George stopped digging and said, "Homer what is going on?"

Homer looked around and said, *"We's coming to help ya'll with the digging and the new ground."*

"What about the planting?"

"It's all done, Mr. George," Homer said.

"All the cotton?" Homer nodded yes.

"All the corn?" Again, Homer nodded.

George took off his hat, wiped his face on his sleeve and looked out at the seventy plus slaves standing behind Homer with digging tools in their hands.

"Amos," George said spotting a slave he knew standing nearby. "Do you know what today is...what the date is?"

"No's sir, I don't rightly knows for sure," Amos answered looking bewildered.

"It's May fifteenth," George said. "I was hoping to have the crops planted by the first of June and ya'll finished by the fifteenth of May."

All the slaves looked at George and wondered what he was going to say next. Was he going to be happy or mad?

"Homer," George said addressing his field boss. "I need you to take a few men and dig us a hole behind the main house. Make it about four feet by five feet and about two feet deep. Get us a pile of fire wood and stack it near the hole. Homer, you know those two half grown hogs; the white one with the brown spots and the brown one with the black spot on its nose? Burn the wood down to coals in that pit, slaughter those hogs and put them on a split over the coals; because we are going to have us a day off and a barbeque tomorrow."

The slaves all grinned, then started to laugh and dance around. George held his hands up to signal quiet. When they had quieted down, he spoke again. "Amos, how many hours till dark do you think?"

"I's recon' maybe three, four hours, Mr. George." Amos said scratching his chin and looking at the sky.

"It sure is hot today ain't it?" George said.

"Yas'sir, it so're is hot," Amos said.

"Wait!" George said, "Did you hear that?"

Amos looked puzzled, *"I's didn't hear nothing."*

George smiled, "I did! I hear Crooked Creek calling, and it said it sure was nice and cool down in the creek. Last one in the creek is a dirty dog!" George threw his hat down and took off running down toward the creek!

He looked back to see an army of slaves, men, women, and children, laughing, skipping and running down to the creek. When they arrived, George kicked off his boots, stripped off his pants and shirt and dove into the deepest part of the creek...which was only about five feet deep. He was followed by the slaves who started a splashing war amid the laughing and shouting.

After a while, George pulled himself out of the water and lay on a big rock to dry off a little and watch the frolicking slaves enjoying the water. It was there that Mrs. Pruitt found him.

"So this is what is going on; I wondered what was happening. Hannah came into the house, and told me to come on down to the creek. All the household slaves and the ones around the sheds were all walking this way. What are we celebrating?" Mrs. Pruitt asked.

"The crops are all planted!" George said. "Two and half weeks early before the first of June, so I thought the slaves deserved to take the rest of the day off and we are going to take tomorrow off and have us a barbecue."

George saw her glance at him in his long handle underwear, and he gave her a big grin. "Since it is so hot today, we decided to cool off a little in the creek. Why don't you join us?" George asked.

"Oh, I don't think I could do that. It wouldn't be proper for the owner to be swimming in the creek with the slaves; besides Mr. Pruitt would not approve," Mrs. Pruitt replied.

"Well, I do believe Mr. Pruitt is gone on another of his politicking trips isn't he?" George asked. Mrs. Pruitt nodded. "Well then..." George grabbed Mrs. Pruitt by the waist and threw her over his shoulder and started toward the creek. She howled and screamed, but couldn't avoid the giggles.

"Don't you dare!" she yelled just before George dropped her into the water. She came up spitting, wiping the wet hair out of her face and started splashing water at George. She was giggling the whole time. They spend the next twenty minutes playing and dunking each other in the water, and fighting a splash war with the slaves. When they finally were exhausted, they climbed back on the rock and watched the slaves playing in the water.

"Mr. Kilgo," she started to say, but George stopped her and said, "It's George." She nodded.

"George, I think you have done a wonderful job with the slaves and the plantation, and I know Mr. Pruitt will be very happy with things when he returns," she said.

"I am kind of happy the way things have turned out so far. I consider it a small miracle, but we have a long way to go. So much could still go wrong. There could be a drought, or a hail storm could destroy the crop, or the bugs could destroy it. I'll rest easier when I see those bales of cotton loaded on the wagons going to market," George said.

Mrs. Pruitt just smiled. "Well, let's just enjoy the day and the company, and worry about all that tomorrow." George nodded and smiled back.

Mrs. Pruitt had been trying for several months to get George to bring his wife and family over to the plantation so she could meet them. It was hard to find a time when Mr. Pruitt could also be there because he was spending more and more time traveling and politicking. He saw the national political situation as critical to his father's goal of becoming governor. Mr. Pruitt was trying to use the threat of freeing the slaves to get people to support his father.

Finally, a time was found and George brought the whole family over to meet the Pruitts. After a wonderful lunch, the younger kids were playing in the yard under Liz's supervision, while Mrs. Pruitt and Emme were sitting on the front porch watching them play. As usual, Hannah was sitting nearby in the background, but near enough to see and hear.

George, Mr. Pruitt and Will were out back shooting George's rifle and practicing throwing Matoomba's spears and orinkas, as Matoomba instructed them.

Mrs. Pruitt had served some wine after lunch, and it had loosened the ladies tongues. Emme spoke at length with the other woman about her "female" trouble and how it limited her relations with her husband. She mentioned that it seemed things were getting worse lately.

Finally, she said, "I love my husband, but I know that I can't meet all the needs of a man like my husband. I know that you...two, she said, including Hannah, whom she turned to look at, are around him more now than I am. I see how he looks at other women...I see how he looks at both of you, when he thinks I am not watching. I know he is attracted to you both. I don't know what your situation is with your...mates, husbands or boyfriends... it just pains me to know that he has...ah...needs that are not being met." Emme looked carefully at the other women to see if they were getting her meaning. When she was sure they were following her thoughts, she continued.

"I...know George is a good man and a good husband; but he is just a man, and sometime men are weak. I don't want him to turn to the whores at Looney's Tavern to...ah...meet his needs...if I can't meet them," Emme said looking from Hannah to Mrs. Pruitt. "What I am saying is I won't be upset if he should seek...ah...companionship elsewhere. I can't fault him or others he might get...ah...involved with."

Finally, Emme stopped talking and took another sip of her wine. Mrs. Pruitt cleared her throat and said, "I...ah can relate and I share your feelings. I know my husband has been with other women...when he is on his trips. It really hurt me the first time I realized it...but now...I have come to accept it. He is a man, and a weak one in some ways. When he is here, he spends too much time drinking...and sometime he neglects... his husbandly...hmm ...chores. I think he drinks because he... knows...he can't give me the thing I want most...a child. My husband is an only child and once, when his mother was quite drunk, she let slip that she was not sure her husband, Jim's father, was capable of fathering children...that he might not be

Jim's father. I...we...have been trying for a child from the beginning of our marriage, and I have come to realize that Mr. Pruitt in not capable of fathering one."

Hannah had sat silent all this time. Mrs. Pruitt looked over at the slave girl and saw tears streaming down her face. "What is it Hannah? Is something wrong?" Mrs. Pruitt asked.

Hannah burst out crying, stood up, put her arms around Mrs. Pruitt and started to sob softly on her shoulder. After a few moments, when she could talk, she sobbed out, *"I's didn't want to do it. I's told him no, that it wasn't right a dozen times, but he wouldn't listen. I's so sorry! Please don't hate me and send me away!"*

Mrs. Pruitt pulled Hannah off her shoulder and looked her in the face. "I suspected as much for some time now, but thank you for telling me. Don't you worry; I will never send you away." Mrs. Pruitt stroked the girl's hair and face. "It's okay. I know you couldn't help it."

Hannah burst into another crying fit. *"That's jus' it Mrs. Pruitt...sob... sob...I's didn't like it at first. When Mr. Connors broke me, it hurt something awful...sob...he was mean to me and hurt me...but Mr. Pruitt he's nice and didn't hurt me. I's guess I's jus' a whore, and I's going to hell...cause...sob...I's starting to like it...sob...sob...I'm sorry!"*

The two older women exchanged a look. "Hannah it's okay, you are not a whore, and you are not going to hell. You are just becoming a woman, and are finding out about a woman's...ah desires. You are...it's... perfectly normal," Mrs. Pruitt said.

They stopped talking then because Liz had noticed something going on and had come closer so she could hear. "Is everything alright?" Liz asked.

"Yes, everything is fine," Mrs. Pruitt said, "Hannah, why don't you take Liz and show her around a little."

"Yes, Mrs. Pruitt."

When they left, the two women didn't say much else. They sat on the porch and watched the boys play for a few minutes, and they talked about other things until it was time for the Kilgos to leave. When they had said their goodbyes, Mrs. Pruitt and Emme shared a long hug; and a look passed between them that said a lot more than goodbye.

CHAPTER ELEVEN

E vents were happening fast across the nation that summer. Abraham Lincoln was leading the Republican race and looked to likely be the new President. Southern Democrats were splitting their votes between candidates, while a third candidate divided voters even more. Southerners considered Lincoln an abolitionist; and vowed that if he were elected, they would secede from the union.

Jim Pruitt was traveling the state trying to work up support for his father; but also trying to work himself into an appointment, as an officer, if war broke out with the North. When Lincoln was elected in November of 1860, the South took steps to secede from the Union...with the first seven states doing so in February...before Lincoln was sworn in that March. An immediate and forceful reaction by President James Buchannan may have stopped the coming war, but he waited to let the next President deal with the problem.

The hill counties of North Alabama were caught between the slave owners of South Alabama and the slave owners of the fertile Tennessee Valley. Having no slaves of their own, these poor farmers just wanted to be left alone. When Alabama called for a convention in January of 1861 to vote on seceding from the Union, Winston County selected Chris Sheets to go and vote 'no' on seceding. He did so, was thrown into jail, beaten, and given another chance to vote to secede. When he again refused, he was thrown back in jail. None of this went over well with the people of Winston County.

Alabama seceded from the Union along with other Southern States and began building a government and organizing an army. Fighting broke out in April at Fort Sumter, and the Civil War began.

Mr. Pruitt received an appointment as a Captain in the Confederate Army, and was in charge of recruiting troops from the North Alabama area. At first, he went around making speeches and asking for volunteers for the army. As things progressed, the South passed a conscription act and called for loyalty oaths from those in Winston County who voiced their opposition to the war and seceded from the Union. Things began to heat up in Winston County.

George and Mr. Pruitt had gotten along great up until that point. George was able to increase the number of bales of cotton raised on the plantation and had earned a nice bonus as a result. He was able to use the money to add the extra bedroom to his house, and buy a couple of more cows and hogs.

Mr. Pruitt assured George that as long as he was working for him, George had nothing to worry about and would not be conscripted into the army or bothered by the Home Guard or the Partisan Rangers. These two groups were active in Winston County; both tried to recruit men into the Southern Army. Later, both groups would start trying to force men into the army at the point of a gun, with the choice of joining or dying.

"George you don't have to worry about the Home Guard or getting drafted. I have put out the word to leave you and yours alone." Jim Pruitt said to George on one of his visits back to the plantation. George felt a little better but still worried about what might happen in the future and where the war would lead them.

Shortly after the Kilgo family's visit to the Pruitt Plantation, George had been lying in bed one night after a hard day working on draining the swamp when there was a light tapping on the door of the overseer's cabin. George opened the door to find Hannah standing there.

"Hi, Hannah. Does Mrs. Pruitt need something?" George asked.

"Non' sir, cans I comes in before everyone sees me and tongues starts a wag'n?"

George stepped back and let her come in. He looked about outside, and didn't see anyone who might have observed her coming in.

"Mr. George, I's been thinkin' a lot ever since your wife talked to me and Mrs. Pruitt the other day," Hannah said. "I's finally figured out what's I's needs to do." Hannah pulled her shift dress top down over her shoulders and with a little wiggle let it fall off to pool at her feet on the floor. She was gloriously naked. George couldn't stop his eyes as they traveled the length of her light brown body.

"Oh, my sweet Lord!" George proclaimed. "What...?"

"Sh..sh.." Hannah said putting her finger to George's lips. "Yo'ur wife says she couldn't be meet all you'se needs, and it tooks me awhile to figure out jes' what she was sayin', but now I knows she was askin' for some help...and I's here to help." George couldn't argue with that even if he wanted to...which he didn't.

In July, George was working in the fields with the slaves

chopping cotton when two men rode up. "Howdy, George," the men called out. When George came up and shook their hands, they told him of a meeting that Saturday night at Looney's to discuss what to do about the way Winston County was being treated; how Chris Sheets their representative was being treated, and what to do about the activities of the Home Guard and Partisan Rangers.

"George, we need you to come to the meeting and try to talk some sense into some of the hot heads. Pat Woods and Rupert Johns are talking up raising a militia to go to Montgomery; break Chris Sheets out of jail, and take down the Home Guard. The dang bunch of fools is going to get killed or worse; they are going to bring the whole damn army up here to the county," one of the men said. The men rode off after George promised that he would attend the meeting.

When George arrived Saturday at Looney's, there were several dozen horses tied up around the tavern. George could hardly get inside since there were so many people gathered. They lined the upstairs balcony, and stood all up and down the stairs. The windows to the tavern were open and people stood just outside so they could hear what was going on inside.

A few were sipping beer, but George soon found out Bill had cut off all beer and whiskey sales a couple of hours before the start of the meeting. As it was told to George, Bill had said he didn't want a bunch of drunks starting trouble. People milled about talking in small groups.

When the meeting started, the local preacher started things out with a prayer; and then turned the floor over to Chris Sheet's brother, John, who told of getting a letter from his brother in the Montgomery jail. Chris said he had been beaten and threatened once again, but still refused to agree to the resolution to secede.

One after another, various men stood up front and discussed what they thought the people of Winston County should do about the way they were being treated. Most wanted some kind of action taken, but they couldn't agree on what. Suggestions ranged from raising a militia to try and break Chris out of jail, to sending the governor a letter of protest saying the county just wanted to stay neutral and be left alone.

George sat and listened to the hot heads and the more timid all say their piece. He kept his mouth shut and didn't say anything until he was put on the spot.

Winfred Sheets, one of Chris Sheets' cousins, spotted George and called out to him, "George Kilgo, what is your opinion on what we ought to do? You are a small farmer just like the rest of us; but you also work for a slave owner, so you surely have heard your employer talk about this issue. Please tell us what you think would be best."

George shifted around uncomfortably. On one hand, he wanted to agree with being neutral, but he knew those favoring secessionist would never let them be. You were either for the South, or you were against it. There was no middle ground to them. He hesitated to say anything at all.

Richard Payne, who was pro-secession, spoke up and said, "Are you afraid to say?"

George knew he had to speak. "No, I'm not afraid to state my beliefs; I just don't know that what I think or what you think is going to make much difference. The only ones whose thinking is going to make a difference, are the big land owners and big slave owners. They out number us in both numbers and power. They have made their decision to secede, and nothing we can do now is going to change that. Go ahead and pass your resolution and ask to be neutral, but I fear we are going to be forced to choose sides, and I fear we are going to be pitted against each other... neighbor against neighbor; and Mr. Payne, **I am afraid** of what that will mean to us and our families."

There were a lot of heads nodding in agreement. Someone shouted, "Well, if the slave owners can secede from the Union, why can't we secede from the State of Alabama?" Someone else said, "I hear there is talk of the hill and mountain counties of East Tennessee seceding from the rest of the state. Bill, you have people living in the mountains in the East. What do you hear from your people?"

Bill Looney stood and said, "My people are all part Indian, and they don't want to fight to free the slaves, because they are slaves themselves to the white man. They will try to sit this war out if they can, but like George says, I don't know if that is possible. We all know that the Home Guards are rounding up men and forcing them into the Confederate Army. I heard the Confederates are starting to form irregulars into groups called Partisan Rangers, like Mosby has up in Virginia."

The talk went on and on for more than two hours. Finally, they agreed to send a resolution to the governor proclaiming their desire to be neutral and to be left alone. They also asked that Chris Sheets, their duly elected representative, be freed and allowed to return home. As the final vote to accept the resolution was being taken, Payne shouted, "Now let's vote on the Free State of Winston!" Everyone was tired and ready to go home so he was ignored, and no other votes were cast.

George went back to the Pruitt Plantation. It was July and the crops were all planted and coming along well. The cotton had to be hoed to get the weeds out and chopped to thin it out, but it looked like they were heading for another excellent harvest.

Mr. Pruitt was around less and less. At first, he came home every three weeks or so; but neither George nor Mrs. Pruitt had seen him in over a month. His last letter to his wife was three weeks ago, and he was in Mississippi somewhere recruiting more men into the Confederate Army.

A month after the meeting at Looney's Tavern, a rider came to the Pruitt Plantation where George was working in the field. "George did you hear about what happened at Looney's yesterday?" the man asked.

When George said no, the man continued. "Home Guard, about twenty of 'em, came looking for Bill. Well, he wasn't there, had gone to Double Springs with Chuck to get supplies. The Home Guard forced their way into the tavern, started to beat Senie to get her to tell where Bill was. They shot Shorty dead when he tried to intervene to protect Senie. George...they raped Senie, and burned the place to the ground."

"Good grief!" George said. "What is the matter with people? Has everyone gone crazy! What about Bill?"

"He went crazy when he got back; threatened to kill them all! George, he is running around looking for someone to kill. Johnny Two Feathers asked me to come and get you to see if you can calm him down." George left and rode to the tavern. There was nothing left but the chimneys and smoking ruins. Johnny Two Feathers was sitting on a log across from the ruins.

"George," Johnny said when he saw George. "They almost killed my Senie, raped her, and burned the tavern. They pistol whipped me. Shot Shorty dead on the floor. I wish they had killed me. I want to go to the other side, to be with my wife; but I can't go until these men pay for what they have done. George, Bill is going to hunt them down, but I fear he will just get killed. He is not thinking right. Please find him and talk to him." George noticed that Johnny had a bandage on his head and a huge bruise on the side of his face.

"How...how did it happen? Where were you?" George asked.

"I was in my cabin when I heard the horses. There were about twenty of them. It was Stokes Roberts and his gang. I came out with my shotgun, but one of them hit me with his pistol and knocked me out. The widow Jones' son, Seth, was with them. He is only sixteen. This was his first time to ride with them. Just a dumb kid trying to prove he is a man; he just stayed outside with the horses. He started to get scared when they shot Shorty. When they came out and told him to go in and take a turn with Senie, he jumped on his horse and rode away. He told his momma everything. She made him come back and tell Bill everything that had happened. Seth and his momma begged Bill not to kill him, that he was just a scared kid. He didn't know what they were going to do. I thought Bill was going to kill him. He put a gun to his head, but finally he let him go after he told Bill the names of all those he knew in the gang. He didn't know them all, but Bill's got a list and he is going to kill all of them."

George knew where to look for Bill. It was well known that Ennis Watts was a Home Guard. He lived about six miles west of Looney's so George started by going to Ennis'. When George was about a half mile from Ennis' farm, he spotted a saddled horse grazing along the side of the road. When he rode over to the horse, he saw Ennis lying on the ground. He had been shot in the head with a shotgun. George thought he might have been scalped, but he couldn't tell because there was so little of his head left.

George looked for Bill all that day and most of the next

without any luck. He went to the homes of two other known Home Guards, but none were home. Their families all said they had heard what happened to Senie Looney and to Ennis, and figured that they wouldn't see their men for a while until things cooled down.

CHAPTER TWELVE

The early part of August was hotter than normal. George had finished the ditches and pulled the plug on the swamp. The slaves all gathered with feed sacks and baskets to catch the fish and turtles that were left when the water rushed out of the swamp. A great feast was held with the things they picked up. There were lots of snakes; water snakes and cotton mouths that were killed. Luckily, no one was bitten.

On a hot day after the swamp had been drained a week or two, Mrs. Pruitt ask if George would take her to see it. They rode down and she was amazed at the way it all looked. As they approached, they saw a doe deer running around the edge of the swamp. When they got closer, they could see a small fawn that was stuck in the mud out several feet in the swamp. There were tracks all around where the mother had tried to get to her baby, but was unable to reach it to help it out. The fawn would pull itself up with its front legs; but either the front legs or the back legs would break through the thick mud, and it would fall back into the hole it had made in the mud.

"Oh, the poor thing!" Mrs. Pruitt exclaimed. "We have to

help it. Get your rope and...you know...throw it over it and pull it out."

George tried several times to throw his rope hoping to get it over the fawn's neck and pull it out, but it was just out of reach, and was moving around too much. "I'm sure it will be alright," George said.

"We can't leave it! If you can't get it, then I will," Mary Pruitt said pulling off her shoes. Before George could stop her, she started walking across the mud toward the fawn.

"Wait! You're going to sink up, and then I'll have to rescue you!" George said.

Mary took about three steps before she broke through the surface mud and sank up to her knees. "Ah...it's cold and wet!" she said. The farther she went, the deeper it got; soon she was thigh deep and struggling to stay upright. She had started out holding her dress up, but now she had to let it go as she struggled to stay upright. She was squealing and grunting as she tried to get to the fawn. "George!" She yelled as she sank up to her waist. In spite of himself, George started to laugh at her.

"It is not funny! I can hardly move!" Mary sank up to her chest just as she reached the fawn. She put her arms around the fawn and at first it bucked and jerked trying to escape; but in a few moments it stop struggling, either exhausted or it realized someone was trying to help. Now that Mary had the fawn in her arms, she weighed more, and they both sank deeper. "George! Help me! Please!" She begged.

George grinned, "I don't know, I think I should leave both of you to find your own way out. I tried to warn you."

"Please throw your rope."

George tried, but it was too short to reach them. "Crap!" George slipped his boots and socks off, and took a couple of steps out into the mud. From this position, he could reach them with the rope.

"Mary, put the rope over your head and under your arms," George said. Mary did as instructed, and George started to pull. He had to put all his weight into it and soon was sitting down pulling. He had a hard time breaking the tension of the mud and pulling them toward the edge of the swamp. After several minutes, he finally had them near the edge. The fawn got on firmer soil and bolted away leaving an exhausted Mary and George laying in the mud watching it run into the woods.

"Well, I hope that was worth it." George said standing up and pulling Mary to her feet. They were both covered with mud; Mary all the way to her shoulders and George to the waist.

"I guess we need to take a trip to the creek and wash off," George said.

Mary started to get on her horse, but George stopped her.

"Don't! You'll just mess up your saddle. It is only a short walk to the creek," he said.

They walked the short distance across the field and down the slight hill to the creek. Mary waded in until she was up to her waist, and started to rub at the mud that coated her body.

George just stood back and admired her from a few feet away. The way the mud clung to her shape and the way the water molded to her, she looked amazing.

Mary finally figured out that he wasn't joining her, and she turned around to see what he was doing. When she saw him, she smiled and said, "You're never going to get clean standing there. Come on in."

George walked out a couple of feet, grabbed her by the waist and took both of them under in the deeper water. They both came up spitting water and laughing.

"Oh, you brute!" Mary said laughing and splashing water

on George. Soon they were in a wrestling match trying to see who could dunk the other. All at once they found themselves face to face. Slowly, both moved into a kiss that they both wanted.

Mary pressed her body closer to George and pulled him as close as she could. George picked her up and she locked her legs around his waist, never breaking their kiss. George carried her to the edge of the creek to the sandy band, laid her down and crawled on top of her.

Neither one could stop what happened next as their passions took over. Mary had been long neglected by her husband, and George hadn't been with Emme in months. Even though he had been with Hannah he had lusted after Mary Pruitt for a long time. Mary pulled at George's pants while he pulled up her dress.

"My Gosh, woman, where is your underwear...your pantaloons? Have you been naked under there all this time?"

"No," Mary said sheepishly. "I lost them in the mud."

Later, as they lay beside each other, George looked into her face and saw a tear roll down her cheek.

"I'm sorry, Mary...I...didn't mean..."

"You've made me an adulteress, but I'm not sorry! I knew this would happen from the time your Emme told me and Hannah that she couldn't...ah...give...meet all your needs," Mary said. "Maybe I knew it the first day we met, when you fixed our wagon wheel."

George looked at her in wonder and amazement. He didn't know what to say.

Mary smiled and said, "Now, please give me a baby, George. I want one more than anything, and my husband can't give me one. Please! I need you again."

That was the beginning. George felt guilty, but he couldn't seem to help himself around her. Soon after George was with Mary, Hannah came to him and let him know she wouldn't be visiting him anymore. George didn't know if Mary Pruitt had said something to her or not. Hannah just said she was glad he was feeling better, and she had a new beau. Between Mary Pruitt and his occasional trip home, when Emme was able to make love, George had more women than he could handle.

No one had heard from Mr. Pruitt for about three months. One afternoon, George was getting ready for supper with Mary when he heard a knock at the door. A young slave said, *"Mr. George you'se needed in the big house right now."*

George frowned, "Okay, I'll be there in a second."

Just as George went up the steps and entered the back door of the house, he was struck from behind. When he awoke, his hands were tied behind his back, and he was lying in a pool of blood. One eye was swollen shut and his head was throbbing. When he could focus his eye, he saw Mary sitting in the corner of the room. She had a blue bruise under one eye and a busted lip.

Jim Pruitt was sitting at the table with a bottle of whiskey. He was wearing his uniform, and looking at George. "Well, you are finally awake. I was beginning to think I would have to pour a bucket of water on you," Pruitt said. George tried to speak, but found his throat very dry and was not able to talk.

"You didn't really think you could sleep with my wife and get away with it did you, George?" Pruitt said glaring at George over the glass of whiskey.

George finally found his voice. "I didn't really think about it. It just happened. I didn't plan for it to happen, and neither did Mary."

"Oh, so it is Mary now, is it? Not Mrs. Pruitt, but Mary!" Pruitt said raising his voice louder and louder.

"Well, I can see that we need to break up the happy

couple. I can take care of that easily enough. I have sent for the Home Guard; and when they arrive, we will ship George here to the front lines. I will put in a good word for him and make sure that he gets to see the war up close, real close. What do you think about that my dear?" Pruitt said to his wife.

Mary just sobbed. George strained against his bindings. Pruitt just laughed and took another drink of the whiskey, draining his glass. He stood up and walked over to George, and kicked him in the ribs. George groaned and lay there fighting for breath.

Sometime later, George heard horses outside. Pruitt rose and went to the door. When he came back, he had Connors and his brother with him. "I didn't expect to see the Connors again, but I guess this war forces all of us to do things we didn't think we would ever do," Pruitt said.

"Now George, they are going to take you along over to the Houston jail where there are six other men, just like you, who are going to decide if they want to get hung, or if they want to join the Confederate Army. I'm going to have my wife, and then I am going to go back to the war. There is going to be a big battle soon; and then, the South is going to be left alone," Pruitt said.

Connors took George's rifle from his saddle holster along with George's colt, holster and gun belt. George was carried out to his horse and thrown up on the saddle. The Connors and eight men rode off with George into the fading daylight. They had ridden a few miles from the plantation when a man appeared in the distance. In the fading light, the riders could barely make him out. He sat on his horse, raised his rifle and fired at the riders; then, turned his horse and rode away.

The leader of the Home Guard shouted at the Connors brothers to stay with George, and he and the other men rode after the bushwhacker. The Connors brothers pulled their horses around on either side of George, and sat there looking after the other men. Suddenly, Connor's brother let out a gasp. The back of his shirt suddenly split and something pushed through it...he fell to the ground. As George turned, he saw the shaft of Matoomba's spear sticking out of the man's chest. Connors looked at the spear; but before he could do anything, an arrow flew through the air and struck him in the neck. It traveled half way through, sticking out of both sides of his neck. As Connors reached up to grasp at the shaft, another arrow hit him in the chest. He groaned and fell backward out of the saddle, joining his brother's body on the ground.

George squinted out of his one good eye to see Matoomba and Bill Looney come riding out of the woods. Bill got down off his horse and cut the leather straps tying George's hands. "George, good to see you," Bill said.

"Good to see you, too," George said. George turned to Matoomba, "Thank you."

"Matoomba... be sorry.... he hunting and.... not protect you till this hour," Matoomba said in his broken English.

"Well, your timing was perfect," George said.

"Damn lucky that Matoomba found me as he was heading this way," Looney said.

Matoomba walked over to the body of Connors' brother and pulled his spear out.

While George watched, Bill went to both bodies and grabbing them by the hair, quickly scalped both men.

"You taking scalps now Bill?" George asked.

"No, these scalps are not worthy to be hanging in anyone's lodge. I just want the rest of them to think about me when they lay down to sleep each night," Bill said as he took the scalps and using the point of his knife shoved the scalps into the mouths of the dead men.

George went to Connors' horse and got his weapons. He looked down at Connors with the arrows sticking from his body.

"Hella'va shot, by the way...got him right in the throat so he couldn't cry out," George said.

"Naw," Bill said. "I was trying for his chest. I had to use Johnny Two Feathers' bow, and it don't shoot worth a crap. Mine burned in the tavern.

"Ah...I'm really sorry about Senie...she is a sweet lady and didn't deserve that," George said. "How is she?"

"Not good. She cries all the time and can't sleep. It's okay, I'm going to make them sorry for what they did," Bill said squinting his eyes. Just then a loud bird whistle was heard.

Bill shouted, "Come on in!" A man walked out of the woods leading a horse.

"This is my cousin, Eddie Whitepony; he is the one who led the others off so we could rescue you. Oldest Indian trick in the world. I can't believe they keep falling for it."

George nodded and said thanks to Eddie. Bill came over to George. "George, you know they are going to go after Emme and your kids now," Bill said looking into George's face. George went pale with the realization that Bill was probably right. George turned to Matoomba.

"Matoomba, you remember when I took you to my farm a while back? Do you remember the way there? Well, I need you to go there right away. I need you to tell my wife to take the kids and go north to Tennessee. Tell them to let the livestock out, and just go. They have to leave right away. Tell her to write to Mr. Halston at the store in Double Springs, to let him know where she is...I will find her. Do you understand?"

Matoomba nodded. "Repeat it back to me then," George demanded. Matoomba repeated it back in his halting English, then jumped on his mule. *"Matoomba... will guard... your family,"* Matoomba said.

"No, they will be alright if they leave right away. You need to go back and protect Mrs. Pruitt," George said.

"Men, we need to get going, those Guards are going to figure out they are chasing their own tails pretty soon and come back," Eddy said.

"Go... safely... my friends," Matoomba said as he rode away.

The men mounted up and started to ride, with George going in one direction and the other two men in another for a step or two. They both turned back at the same time. "Where are you going?" Bill asked.

"There are six men in the Houston jail that will hang soon if we don't save them; that is where they were taking me," George said.

Bill hesitated then said, "What do you want us to do?"

"Well, we can't just let good men die," George said looking at the other two men.

Bill looked at Eddie who shrugged his shoulders. "Okay, let's move."

They rode hard for two hours in the dark. Finally, they arrived at a small group of buildings; two houses, some barns and out buildings. On one end of the group of buildings was another log building. Getting off their horses, they crept up to the log building. It was a moon lit night and they could see pretty well. Bill told the others to wait while he crept forward until he could see into the house nearest the log jail. When he came back, he told them that there were three men in the house. Only one was watching the jail; and he was sitting in a chair leaned back on the porch of the house, watching from a distance and dozing from time to time.

"I will try to take the man on the porch as quietly as I can while you keep your guns on the door of the house. If we can take the men out of the jail without waking up every one, that would be best," Bill said.

They moved into position while Bill crept up on the man on the porch. When he was beside the building, he threw a stone to make a noise off to one side. The man on the porch heard it; and he got up, stepping off the porch looking for the source of the noise. Bill came up on him from behind and grabbed him, covering his mouth, while holding a knife to his throat.

"You make a sound and I'll cut your throat," Bill hissed at the man. Bill walked the man over to the log jail and around the side of the building. Bill called to the men inside. "Hey, wake up! We are here to get you out." Pressing the knife tightly to the man's throat he asked, "Now, who has the key?"

"It hangs on a nail just inside the door. I swear I don't have it," the man said.

"What is your name?" Bill asked.

"Abe Watson," the man said.

"You ain't on the list," Bill said. "Do you want to live?" The man nodded his head. "You do just exactly what I tell you to do, and you might live. Do you understand?" Again, the man nodded his head. "Can you get the key without tipping the others off?" The man nodded.

"Then you go get the key. If you tip off the others, you will all die. I got a dozen men in the woods with their guns trained on the house right now, and some of them are itching to kill them some Home Guards. Do you understand?" Again the man nodded. Bill led the man back to the porch, and he let him go in. He couldn't hear what the man said or what excuse he gave for the key but in a moment he came out with a set of keys on a large ring. With Bill holding the knife to him again, he went to the jail and unlocked the door. The men inside poured out; Bill pointed to his lips and urged them to be quiet. They moved toward one of the barns nearby where their horses were being kept.

They led the horses out and away from the house and jail. Only when they were several hundred yards away did they start mounting up to ride away. A couple of the men wanted to kill the Home Guard they had taken with them, but Bill said to let him go.

Bill pulled the man close to his face and hissed. "You wait until we have been gone ten minutes, then you go back and tell them Bill Looney is coming for them. One night soon, they will wake up to find me standing over their beds with my knife; and I'm going to slit their throats, and then I'm going to eat their hearts for what they did to my wife! Now, go tell them!"

"Mr. Looney, I swear none of us were involved in what happened at your tavern. That was Stokes Roberts' bunch. We don't ride with them, and we don't like them! I swear!" the man said.

"Where are you taking us?" the men asked.

"I don't know; where do you want to go?" Bill asked the men.

They looked at each other. "I don't guess we can go back to our homes, the Home Guard will just get us again," one man said. "I damn sure ain't going into the Confederate Army and fight for someone who was going to kill us," another one said. "I'd rather fight for the Union, but how will we get to their lines? These hills are gonna be crawling with Home Guard by morning."

George looked at Bill. "Bill, you know they are right. If you don't guide them, they will be caught again." Bill gave George a look, then shook his head.

"Damn it! I need to take care of some of my own business.

I don't have time to babysit this group; there are men out there who raped my wife."

George just looked at Bill for a minute without saying anything. Finally, Bill said, "Alright, follow me. I'll take you to the Union lines; but you have to listen, and do just what I tell you. The Home Guard will be watching the roads, and we have to travel fast and at night."

They rode the rest of the night, headed northwest toward Mississippi. As soon as the first signs of daylight appeared, Bill moved off the road and into the woods. He led the bunch down a steep hill, so steep that they had to get off and walk the horses the last hundred feet. At the bottom of the hill was a large bluff that opened back into the hillside about fifteen feet where it was dry at the back end.

"We will camp here today. We have to be extremely quiet. No rattling pots and pans, no loud talk. You can build a really small fire deep in the bluff to cook something on, but no green or wet wood that will smoke," Bill said. "We will post two lookouts on the road a quarter of a mile in either direction. If you see something, you haul butt and come back here and warn us. We don't want a fight because we will be out numbered and out gunned; but if we have to, those who are armed will make a stand while the others get away, down the hill and then along the creek. If we get separated just go north-west till you get to Corinth; that is where the Union army should be." The men all nodded that they understood.

This was the first of six camps they would make before they reached the Union army lines. Always, Bill seemed to find a bluff or cave for them to hide out in during the daylight hours. At night, they rode along the road or just off the road. At times, Bill would make them stop and he and Eddie would go on ahead and check to see if the road was clear. Most of the time, they were safe; the Home Guard was afraid of being out in the dark. Too many people hated them, and they were under constant danger of a lone bushwhacker taking a shot at them; then disappearing into the night.

Twice, Bill pulled the group to a halt. He would suddenly stop and hold his hand up in the air. He would listen for a moment; then, motion for all of them to move into the woods and down the hill to their right. Not two minutes after they left the road, a large group of Home Guard or Partisan Rangers would come riding up the road right by them.

It was like Bill had a sixth sense about things, or he had super good hearing. George and the other men couldn't hear the horses and riders coming, but Bill either heard them or sensed them.

George couldn't understand how he always found a bluff to sleep under either. Finally, on the next to last night, George asked him how he did it. "Bill how do you find these bluffs and caves? Have you been this way before?" George asked.

Bill smiled and said, "I don't know if an Indian should share that knowledge with a white man. Wait until about daylight and I'll show you."

They rode along until the first sign of light. When you could see a little, Bill slowed down the group and George could see him looking at the trees along the road side. Finally, he spotted something and pointed it out to George. It was a sapling that was bent into an "L" shape with the flat part pointing up the road.

"This is a trail marker left by Indians long ago. They tied the sapling over with rawhide to mark the trail and point the way to go. Soon, it grew that way. The rawhide broke or grew into the tree. Most of the roads follow them now. There are also ones that point out shelters, bluffs or caves like this one. See how it is twisted and points down the hill while that one (he pointed to another one nearby) points out the trail. They are hard to see in the dark; but when it starts to get light, I begin to look for them." George shook his head. No wonder the Indians could survive and hide in the woods.

After six nights, Bill told them they were really close to the Union lines. That morning, he told them to break camp, but to wait for him as he would approach the Union lines alone...if they all rode up, the Union would open fire.

"George, you and Eddie come with me. I want you and that long range rifle watching my back," Bill said.

They rode up to the road from the cave where they had spent the previous night. About a half mile up the road, Bill waved them off their horses. They tied the horses and walked up the road a hundred yards or so. Bill pointed to a line of trees across a field to their left. George looked, but he couldn't see anything.

"The boys in Blue are camped up ahead. Their pickets are in that line of trees," Bill said.

"I don't see anything," George said.

"Look carefully at the openings, and watch for shadows crossing the openings." George looked and sure enough he could see movement. An opening would go away, and then re-appear.

"The trick is to get close enough to talk to them without getting spotted and start them to shooting," Bill said. "Let's move along this tree line a little closer, and then I'll go on up and shout at them."

They moved up about another hundred yards. Finally, Bill said, "I'll get closer and tell them who we are. I think they will be okay, but if they start shooting and come riding out at us, we'll need to high tail it out of here and back to our horses."

George and Eddy watched as Bill moved slowly through the grass and weeds in the field until he was only about two hundred yards from the men that George could clearly see now. They were moving around talking and not paying much attention to what was happening around them. They clearly weren't expecting anyone to sneak up on them.

"Hey! You men in the trees," Bill shouted out. George could see the men scrabbling around grabbing their guns, and looking for the source of the voice. Finally, one shouted back, "Where are you? What do you want?"

"Well, I ain't about to tell you where I am so you can shoot my head off," Bill said. George looked from the men back to Bill, and he had to look hard to see Bill. He had flattened himself down in a batch of brown weeds, and his buckskin pants and shirt just seemed to disappear.

"What do you want?" The voice asked.

"I don't want to hurt you or I could have done that already. I have got a dozen men who want to come in and join the army," Bill said.

There was silence from the other side while they discussed what to do next.

"How do we know this ain't a trick or an ambush?" the voice asked.

"Think about it. If this was an ambush, we would have come in shooting and not talking," Bill said. There was more silence; then, finally the voice said, "Okay, show yourself; and then we'll know this ain't a trick."

"And get shot by some trigger happy young buck out to make a name for himself...I don't think so," Bill said. "Have you got a sergeant or an officer in there?"

"No, we just got a bunch of privates," the voice said.

"Well, send someone to get us an officer or a sergeant, and I'll take my chances," Bill said.

Silence. "Okay, give us about five minutes and we'll get someone."

George could see a man moving away from the group. A few minutes later, a new voice answered, "This is Sergeant Brooks. Who are you?"

"Name's Bill Looney. Look sergeant, I got a bunch of men from North Alabama who have been chased out of their homes by the Home Guard, and they want to join up with the Union. We ain't crazy about getting killed by some jumpy Union soldiers. Can you give me your word you ain't going to start shooting?"

"Okay, I give you my word. Now come on out."

"In a minute...where you from Sergeant?" Bill asked.

"What the hell's that got to do with anything?" the voice asked.

"Well, if'n you kill me, I want to know which part of hell to look for you in," Bill said.

George could hear the sergeant laugh. "I'm from Brownsville, Kentucky."

"Well hell, that's nearly in the South," Bill said as he stood up with his hands in the air. George could see the men were surprised that Bill was so close to them.

Bill walked toward the line of trees; when he was about twenty steps away, a man stood up and walked out to meet him. The two men talked for a few moments; then, Bill turned toward George and Eddie and shouted, "Go get the others. It is safe now."

The men were taken to the main Union camp. Their weapons were taken from them, and they were looked at closely by the Union soldiers as they walked among them. They were a sorry looking lot. Most had been riding bareback for six days, sleeping on the ground, without any bedding, and hadn't bathed or had much to eat in all that time. First, they were met by a captain. He led them deeper into the Union camp. Finally, they were given something to eat, and led to an area where they remained under guard for a couple hours.

Later, Bill and George were escorted to another area where they were led to a tent and told to wait.

"Who are we waiting for?" Bill asked.

"Black Jack Logan," the soldier said.

"Who is that?"

"In my book, he is the best damn General in the Union army," the soldier said. "He led the charge up Nobb Hill that turned the tide in the Battle of Corinth. Got wounded twice, but continued to lead the attack. I'd follow him into battle anywhere."

About that time, a tall dark haired man with a black beard and an obvious limp came into the tent. He extended his hand to the men, asking their names and where they were from.

"Gentlemen, it is a pleasure to met you. I have heard a lot about you in the last two hours," Black Jack said. "I understand that you brought in a number of men who want to join the army."

"Yes, sir. I don't know how you feel about southerners fighting for the Union, but these men have been run off from their homes by the Home Guard, and they want to fight back," George said.

Black Jack nodded his head. "I have found that our southern boys are excellent fighters and horsemen. I am actually raising a regiment of men from Alabama called the First Alabama Calvary. I will be pleased to have these men join that group."

"What about you men? Do you plan to join also?" Black Jack asked.

George looked at Bill. "I...ah...had hoped to stay out of the war. Until a couple of days ago, I thought that was possible... but now..." George said.

"I got my own war to fight, and I don't have time to fight anyone else's," Bill said.

Black Jack nodded his head. "I heard something about what happened to you and ...your wife. Damn shame! Those are the kind of men I am fighting this war against. People who would tear this country apart...who don't seem to be able to see that slavery is evil and that the country has to be whole to be strong." He continued, "What if I showed you a way that you could fight your war, and also help me fight my war... would that be of interest to you?"

Bill cocked his head to one side. "I'm willing to listen," he said. George nodded.

"Your men tell me that you led them through the hills full of Home Guard without getting anyone killed...that you seem to have some kind of sixth sense to see trouble before it finds you. That is an important power to have. What do you attribute that to? Is it your Indian heritage or something else?" Black Jack asked.

Bill pulled his hat off and ran his fingers through his black hair. "Probably a little bit of my Indian senses and a lot of luck," Bill said.

"And you Mr. Kilgo; what about your family?"

"The Home Guard planned to lock me in jail; and either hang me, or force me into the Confederate army. Bill rescued me and these other men. My family...all these men's families are in danger now. I sent my family North hopefully behind Union lines...I don't know if they made it out or not. I can't join your army until I know if they made it to safety," George said.

Black Jack nodded and was silent, thinking about all this for a few moments. "Men, I would like to propose that we help each other. Mr. Looney you want revenge on the Home Guard for what they did to your wife and tavern; and Mr.

Kilgo, you need to be sure your family is safe. If you men will come to work for me, I think I can help you both," he continued.

"I need men to fill out the First Alabama Calvary, and if I don't get the men from North Alabama; then, the Confederates will get them and they will be forced to fight against us. I need someone to lead those men to our lines. I believe you two are the men for that job. If in the course of recruiting those men...you happen to find some of the Home Guards that you want, Mr. Looney you feel free to handle them anyway you see fit," Black Jack paused again.

"Mr. Kilgo, I will put out the word all along the Union lines to be on the lookout for your family. I can help them find a way to cross into our territory, and help them once they are on land under our control." Black Jack paused to let what he had said sink in. "I will also sweeten the pot. I will pay you regular army wages...sixteen dollars a month, and I'll give each of you a dollar for every man you lead to join my army," Black Jack paused again. "I don't want to deceive you...what I am asking you to do is very dangerous. You know if the Home Guard or the Confederates catch up to you, you will probably be shot or they will hang you. I just think you are too valuable to put in the lines and have you killed in battle."

Bill and George looked at each other; neither wanted to say anything.

"I will give you some time to think about my proposal. Why don't you take a day or two to rest up; then, you can give me your decision," Black Jack said. He shook their hands, and Bill and George were lead back to their men.

What about your cousin Eddie?" George asked Bill.

"Eddie has decided not to join the army. He is going back to the mountains of North Carolina to take Senie to our people. He said he didn't want to die fighting for rights that helped black men, but not Indians," Bill said matter-of-factly. George nodded because that made perfect sense to him.

They spent the next couple of days in the Union army camp. They were shown to a four man tent that they shared with Eddie and another of the men they knew. The food was not that great, but it was better than the jerky and salt pork they had been living on in the caves.

Mostly, life in the camp was boring. There were thousands of men with little to do. The officers made the men train some, but there was just so much of that the men could stand. Mostly, they just sat around, waiting for the generals to plan the next big battle or move. The men spent a lot of time gambling. The officers didn't like it, but couldn't really stop it either. The soldiers gambled on just about anything. They raced and bet on rats they caught, held insect races, pitched rocks into cups, held shooting matches, foot races, knife throws and a dozen other games they bet on. Bill discovered a shooting match and pulled George over there.

"How much does it cost to enter?" Bill asked the man in charge, as about ten men lined up to shoot at targets about two hundred yards away. The big Union soldier looked Bill and George up and down.

"Tis' a buck to enter lads, winner takes all, but you'll be make your own side bets." The big man answered in a heavy Irish accent.

"Look, I got the winner standing right here, but they took our rifles when we came into camp. What will it take to get them back so we can take all your Yankee money?" Bill said. That statement caught the big man's attention.

"You be part of that Southern trash that arrived the other day?" He said glaring at the two men. George was uncomfortable and wanted to move along, but Bill was not afraid of anything or any man.

"Yeah, we can out shoot, out fight, out jump and outsmart any Yankee alive. If you can get my man his rifle back, we will be glad to prove it!" Bill said loudly to all those who would listen. A couple of soldiers started to curse at them and a couple wanted to fight them. The big Irishman soldier just glared at Bill for a few seconds.

"By God Sergeant Swartz! What say we be getting this white trash h's rifle back so we can take his money?"

A small skinny looking sergeant appeared and looked them over. "Let him borrow a rifle," the sergeant said.

"No, No! That won't work! We want to prove that a Southern made rifle is better than your Yankee rifles; and in the hands of a Southerner, it will take all your Yankee money," Bill shouted to the sizable group that had gathered.

"Get's him his rifle!" The big Irishman said to the skinny sergeant. *"Tis time to teach these hillbillies about the superiority of Yankee tradesmen and marksmanship."*

"Okay, come with me, and I'll see if I can get your rifle back," the sergeant said to Bill and George. As they were walking, George turned to Bill and said, "Bill I don't have a dollar. The Home Guard took everything I had when they captured me."

"Don't worry. I got a couple of dollars; and if we play this right, we will have a lot more when it is over. They ain't got anything that will shoot like your new rifle. You just hold her steady and squeeze the trigger slowly," Bill said.

The sergeant talked to a captain who looked them over and then, took them to a tent that held their stuff. "Which gun?" the captain asked. When he gave it to them, along with George's cartridge pouch; he held up the rifle and examined it. "Nice rifle. Don't get any ideas about using it for nothin' but the contest. You are surrounded by forty thousand Union soldiers," he said.

They could hear the shooting from the contest as it went on without them. When they arrived back at the shooting area, the next round was paying their money and selecting their shooting spots. Bill pulled out a dollar from his boot and gave it to the big Irishman who gave them a sneer. Bill and George took up a position while the men near the targets, down range, put up new paper targets. Shooters had to hold their guns free-hand and couldn't rest on anything. George fired thinking he had been right on the center. When the soldier walked the targets back up to them, George had knocked the center out of the target and won twelve dollars. The big Irishman sneered even more as he paid them. *"Lucky shot,"* he said.

Bill paid for the next round and again George won. Now, the Irishman was getting mad. Bill was quick to take advantage of the Irishman's pride and said loudly, "Damn, another lucky shot!" They now had twenty four dollars, and George was ready to take the money and leave but Bill had other ideas. Talking loudly he said, "What about let's sweeten the pot, and make the contest a little harder. Unless of course you don't think your Yankee shooters have a chance to win, and you want to chicken out and stop shooting." The men all started to shout at them.

Bill held up his hand. "Move the target back another fifty yards, and double the entry fee to two dollars. Of course, at this distance shooters will need to prop their weapons." There was a bunch of grumbling and groaning, but the Irishman agreed. The number of men shooting dropped down to eight, but the number of side bets went up since some men were now betting on George. Bill was taking side bets until all their money was gone.

With the target moved to two hundred fifty yards, George still won; missing the center of the target by only about an inch. They shot two more rounds and George won every one of them. Finally, Bill held his hand up again.

"Men, as much as we enjoy taking your money a little at a time, let's just put this contest to an end and move the target back to...five hundred yards. We'll put the fee at five dollars a man." Most of the men dropped out because they didn't want to risk that much, and because some were beginning to believe that they couldn't beat George and his rifle.

George pulled Bill aside, "Damn it, Bill. That is such a long way off, I don't know if I can hit it or not."

"Sure you can. Didn't you tell me that the boy that made that rifle said it was accurate to a thousand yards? Well, five hundred should be easy," Bill said his dark eyes glowing. George was not so sure.

"What if I miss? At least don't bet everything we have won so far," George begged.

A huge crowd had formed now to watch as the men down range paced off the five hundred yards. The targets were just white dots in the far distances. There were only three shooters left. The Irishman called George over and introduced himself.

"Name's Bo McCoy," the big man said holding out his hand to George. *"Sorry about what I said earlier, t'was just blowing off steam."*

"George Washington Kilgo," George shook his hand. "Look this thing is getting kind of crazy. I can hardly see the target. What if we all miss completely?" George *asked*.

"Then, we will re-shoot. Yer are a dandy shot. That man over there is Big Dave Scott of the Fifty-fifth Michigan, and the other man is Hoss Jones of the Twenty-second Illinois. They are the best sharpshooters around here. They both have kills at over seven hundred yards." The big Irishman leaned close to George. *"I be betting a month's pay on ya so don't miss."*

The men all took turns shooting with George going last.

He was getting nervous. This was different than shooting at targets in the back of his place. He could see the targets flutter in the slight breeze, and he wondered if he should allow for the wind. He could see the targets jump when the other men shot, so he figured they at least hit the target. In the end, George decided to trust what Royal Bates had said and held the sights dead on what he guessed to be the center of the target. They were so far away; he couldn't really see the center. George took a breath and let out half of it and slowly squeezed the trigger.

The targets came back, after what seemed like a lifetime. (They actually had to use a horseback rider to retrieve the targets because they were so far away.) Both other shooters had clipped the target near the edges. George had hit about three inches from dead center.

A big cheer went up from those who had bet on George, and a groan from those who had bet against him. A dozen men came over to shake George's hand and pat him on the back. The other two shooters came over to talk with him. One offered to get him on his sharpshooter's team, if George wanted to join his company.

In a minute or so, out of the crowd walked Black Jack Logan smoking a cigar. He congratulated George on his fine shooting. He wanted to hold and look at George's rifle. While they were talking, Bill was collecting their bets. They had made a hundred and twenty dollars to be split between them.

"It's none of my business; but if I were you, I'd turn that money in to the quartermaster for safe keeping. Just like outside the army, we have thieves who will be only too glad to relieve you of that money. The quartermaster will give you a receipt for it and keep it safe. You can get as much as you need anytime," the Major General said. Bill thought about what he had said for a minute.

"I guess you are right. Don't want to get my throat slit. Make it known around camp that I turned it in," Bill said. The General nodded.

"Enjoy your stay, bet and gamble all you want and be thinking about my proposal," the General said as he walked off.

The next day, Bill was at it again. George woke up to find Bill in a heated conversation with several soldiers. "A bet is a bet!" Bill said angrily. The others started to shout and talk at once. George finally figured out that Bill had bet them that he could jump over a large horse, without touching it at all. The horse stood about fourteen hands high and it seemed like a safe bet to the soldiers, so they bet twenty dollars that he couldn't do it. Now, they didn't want to pay.

George was trying to get them to tell him what was wrong, when the big Irishman McCoy showed up on the scene. *"What's the matter, lads?"* he asked.

"I won the bet, and now these Yanks don't want to pay up," Bill said. The soldiers all started to talk at once.

McCoy looked at George, *"Tis what happens when ya don't have someone in charge of the betting. Okay, what was the bet?"*

"I bet them I could jump over this horse," Bill said. "I did it and they start claiming it wasn't fair, and I didn't do it the way I said."

McCoy turned to the others, *"Was that the bet?"*

"Yeah, but he cheated," one said.

"How so?" McCoy asked. *"Did he clear the horse?"*

"Yeah, but...he didn't...do it right."

"And how tis the right way to jump over a horse?" Turning to Bill, *"Maybe ya should show me how ya did it,"* McCoy said.

"Okay," Bill said. "Hold her steady boys." Bill backed up a few feet and took a run at the side of the horse. He planted his feet and jumped up into the air...diving over the horse head first, he flipped in mid air and came down on his feet on the other side.

"Tis that how he did it?" McCoy asked the other men.

"Yeah, but...he never said anything about doing no flip; he just said he would jump it."

McCoy looked at the other soldiers. *"Did he start out with a jump?"*

"Yeah, I guess he did."

"Did he clear the horse?"

"Yeah, but..."

"No buts about it; he jumped, and he cleared it. Now pay up or face the wrath of me Irish temper," the big Irishman said. The men reluctantly paid out the money to Bill.

"That t'ws the damnest thing I ever seen!" McCoy said in his rich Irish accent. *"Still, if'n ya got anymore tricks up yer sleeves ya might want to run them by me first. The boys know I will crack their heads if'n they don't pay up."* McCoy walked away shaking his head.

That afternoon, Bill and George made their way back to General Logan's tent. The General greeted them, and before they could speak said, "George, I want you to know, before you say anything that I have put the word out along the Alabama-Tennessee line to be on the lookout for your family. I sent word to help them and protect them, so you don't have to feel pressure to work for me; I think it is important that a man knows his family is safe."

George gave the General a long look. "Thank you for that, sir; that makes me want to work for you all the more."

"And you Bill, do you want to help bring in those boys from Winston?"

"Yes, sir. As long as you know, I'll be taking my revenge whenever I get the chance," Bill said.

"Understood, just as long as you don't endanger the men," General Logan said.

"I will call for Captain Peterson to brief you on how things are set up with our spies there in the hill counties. I can't tell you how pleased I am that you men have agreed to help. You are going to save the lives of a lot of men," General Logan said, rising to shake the men's hands.

Captain Peterson was a short, redheaded man with a heavy Yankee accent. The Captain laid out a map on the table, pulled out some more papers and spread them out.

"We have several people who are helping us recruit soldiers from the North Alabama and Tennessee hills. These people send us information about the movement of the Home Guard and Southern troops. They also send us messages when they have men who want to get out of the area, and want to join Federal troops," the Captain said.

Pointing to the map he said, "These are the positions of the major Confederate troops. We believe there are four groups of Home Guards operating in the Northern counties. They consist of about twenty men so it is hard for anyone to confront them. There is only one group of Partisan Rangers, and they are staying close to the Confederate troops so you won't have to worry about them as much. I don't have to tell you what will happen if you get caught by the Guard."

The Captain laid a piece of paper in front of them. "We got this two days ago. It says there are four men hiding in a root cellar. We also got information there are four more in two different locations. These are the names of your contacts who will tell you the locations of the men."

"Sometimes, you will need to approach the contacts at night to avoid being seen. Sometimes, you can approach them like just a normal farmer, which is what you need to look like. They will know who you are by you using the code word:

'black,' the Captain explained. Bill and George nodded that they understood.

"Just say something like: We saw a black cat or a black fox on the way over here. That will identify you as part of Black Jack's men. If it is safe to talk, they will agree; but if they can't talk, they will say they never heard of such. You will need code names to identify yourself. Bill, we will call you the Black Fox for your smarts and guile. George, we will call you the Black Hawk, because I understand you have the eye of a hawk when shooting. Use these names to identify yourself to our troops. You don't want to get shot by our boys," the Captain paused to see if they were following. When they nodded he went on.

"The rest of it is up to you. You know how to avoid the Guard, where to hide and how to get back here. Do you have any questions?" The Captain asked. George looked at Bill, and they both shook their heads. The Captain stood up and shook their hands. "You are better men than I am; good luck!"

Black Jack had been standing at the door of the tent listening. "Men I can't tell you how much this will mean to these men who you are going to rescue; what it can mean to their families." The General paused, "This war is taking a sickening toll of lives; maybe you can help save a few."

George and Bill were about to leave when the same Captain came to them and led them to another tent. The men were allowed to pick out a rifle and any pistols they wished to take.

Bill picked out a Sharps Carbine and another Navy Colt pistol to go with the one he already carried. The Captain went over and pulled a sawed off double barrel shotgun from a stack of guns and gave it to Bill also.

"This shotgun is a favorite with our cavalry. The sawed off barrels make it easy to handle and deadly at close range," the

Captain said. He gave Bill a holster for the shotgun to tie on his saddle. "If someone asks where you got these guns, tell them you got them off dead Federal soldiers; otherwise, they will suspect you are a spy."

George kept his rifle since it was as good as the Sharps. He took a second Colt revolver, but didn't get a shotgun because of the added weight. George was sworn into the Union army, but Bill refused to be tied down by being in the army.

CHAPTER THIRTEEN

The men left and rode four days to their first meeting place. They approached a farm house outside a little town near Russellville. The shutters were closed; when they called out, gun barrels appeared out the slots in the shutters. "Hold it right there, boys! State your business!" a voice called out from inside the house.

"Hold steady with the guns," Bill called out. "We were just wondering if you had seen any black foxes around here." There was a silence; and then the door opened a crack.

"Come in closer. We see black foxes all the time. Who sent you?" the voice asked.

"Black Jack," Bill answered. The door swung open, and a man and woman appeared.

"Come on with me. There's no time to waste. We heard the Home Guard was searching every house around looking for some Tories," the man stated. He went into the house, pulled the kitchen table to the side, and pulled open a trap door in the floor. Four heads stuck up out of the floor.

"Come on up, and hurry! We need to get you out of here before the Guard comes." Bill and George told them who they were, and they were there to take them to the Federal lines. Among the men were a farmer, his brother and their two teenage sons. They explained that their names had been posted in town with orders to report to the Confederate army enrollment center by a certain date or be subjected to arrest.

"We ain't going to fight for the Rebs; please, help us get to the Federals. We have been hiding out for a week now; and the Home Guard has visited our homes and harassed our families. We're ready to fight, but just the four of us don't stand a chance against the twenty Guards that are riding around here."

"Don't worry. We will get you to the Union lines. Now, where are your horses?" Bill asked.

When the men had recovered their horses hidden in the woods, they all rode off toward their next contact. The bunch had to ride off the road. There was only one road in and out of the farm, and they were worried about meeting the Home Guard. Their fears came true. They were moving parallel to the road when Bill suddenly signaled them to dismount and be quiet. Not a half minute later, about twenty riders galloped by on the road headed toward the house they had just left.

Bill followed Indian markers, and found a bluff to hide in the rest of that day. That night, they rode all night to their next contact. While the men and their sons hid, Bill and George rode to the next contact a country store. After watching for an hour or so, Bill believed it was safe to approach the store. While George waited and watched the door, Bill went in, and had a conversation with the store owner. Afterwards, a young boy led them to a barn where two men were hiding in a pile of hay in the loft.

Bill led the party of eight to the next hiding place, and the next, until they were nearing the Federal lines. As they made their way in the dark alongside the main road, Bill suddenly stopped and signaled them to hide in the woods. Bill and George crept forward. "Do you smell it?" Bill asked George. George shook his head. "I smell a camp fire."

When they had moved a couple of hundred yards, they spotted a small fire up ahead. They snuck in closer and could see two men huddled around the fire cooking. They split up and made their way to either side of the camp.

"Hello, to the camp!" Bill called out. The men scrabbled for their weapons and took cover. "Who are you, and what are you about?"

"Name is Guthrie, this here is my brother. Who are you?" the man called back.

"We are just fox hunters, hunting for black foxes," Bill called out.

"Thank God!" the man said standing up. "We were trying to make our way to the Federal lines. We heard about you from Hap Johnson over at the store. He said ya'll might be up this way. We want to join up, but have been afraid we were going to run into the Home Guard before we found you or the Feds."

"Well, building a fire wasn't the best way to keep from attracting the Guard," Bill said as he and George walked into their camp. The man looked sheepish. "Never mind now," Bill said. "Spread the fire out so it will die, and ya'll come with us."

Bill and George went about meeting and taking men to the Union army for the next twelve months. During that time, they avoided meeting the Home Guard, although they had a number of close calls. Bill's intuition always somehow warned them when the Guard was closing in.

It was early 1863, and things were not going well for either side. The first two years of the war were spent with both sides winning and then losing battles. General Lee was beginning to realize that time was on the Union side, and he was determined to force the issue by invading the North.

George was able to sneak by the plantation a few times over the next few months to check on Mary Pruitt. She had not heard from her husband since the night George was captured. Jim had brutally raped and beat her until she passed out. When she awoke Tee was bathing her face with water. Her face was swollen badly but other than bruises on her body she had survived.

"George!" Mary cried out when she saw him. George had met her down by the creek after sending word by Matoomba for her to meet him.

"I thought I would never see you again!" She said as she rushed into George's arms.

"I was worried that Jim might have killed you." George said smothering her with kisses. "I was so relieved to hear you were OK."

"He beat me until I thought I was going to die...until I passed out. Lou Johnson's son, Seth, came home after getting his arm shot off and said he saw Jim with Lee's army in Virginia. George, I pray that he gets killed in the war! I know that makes me a terrible person and goes against my Christian faith...sob.... and I will probably go to hell for being with you and thinking such thoughts but I can't help it." Mary sobbed into George's shoulder.

"It's alright. I admit to having the same thoughts."

"What about Emme and your children?" Mary asked when she had stopped sobbing.

"I got word that they were safe and behind Federal lines somewhere in the Nashville area. I have written to her but I have been on the move so much I haven't gotten any mail." George explained.

"Then you will want to see these." Mary said pulling two letters from the pocket of her apron.

George opened the letter with shaking hands. Mary said, "I will leave you alone to read them." She walked a little ways away and sat on a large rock near the creek bank. It was a good thing because George's eyes filled with tears as he read about the families harrowing trip north to union lines.

The first letter was mailed in Athens, Alabama and the second from Pulaski, Tennessee. George finished reading and then turned to Mary.

"They made it to the Federal lines in Decatur and when these letters were mailed they were still on the road and didn't know where they would go or settle. Emme said the children were safe and that a Union soldier had been assigned to help them on orders of General Logan. She seemed to think they would be alright." George said.

"How...when...did you come by these letters?" George asked.

Mary blushed red. "I went to Mr. Halston and lied to him. I told him that you were coming by to see me....he looked at me very strangely and I know he must have heard rumors. He said he didn't think he should give the letters to me, but I convinced him that you would never risk coming into town to the store and he gave them to me." George pulled her up and into his arms.

"Thank you so much! You could have just destroyed them." George whispered into her ear while holding her in his arms.

Mary pulled back to look into his eyes. "George, I would never, ever come between you and Emme and your children. I love you, and I care for you so much but I would never try to take you away from your family. I can't help loving you...and you have given me the most precious gift...but I could never stand between you and Emme."

George kissed her then; George pulled his bed roll off Dolly's back and spread the red wool blanket across the ground.

Later as they lay side by side, George rose up on one elbow and asked what she meant when she said he had given her the most precious gift.

"George, I am with child...I am going to have your baby... the baby I have wanted my whole life." Mary said with tears in her eyes.

George couldn't help but feel the tears starting in his own eyes so he pulled her into an embrace, hiding his own tears.

When they had spent an hour and half together they reluctantly parted. George promised to check on her again if he could. He asked Mary to get word to Mr. Halston to forward any mail to the Federal Army Command in the care of General Logan.

George and Bill carried five hundred and twenty-three men safely to Union lines in spite a reward for both, dead or alive, placed on them by the Confederates. They were called in to General Logan's tent and told that their job as recruiters for North Alabama was at an end. The requests for help crossing to the Union lines had dropped to nothing. Anyone who wanted out of Alabama had already gotten out. Their job shifted to scouts now. Bill was a natural at this because he could move through the woods and fields without being detected.

They were sent into the field to find the location and strength of the Confederate forces, and to find food sources for the Union army. Both endeavors were more dangerous than taking men across lines to join the Union army. Most scouting had to be done in the daylight hours, and the chance of encountering the enemy was much greater.

George and Bill rode into the countryside *toward* the Rebel troops; or at least, where the spies said the Rebels were. Some armies didn't stay put for long periods of time; but instead constantly moved. They were also constantly sending out patrols to seek out the other side.

One of their first assignments was to observe and report on Rebel forces dug in on the banks of the Harpeth River near Franklin, Tennessee. The town, about forty miles from Nashville, was the setting for five of the bloodiest hours of the war.

George was only a few miles from his wife and family. Emme and the kids had gotten out of Alabama safely and were living in a boarding house in Nashville. George didn't know this and wouldn't find out until sometime later.

George and Bill, along with four runners, were on a ridge above the field where the Rebel army of General Hood was gathered. The day before, Hood had sent his men against Union General Schofield in a battle that lasted five hours and cost the Confederates the lives of ten thousand men. Still, General Schofield had felt endangered, and during the night had withdrawn to the city of Nashville, which was said to have the best defense of any city except Washington DC. Now, General Thomas was approaching from the east and looking to attack Hood, who was desperate to gain some advantage after losing so many men.

George and Bill watched and counted the Rebel forces; the number of men, cannons, cavalry, and such, plus their locations. The four runners would, one at a time, take information to General Thomas, who would plan his attack according to the information he received from scouts like Bill and George.

When General Thomas attacked, he caught the Rebels

between his troops and those of General Schofield. The Confederate forces were forced to flee. The problem for George and Bill was that they fled right at them and their ridge. A wall of men dressed in gray came rushing right toward them. Before they realized what was happening, Confederate cavalry was rushing up the slope. They jumped on their horses and rode off, but they had to ride through a party of five Confederates.

Bill's shot gun proved handy as he took out two men with one blast. George shot one at close range with his rifle while on a full gallop. The other two shot at George and Bill with their pistols and missed, but killed one of the runners fleeing with them. Still the bullets were close enough that George could hear them zip by. When they had made their way back to camp, George pulled his hat off to find a bullet hole in the crown of his hat.

After the Battle of Nashville, the war shifted toward the east. General Logan and his forces were sent to Chattanooga, Tennessee where General Grant was determined to drive the Confederates off Lookout Mountain.

Bill and George spent months trying to find weaknesses in Confederate positions around Missionary Ridge and Raccoon Mountain. It was a cold fall and the weather was dreary. Many days the fog was so thick, it made their jobs impossible.

In a three day period, between November 23 and 26, Chattanooga was captured, and the route was opened for Union troops to move down into the state of Georgia.

Bill and George spent time in an army camp in northern Georgia while Union forces moved into position to begin a march through Georgia. Their goal was to cut the Confederacy in two. Bill and George were sent out to find the Confederates and report back on their locations, again and again.

It was dangerous work and only Bill's quick thinking and instinct saved them at times.

Once, they were coming down a road toward a fork, when there suddenly appeared a Rebel patrol. It came up on them so quickly, they didn't have time to do anything except dash off the side of the road. They found themselves in a turnip green patch near the side of a farmhouse. They dismounted and were holding their horses, hoping the Rebs would ride by without seeing them; when from behind them, another group of Confederates approached.

They were totally caught out in the open with no place to run. Bill realized their predicament and seeing the turnips at their feet, immediately pulled his hat off and grabbed up a handful of turnips greens. Bill grabbed George's hat and handed it to him, and he quickly followed Bill's lead and started to pick turnips. When the Rebs approached them, Bill threw up a wave and shouted, "We are going to have turnip greens for supper tonight boys!" The group of Confederates rode by them a few feet away. Because they were dressed like many Confederate irregulars, without any real uniforms, and because of Bill's southern accent, the soldiers rode right by them. "Pick a bunch of them," one man said, "I'm damn hungry." Only after the Rebels were out of sight, did they remount and ride away thankful to be alive.

Another time Bill had been sick for three days, running a fever and coughing heavily. George had tried to get him to seek a doctor but Bill had dug up some roots, ground them and mixed with some whiskey. It had knocked him out causing him to sleep for several hours. George stood guard for a while but eventually he dozed off also.

George awoke with Bill shaking him.

"Wake up." Bill said. When George opened his eyes Bill said, "George, there are about a dozen riders headed right for us." George reached for ole Stumpy with a panicked look on his face.

"What do we do? Make a run for it? Shoot it out?" George asked.

"I don't know. It is too late for either one I think."

They were on the banks of a creek with the creek on one side and the road about fifty yards away on the other side. George peeked over the log they were lying against and could see the riders turning off the road and heading down toward their position. Bill spotted some poke-berry bushes hanging over the top of the log.

He grabbed a handful and held them out to George. "Here, mash these against your face and make some spots; we will pretend we have smallpox." Bill started pushing a berry on his face and twisting it around and around. George saw what he was doing and started doing the same thing.

"Do you think it will work?" He asked.

"I don't know. It worked in one of the stories my grandfather told about some Indians escaping. We don't have any other choices." Bill said. "You lie down and let me do the talking; just moan, look sick and follow me."

George laid down while he still mashed the berries into his skin, making splotches on his forehead and cheeks.

The riders were almost on top of them now. Bill stood up holding his hands in the air. When the riders saw him they trained their guns on him. Bill called out to them.

"Hold your ground men!" he yelled. The lead riders pulled their horses to a halt about twenty yards away.

"Who are you, and what's your business?" The leader asked.

"Privates Williams and Smith 6th Tennessee Volunteers,"

Bill said using the name of one of the Confederate units they had been shadowing. "At least we used to be. Stay back, we got the pox," Bill said tilting his face up and pulling off his hat. A gasp went up from the riders as they saw the pox sores on Bill's skin. George groaned and sat up turning his face toward the men.

"We were ordered out of the ranks and ordered to follow at a half mile, but we couldn't keep up any longer. Look we ain't had nothing to eat in near two days. Could you boys spare a little food?" Bill asked.

Some of the riders turned their horses and pulled back a little from them. The leader reached into his saddle bags, and pulling out a cloth bag, threw it to Bill.

"Thank you kindly." Bill said. "I don't guess you would have any laudanum would you? These sores hurt something awful."

The man just shook his head. "We heard there was pox in the ranks, but no one seemed to know about it. You boys are the first we have seen. Is it bad...ah...I mean...are there others? The man asked.

"About a half dozen so far," Bill said. "They been sending anyone infected away from the rest of the troops." Bill shook his head. "I sure hope ya'll don't get it. It is not a great way to die." Bill added with a sigh of resignation in his voice.

The man nodded his head. "Good luck to you." The men rode off in the direction they had come from. Bill and George breathed a sigh of relief and quickly rode off in the other direction.

CHAPTER FOURTEEN

N ashville, Tennessee
        March 25th 1863
    My dearest darling George,

    I hope and pray that this letter finds you well and safe and
under the protection of our Lord and Savior. We are safe and
living in a boarding house on Walnut Street in the southern
part of Nashville. When Matoomba came and told us what
happened to you and that we had to get out right away, I feared
the worst. It was very hard to leave behind our little home, but I
understood why you insisted that we leave right away.
Matoomba said you would be alright as you were with Bill
Looney and that I should write to Mr. Halston at the store in
Double Springs when I was settled. I hope and pray this letter
finds its way to you somehow. I have found work cooking and
cleaning at a hotel a half-mile away from Mrs. Wall's Boarding
House. Will went out and on his own found work at a livery
stable, so we have enough money to get by with each month.
The hundred and forty dollars we kept in the coffee can was
enough to tide us over until I started to work. Liz is wonderful
with the younger kids, and we have found another baby sitter

in a wonderful woman named Mary Ann Tucker Sinyard. She is the sweetest person you could hope to know. The poor thing has lost so much in this war. Her husband, Joe Franklin, traveled to Tennessee to join the army much as you did. He was listed among the dead at the Battle of Stone Creek. Mary Ann was left with two young boys to take care of all on her own. Measles took both of the boys shortly after her husband was killed. So many dreadful things have happened to her, the poor thing has stopped talking. She fled the Home Guard much as we did. She makes herself understood by making signs and gestures. She has been a God-send because she has helped with the boys, especially when Liz has to sometimes work in my place. My condition is no worse or better than it was. I still have spells when I must stay off my feet and stay at home. You would hardly recognize little Tom, Sam and John Wesley; they have grown so much. I swear their legs grow a couple of inches every week. Liz is filling out so much it scares me. The boys are noticing her, and there are several that hang around the boarding house trying to catch her eye. I don't know what I would do without Will. He has become such a good and kind young man. He has taken on so much I worry about him. He needs to be a kid, but he has had to become a man. I think I know the reason that Mr. Pruitt turned on you and tried to put you in the army. I want you to know that I am alright if things happened between you and Mary Pruitt. I asked her and Hannah to look after you because I knew I was not able to meet all your needs. Mary Pruitt is a fine woman and the kind of person I would hope you could find if something ever happened to me. She confided in me that her husband was a drunk and very abusive to her. She said he was not able to be much of a husband and that more than anything she wanted to have a child.

I must stop now for it is time to put the little ones to bed.

Between cooking, cleaning and being a mother I am quite busy, and pretty tired each night. I want you to know that I am forever yours. I love you with all my heart and soul. I pray for your safe return and the day our family will be whole and we can return to our happy little farm.

With all my love, your loving wife Emme

GEORGE FINALLY GOT the letter in July of 1863. He now could breathe a sigh of relief that his wife and family were safe. Being separated from them weighed on his mind, but he had little time to think about such things. George promised himself he would write her back as soon as possible.

WILLIAMSON COUNTY, Tennessee

Aug.24th 1863

My dear Emme

I was so pleased to finally hear from you. I got your letter in July so I hope you and the family are still doing well. I am so glad that you have found work and are safely living in Nashville. I am so sorry for everything that has happened. If I had been a better man, none of this would have happened to you. Mr. Pruitt would never have drafted me into the Confederate army, I would still be working on the plantation, and you and the children would be safe at home. I want you to know that you are the love of my life and there can never be another one to take your place. As you know by now, I have joined the Union forces and Bill and I are now working as scouts. We worked to bring men out of north Alabama until most everyone who wanted to got out. Many joined the Union rather than fight for a cause they didn't believe in.

I am pleased that you have found someone to help with the

boys while you are working. I know God had a hand in your meeting with Mrs. Sinyard. I am proud of Will and Liz for helping you so much. Please give them and the little ones all my love. Bill and I are not in most of the fighting, as our job is to report to our General where the enemy is and how many men they have and such. We work for Major General Black Jack Logan, as fine and honest a man as you will ever meet. He treats us and all his men like we are family and grieves with the loss of any of his boys. Scouting is safer than fighting so don't worry about me. Only once have we got caught up in the fight. About a month ago we were watching a battle from high on a hill. Our job was to send runners with messages about any reinforcements we saw coming. Our boys were giving a good fight when suddenly a large Confederate force arrived on the scene and turned the tide against our troops. The General ordered the men to withdraw to the high ground and wait for our own reinforcements. Suddenly we were in the thick of the fighting. Our troops fought their way up the hill and made a stand on the crest. They were followed by a wave of gray Confederates that extended all the way from the valley half way up the hill. General Logan ordered all those troops with shot-guns to the front of the hill. He had them line up in four rows a few feet apart. He ordered the men to hold their fire until the Rebs were only fifty yards away. It was hard not to want to run with that many men coming toward you and trying to kill you. General Logan knew what he was doing because he ordered crisscross firing. It seems that if you fire your shotgun straight ahead you may kill four or five men, but they take all the shot. Others behind them will not get hit and can reach you before you can reload. If you fire at an angle, you may take down as many as ten men with one shotgun blast. Many of our boys had new long double barrel shotguns they just got the week before and had never even fired them. When the Gray Coats were at *fifty yards, our men fired four of the most perfect volleys anyone has ever seen. It seemed ten or twelve men fell on every shot from the shotguns. Huge holes appeared in the Confederate lines. Then our infantry opened up with volley after volley, and the Johnny Rebs broke and ran. A few Rebs made it to our line, but we quickly took care of them with our side arms. Emme, it is with much sadness that I tell you, I killed at least a dozen men that day. I have killed before with my rifle at long range, but never have I looked into the face of a man as I took his life. Some men had a surprised look on their face, others looked angry, and some just looked calm, like they knew they were going to die. I marvel at how men can keep charging forward knowing that they are going to die. I don't mean to worry you as this in not the situation we are usually in. I know I am writing too much, but I don't know when I will get the chance to write again. Please kiss all the children for me. Know that whatever happens, I am in God's hands and that I love you more than life.*

Your loving husband George

GEORGE AND BILL were pushing well down into the state of Georgia now. Confederates were falling back toward Atlanta, looking to make a stand there. General Grant had left to return to the fighting against General Lee in Virginia. General Sherman had taken over as commander of the Southern Union Army. He was not as well liked as Grant, but most soldiers considered him a good general. General Dodge was also under General Sherman and General Logan under him.

The year of 1863 seemed to melt away into an endless drone of warfare. George, Bill and the other scouts divided their time between hair-raising, dangerous, trips into Georgia and months spent in an army camp, filled with boredom. The biggest danger in the camps was being killed in a fight over gambling or getting some disease from the makeshift camp life. They basically lived in tents that were sometimes made a little better by building log attachments to them.

The food was terrible and consisted of salt pork, salt beef, potatoes, and a little dried fruit or vegetables if they were lucky. Everything was cooked in lots of grease to give it some flavor; otherwise, it had none. Bread was usually hardtack that was hard enough men sometimes threatened to put it in cannons and shoot it at the enemy. George and Bill ate better when they were on scouting duty because they could find their own food on the area farms. They carried rations with them, and the farm people would share if they had any food but the southerners ran out in the later years of the war. Bill and George found themselves sharing their food with the starving people more often than not.

If Bill had an hour he could find something to eat. Many times not wanting to risk shooting a gun, Bill would kill something with his bow. He also knew how to use a split green willow stick to push into an animal den and twist out some animal. They ate squirrels, possums, rabbits, birds and even snakes. At first George balked at eating snakes but soon learned to like the rattlesnakes that Bill could always seem to find when they couldn't find anything else.

In the spring of 1864, General Sherman decided to begin his final conquest of the state of Georgia and his drive to divide the South into two parts. Atlanta fell to Sherman in July of that summer. Now Sherman did something that no one expected. He turned his troops loose to march to the sea with the orders to destroy anything that might give aid or comfort to the Confederacy. Sherman's men followed his orders too well, burning and looting everything in their path.

George and Bill were returning to the Atlanta area after

scouting ahead toward Macon. They came upon Union troops looting a small village. Part of the town was burning, and men were driving wagons loaded down with loot. At one farm, a sergeant and his men were standing over the body of a farmer and loading the contents of the farm house onto a wagon.

"Sergeant, what the hell are you doing?" Bill asked.

"Just following orders," the sergeant said, "destroying everything that might help the enemy."

"But you are looting, how does that follow orders?" Bill asked.

"Well, these people might use this stuff to help the enemy, so we are taking it," the sergeant said. "Look, you can take your share if you want."

Bill was just shaking his head when the farmer's wife and young son came rushing out of the house. The wife had a shotgun in her hands and she aimed it at them and screamed, "You damn Yankees!" The sergeant pulled his pistol and shot her dead before she could fire the shotgun. When the son, who looked to be about ten, saw his father dead and his mother shot down, he started crying and grabbed up the shotgun. He too was gunned down before Bill or George could stop it from happening. George had screamed, "No!" but it didn't stop the boy from being killed.

"Now if those farmers hadn't resisted, no one would have had to die here," the sergeant said. He pointed his pistol at George and Bill.

"Is anybody else going to have to die here today?"

George could see Bill gritting his teeth and was afraid Bill was going to cause a shoot out with the sergeant and his men who were now standing around with their guns drawn, looking at Bill. Finally, after a long few seconds, Bill wheeled his horse and they rode away. They rode in silence for a long time.

CHAPTER FIFTEEN

George and Bill met a line of Union army headed their direction. They asked where to find General Logan and were directed about a quarter mile to their right. General Logan and his staff were moving forward, toward the village that was now burning.

When they got close to the General, Bill told him about what they had seen. The General asked them to ride a little ways ahead of the others. When they were out of sound of the others in the General's staff, he spoke to them. "I know what you saw was upsetting, and it is not right, but there is little I can do about it now. A few other officers and I have tried to rein in the men, but General Sherman's staff has made it clear that they don't want to stop what is happening. I believe they are trying to break the will of the Southern people," General Logan explained. "I don't agree, but I don't know what to do at this point. I have sent a message to General Grant about what is happening, but I don't hold much hope for him to take some action to stop Sherman," General Logan said. He looked at Bill and George, then said, "I know you boys just got back, but if you want to do something...here is what I think you could do to help."

"If you can...ride hard and get ahead of the advance troops who are doing the most looting and killing. Warn the people in the towns and villages what is coming. Tell them that an army, sixty miles wide and a hundred forty thousand strong, is headed their way and their orders are to destroy anything and everything that the Rebels might use in the coming winter," the General went on. "If you can manage to get to the Confederate lines, ask for an officer and let him know what is coming...they will probably have to fight anyway, but if they could just fall back...hundreds maybe thousands, of lives could be saved."

George and Bill both looked at each other, and then at the General.

"I have got to meet with some of the other officers in a few minutes," the General looked at them. "God speed, Gentlemen." Then the General rode away.

Bill and George rode over to the mess wagon, asked for some more food; then turned back in the direction they had just come. After a week of hard riding, they were finally a day ahead of the advancing Union troops. They rode into the center of the first town they came to and looked for the mayor or sheriff. They found the mayor. They told him just what the General had said was coming that way.

The mayor just looked at them like they were crazy. "These Union troops have to know we won't resist them. Surely they will spare us if we don't fight them," the mayor said.

Bill and George both shook their heads. "Mayor, you have to understand they are going to burn and loot, and they don't care if you resist or not. Their orders are to destroy anything that might help the Rebs during the coming winter. Believe us; they will burn everything, even churches and homes. They will rape and kill. They are out of control and bitter after four years of war, and their officers can't or won't try to stop them, Bill said. "Tell your people to get out now and take what they can...what they want to save. Please send word to all the other towns around. We have to go now." George and Bill rode away and repeated the warning to every farm and village they came to.

Finally, they came to what they knew was the edge of the Confederate lines by the number of wagon tracks they saw along the road. Large numbers of wagons had passed this way not too long ago. Now, they crept along fearful of encountering a Rebel patrol. Bill's instincts were on high alert now. He could feel the danger in the air. When they finally saw the fires of the Confederates' camp, they rested until morning. They talked about the best way to approach the Confederate lines and decided to use the same tactics they used the first time they approached the Union lines back in Mississippi.

In the morning, they moved along the lines until they found a group of skirmishers a little ways out from the main line. Bill approached, while George hung back watching and guarding his back as they had done before. When Bill was within shouting distance, he called out to the men. "Hey, you guys in the skirmishing pits." There was a scramble in the pits as the men all jumped to get their guns and try to find where the voice was coming from.

"Show yourself!" The men called out.

"I don't think so," Bill called out. "I need to talk to an officer."

There was quiet and then the men called back, "We don't feel like bringing an officer up here so you can shoot him."

"Look, if I...we...wanted to shoot anyone we could have done it by now. This is important. We have a message from a

Union general, but we don't want to get shot either. We can't talk to anyone except an officer, so get us someone to talk to and don't try to send someone out to flank us because that will just get someone killed," Bill said.

There was another period of silence and then the men said, "Okay, give us a few minutes." Finally, after what seemed like hours to George, the men called out that they had an officer there.

"State your name and rank," Bill called out.

"Captain Foster Bechum of the 6th Georgia Infantry; and you, Sir?"

"Bill Looney, scout of the 1st Alabama Cavalry," Bill answered from his hiding place. "Can we talk? I have an important message for you from my General."

"Okay, how do we do this? I don't want to get shot," Captain Bechum said.

"Me neither, Captain. I've survived three years of this hell, and I would like to live to see another day. Do you trust your men to obey and not shoot?" Bill asked.

"Sergeant Swan, do I have your word that you will personally kill any man who disobeys my orders and shoots this man?" Captain Bechum asked.

"Captain, you have my word," came the answer from behind the pits.

"Mr. Looney, that is the best I can do, now what is your guarantee?"

"George, you heard the Captain, now do I have your word that you will kill the Captain if someone on his side shoots me?" Bill called out to George.

"You got my word Bill, in fact, I got him in my sights right now," George shouted back. At first the Captain flinched and ducked his head a little; then he laughed.

"Okay, scout, I'm coming out; you do the same," the

Captain said standing up. Bill stood up and they started walking toward each other. When they reached a point about sixty yards from the skirmishers pit, the two men shook hands. They stood there and talked for at least ten minutes. George could see the Captain shaking his head and Bill talking and talking. Finally, the two men shook hands and walked away.

When they had ridden a ways George asked, "How did it go?"

Bill looked at him, "Alright I guess, the Captain is going to pass the word along, but he is not hopeful that anyone will believe him. He says even if they do believe him, he doesn't believe they will fall back without a major battle."

"Damn! We tried; I guess that is all we can do," George said.

They rode back toward their own lines. They were much closer now as the lines had advanced. Now, long before they reached a town, they could see the smoke of the burning buildings. They met Union soldiers driving wagons filled with loot. They saw farmers being buried by their families and fresh graves along the way. Stores burned, churches, farm houses, barns, taverns and all manner of buildings reduced to burned out shells with just the chimneys standing.

Mostly, they rode in silence, both lost in their own thoughts. Finally, Bill said, "I don't know about you, but I didn't sign up to be burning and looting from folks. What the soldiers are doing just ain't right."

George nodded, "I think we need to talk with the General again about all this."

When they arrived at the temporary Union camp, the General was busy in a staff meeting, so they went to a tent to rest and get something to eat. While they were resting, Bill went to the mail tent and came back with two letters for George.

The first letter was pretty much like the first George had received, and all about the family's daily life in their new home in Nashville. The second broke George's heart.

Nashville, Tennessee
May 22, 1864
My dearest George,
I don't know if you have received my letters as I have been writing to you almost every week, and I haven't received any letters from you since your letter of August last year. We have heard of mail wagons being blown up and mail bags being lost on several occasions, so I fear we are not able to communicate as I would wish. It is with a sad heart that I must tell you my health is much worse. I have been going downhill since the fall. I have taken to my bed and been there most of the last months. I am very weak, and I fear this may be the end. I don't mind going to the other side as I know I will be with the Lord. I just hate to leave the children behind to such an uncertain fate. I know Mrs. Sinyard will do her best to take care of them; it is just such a big job for someone in her condition. I have made her promise me that she will do her best to keep the children together. There are a lot of orphanages here in Nashville, but they are so full of children and their conditions are not the best. Will and Liz will be alright if I pass, but I worry so about little Tom, Sam and John Wesley. My darling, please promise me that you will remarry and find a good mother for my babies. I don't wish to die, but now I sometimes dream of death when I sleep. It sometimes seems preferable to the pain that I am in now. The doctor comes around every couple of days and gives me some medicine to ease the pain, but it makes me sleep all the time, and I want to spend as much time as I have left with my babies.

Before I became so sick, I tried to volunteer at the local hospital, but after one day I couldn't go back. I just couldn't stand to see those poor men with their legs and arms shot off. Some were so badly burned and scarred that it broke my heart. I kept seeing your face when I looked at them, and I spent most of the day in tears. If this is my last letter to you, I want you to know that you have been the best husband I could wish for. You have loved me with more passion and treated me with more respect than I deserve. I love you with all my heart and all my being.

Your loving,
Emme

GEORGE READ and re-read the letter. He couldn't believe what he was reading. He couldn't think about living without his Emme. He knew he had to leave, to go to her and the children, even if he had to desert the army.

George and Bill went to see the General again. They told the General about their concerns with what was happening. He agreed that things were out of control and that bad things were being done that should not be happening. Finally, George let him read Emme's letter. The General had to blink quickly when he finished reading and George could see his eyes misting.

"George, I believe you need a furlough. I will make it for three months, and we will see how things go from there. I am really sorry about your wife. I hope you get there in time to see her and you are able to take care of your children," the General said. Turning to Bill he said, "Maybe you need to go with George to make sure he gets to Nashville safely. I really need both of you back as soon as you can. You men are the best scouts I've got," General Logan said. "It has been a pleasure to serve with you. Good bye." The General shook the men's hands.

George and Bill just nodded. Neither knew how this worked, but General Logan turned to his second in command and had him get the proper papers ready. In a few minutes, George had the furlough papers and they were drawing supplies for the trip ahead.

They rode steady for five days to get to the Georgia-Alabama line. The shortest route to Nashville went right through a corner of Alabama. The trouble with that route was that it took them through territory still patrolled by the Home Guard. Bill was fine with that because he had a score to settle with a bunch of them. George didn't care about that; he just wanted to get to Nashville by the fastest route. If that meant going through a little corner of Alabama, then that was the way they would go.

George and Bill slowed down when they crossed into Alabama. The whole area had been skipped over by the Union because it was so remote; except for one ill-fated raid by Colonel A. D. Streight, the Home Guard was free to roam and do whatever they wanted.

It was now clear to a lot of people that the South was going to lose the war. The Guard was worried that they were going to become the hunted, just as they had hunted people to force them into the army. They still roamed the roads; only now they were trying to punish and drive out all the families of the Tories, and those who might come after them when the war was over.

They were approaching night of the second day in Alabama, when Bill threw up his hand to stop. "Do you smell that?" he asked George.

George sniffed the air, but just shook his head.

"Stay here. I smell a campfire," Bill said.

When Bill returned a little later, he was shaking. "George, there are seven men over there, all Home Guards. I listened, and at least three of them are on the list. I recognized their names."

George shook his head. "Bill, there are seven of them. How...can we take on seven men? Even if we surprise them in their bed rolls, there are seven of them."

Bill said, "We can't surprise them in their camp. They are too smart for that. They will be sleeping spread out so they can't all be taken at night."

George looked at Bill. "Can't we just pass on by? I really need to get to Nashville to see my Emme before she dies."

Bill paused and gave George a look. "George, these are the men who raped my wife," Bill said.

George took a deep breath. "Okay. How do we do this without getting killed?"

"Let me look things over a little. You watch them, and I'll be back in a little while."

George crept along so he could see into the camp. The men were passing around a bottle and drinking. They seemed to be talking about someone they had killed recently. They were laughing about how the man died begging for his life. George felt his temper rising. Bill came back, got George, and took him a half mile or so down the road.

"They are traveling north, and tomorrow they will come this way. There is a little rise and a curve about six hundred yards up the road. I want you to shoot from there, and then ride away. If you can, get them to chase you like Eddie did the day we rescued you," Bill explained. "If you can get one of them, that will leave six for me to deal with. I will set an old Indian trap for them about here. I'll use a rope to trip their horses. That should take a couple down; I'll use the shotgun first, I should get a couple. That will leave four. If they fall off the horses, that will give me a little time. I should be able to take them," Bill explained. "Just ride back as soon as you hear the shooting; in case I don't get them all, you may have to help mop up," Bill said. They worked for an hour in the moon light setting Bill's trap.

George spent the rest of the night trying to sleep. He only dozed off a couple of times. When first light came, he went to find Bill who had been up for a while. George took his position and waited for the Guard to come down the road.

An hour after daylight, the Home Guard came into sight, trotting their horses down the road. George took aim with Ole Stumpy. It was an easy shot. The men were riding in twos, with one riding alone up front. George aimed at the man in the lead and squeezed the trigger. The roar of the fifty caliber rifle shook the morning silence. The bullet flew true and the man flipped backwards off his horse. George rode up into the road so they could see him; turned Dolly, and took off down the road away from them. They fired a volley of shots after George, but he was too far away for their guns.

As expected, the men spurred their horses and gave chase to the bushwhacker. This was not the first time someone had taken a shot at them, and they were determined to catch and kill the shooter.

They had just reached a full gallop when Bill sprang his trap. Bill had hidden his ropes, tied together, covered in dirt, and stretched across the road. Bill stood in the woods off the road. The rope was tied to a four inch-thick limb that was placed between the forks of a tree. As the horses approached the rope, Bill dropped the limb, which pulled the rope tight about knee high on the horses.

The horses hit the rope, tripping them and throwing some of them over into the road. Three horses went down; two threw their riders. One horse fell on the man riding it, trapping his leg under the horse. Bill came out of the woods with the sawed off shotgun in his hands. He blasted the men who remained on their horses because they were the most dangerous. The first blast took one man down; the next knocked another one off his horse.

Bill dropped the shotgun and pulled both of his hand guns. He shot the remaining horseman who was trying to pull his handgun. Walking around the horses, he shot the two men on the ground, one after the other, before they could recover from their falls. Bill walked over to where the man was trying to crawling out from under the horse penning his leg.

"Who...why...?" the man asked.

"I'm Bill Looney! Does that tell you why?" Bill asked.

"Bill Looney, you killed my brother! I hope you burn in hell!" the man said.

"Oh, I'm sure I will. You and your brother raped my wife, so when you get there, tell them I'm coming; but I'll be sending a few before me," Bill then shot the man in the head. Bill walked around and put another bullet into each of the men just to make sure they were all dead.

When George came riding up, Bill was busy scalping the men and stuffing their scalps into their mouths. Two of the three horses that fell had broken legs so George had to shoot and kill them.

"Do you want to move the bodies off the road?" George asked.

"No, let them lay where they are. I want everyone to know what happens to Home Guards." The two men mounted their horses and rode away. After a little while, Bill stopped and turned to George. "This is as far as I go," Bill said. "I ain't going back to the army. I've got no stomach for what is going on now, and I've got unfinished business with about a dozen more Home Guard."

"I think the General knew we wouldn't be back. When he shook our hands, he didn't say see you later, he said good bye, I'm pretty sure he knew we were finished," George said. He offered his hand to his friend. "Be careful, don't let your temper and need for revenge get you killed."

"Don't worry," Bill said. "I ain't ready to go yet; too many bad guys to kill first." Bill turned and rode away headed southeast.

George rode hard for over a week, sleeping on the ground at night and sometimes dozing in the saddle, just letting Dolly walk along the road. Here in Tennessee, there was no danger from the Home Guard because there were too many Union patrols and troops. Twice he was approached by Union patrols. As they approached, he called out "Black Hawk and Black Jack" to let them know he was Union. They looked at his furlough papers and let him go on.

CHAPTER SIXTEEN

He finally reached the outskirts of Nashville, after what seemed like a month. He needed a bath after days and days without one, but he wanted to see his wife and kids. George asked for Walnut Street and soon found Mrs. Wall's Boarding House. He rode up and started to walk into the yard of the house. There were several children playing in the yard. A curly headed boy was chasing a click-n-wheel around the yard, while another boy was on his knees playing in the dirt near the base of a large tree. George recognized Sam and John Wesley even though they had grown a lot. Sam lost control of the wheel, and it fell to the ground. He looked around and saw the man looking at him. The man looked familiar; yet he didn't.

George had not shaved in almost two years. He used to shave every Saturday because Emme didn't like the way the beard felt on her face. George was wearing the old black felt hat he had left with two and a half years ago. It was now bleached out in places and more gray than black. He wore an old brown shirt and a dark brown pair of pants because they helped him hide.

The boy looked at George and cocked his head to one side. George couldn't help but see how much he looked like his mother. He had the same eyes and forehead. Finally, the boy said, "Daddy?" It was more of a question than a statement. Then, he was running full force as he jumped into his Daddy's arms nearly knocking George over as he hugged him.

John Wesley had turned when his brother spoke, and now he looked carefully at the two as they hugged. He vaguely recognized the man, but when George pulled off the hat, it hit him that this was his father. He let out a scream, and ran to join in the hug.

George looked up from the group hug and spotted a woman sitting on the steps of the house. She was tall and thin, with light brown hair and pretty features. She was holding a sleeping boy that George knew must be Tom. Tears were running down her face as she tried not to cry at the scene before her.

Sam pulled back from the hug and looked his Dad in the eyes. "Momma is gone," he said choking back tears. "She died last month. She said she wished she could see you again; but... she was just too tired, and it was time for her to go to be with Jesus."

George felt the tears rising to his eyes. "It's okay. I'll see her...we will all see her again someday," George said in a choked voice to the boys. He picked up John Wesley and put him on his hip as he put his arm around Sam. They walked over to where the woman sat now covering her face and crying softly.

"You must be Mary Sinyard. Emme wrote me about you helping with the children. She said you were sent by God to help her and she thought the world of you," George said extending his hand to the woman. She took his hand and pulled him down into a hug, which turned into crying on his shoulder.

When a few moments had passed, she let him go. "Where are Will and Liz? George asked running his hand through the hair of the sleeping Tom. That set off another round of crying by Mary Sinyard.

"They had to go live at another place," Sam said. "Mrs. Sinyard pitched a fit, but in the end there weren't nothing she could do. Mrs. Walls said that without Momma paying, they couldn't live here no more. Mrs. Walls called a man she knew; he came and took Will and Liz away to work for him in his factory. I got a letter from them, and they said it was terrible there and they were thinking of running away. That was three weeks ago, I guess, I ain't heard a word since," Sam said breathlessly.

Mary Sinyard started making motions and hand gestures with a pained look on her face. "She says she is sorry that she failed," Sam said. He closely watched as she made a bunch more gestures and signs. "She says she promised Momma that she would keep the family together, and she just couldn't." Tears started to flow down Mary Sinyard's face again.

George put his arm around her shoulders and said, "It's alright, I'm sure you did your best. It's okay; we will go and find them."

A short, fat woman, dressed in a blue and white dress, came to the door of the house. "Who are you, and what are you doing with those kids?" she asked.

"I'm George Kilgo and I'm their daddy. Are you Mrs. Walls?"

"I am. I'm sorry about your wife. She was a sweet lady and a hard worker," the lady said. "I'm sorry about your older kids, but I just couldn't afford to keep them here without someone paying. I charge eight dollars a person per month and four dollars for kids. Now your two oldest are old enough to be charged as adults, and I just couldn't afford to let them stay here without paying. Your boy offered to pay what he was making, but it wasn't enough for both your boy and girl to stay. When the hotel wouldn't let your daughter take your wife's place cooking over there; well, I just had to let them go," Mrs. Walls stopped talking to see how George was taking what she was telling him about sending his two oldest children away.

George could feel his face turning red. He wanted to slap the woman for her cold heartedness. Mrs. Walls continued to make her case. "I did send them to a friend of mine who I knew could give them jobs, and let them live over there. So it wasn't like I just threw them out."

George just gave her a stare. "And where would this place be?" George asked almost biting his tongue to keep from lashing out.

"Mr. Wise has a factory over about ten miles out of town to the east, down the Wallace Pike Road. He said he could use them and give them a place to live in his housing," Mrs. Walls said.

George nodded and said, "I need a bath and a place to stay tonight. Do you have a room available?"

"Of course, two dollars for the bath and four dollars for the room," Mrs. Walls said smiling. George pulled the money out of his pocket and paid the lady, although he wanted to hit her. She had a room for rent, but not one for his two oldest kids. After a bath and shave, George felt like a new man. He left his boys in the care of Mrs. Sinyard, and went to find his oldest.

He found the factory just as Mrs. Walls said. It was a two story building made of brick with several chimneys sticking out the top. Inside the door, George could see a bunch of women sitting at machines sewing what looked like blue military pants and tops.

George asked for the boss and was pointed toward a tall, heavy set, man walking the rows between the machines. As George approached, he was cursing at a young girl who couldn't have been more than nine or ten years old. She had messed up on a pair of pants. "You stupid little bitch! Can't you do anything right? Take the stitches out and do it again!" he shouted at the cowering girl.

George walked up to him and stared at him until he felt George's presence and turned around. "What do you want?" he asked sharply.

"My name's George Kilgo, and I'm looking for my daughter, Liz. Mrs. Walls said she was working here," George explained.

The man looked George over. "Kilgo, you say...yeah, I think she is over in the corner...there," he said pointing to the left back corner of the building. "She'll be able to leave in about twenty minutes when the ending whistle sounds," the large man said.

"Oh, she'll be leaving now," George said with a flatness and edge to his voice that he meant for the man to hear. "We'll also need to collect her pay. She is going home with me, and she won't be back."

"Pay day is Friday. You'll have to come back then," the big man said standing tall and looking George in the eye, challenging him.

George reached up and rubbed his newly shaved chin. "No, that won't work for me; I'll be gone by then, and so will you if I don't get her pay," George said as he pulled his Colt revolver, cocked it and pointed it at the man's face.

A loud gasp went up from the women working, and suddenly a silence started as the women stopped working the machines. It started with those closest to them and then spread throughout the shop. Two men who were also walking the aisles and were maybe foremen, saw what was happening and started toward George. He pointed the Colt at the nearest one, but never took his eyes off the big man standing in front of him. "If I were you, I'd stop...unless you want these women to see you die," he said calmly to the men as he shifted the Colt to the other man.

"Daddy!" Liz screamed from the back of the shop. She came tearing up the aisle toward her Dad. Liz grabbed George around the waist and gave him a big hug. "Where is Will?" George asked Liz. "Mr. Wise sent him off to another factory," Liz said. George swung the big revolver back to the big man standing in front of him. "What is your name mister?" George asked.

"Henry Wise," the man said. "I own this factory. I...I sent your son to another factory I own a few miles away in another town."

"Well, Mr. Wise, do you or do you not, owe my daughter some wages for her work?"

"Yes, of course."

"Then I'm asking nicely that you just give her what she is due so we can all leave quietly. Don't you think that would be the best for all parties?" George asked.

"Okay, okay...I guess we can make an exception this once," Mr. Wise said.

"Now you are living up to your name," George said. The man just looked puzzled for a second, then it hit him what George meant. They went to the office at the rear of the shop; but not before Mr. Wise shouted for the women to get back to work, and the noise of the machines started again. Mr. Wise tried to hand George a few dollars and some change, but George who still held the gun in his hand pointed to Liz.

"Is that the right amount?" George asked Liz who nodded.

"We'll be leaving now," George said. "Walk us out, won't you please."

When they were outside, George turned to the man. "Now, where is this other factory where you sent my son to work?"

While he was talking to George, Liz slipped away to get her few things from the long dormitory building behind the factory. After getting her things, Liz climbed up on the back of Dolly behind George, and they rode off to pick up Will. As they rode, Liz filled George in on all that had happened in the last few months. She told him about her mother's illness, and how she had suffered before she died. How she left George a letter that Liz had in her bag. Liz told how Mrs. Sinyard tried to keep the family together, but Mrs. Walls wouldn't let them stay unless they paid the full adult rate. How she tried to work at the hotel in her mother's place; but when she couldn't cook all the stuff they wanted her to, they let her go.

According to Liz, Mrs. Walls got paid for sending them to Mr. Wise's factory. Liz said there were lots of girls like her that worked there, and they were treated like slaves. We only made thirty-five cents a day, so we made about $8.50 a month and Mr. Wise charged us five dollars a month for room and board in the dormitory.

"I sent what money I had left to Mrs. Walls for Sam and John Wesley," Liz said. "The food was terrible and never enough of it. But...Daddy, the worst thing...was Mr. Wise and the foremen...Daddy they were always rubbing up against us, and when they were showing us how to sew something...they put their arms around us and...you know...grabbed us," Liz said shivering. "The reason they sent Will away to the other factory was because he told Mr. Wise if he laid another hand on me, he would find a way to come into his house and cut his throat. I think that scared Mr. Wise a little." George gritted his teeth. He wished Mr. Wise had tried something now so he could have put a bullet in his head.

They rode for over two hours before they arrived at the other factory. It was similar to the other one. They found Will working in the back loading up bundles of clothing. George had little trouble convincing the boss here to pay them Will's wages. The boss bragged on Will and said he was sorry to lose him. They rode triple on Dolly back to Mrs. Wells' house to spend the night. The boys were asleep when they arrived as it was late. Liz gave George the letter from Emme, and then they left him alone.

N ASHVILLE, *Tennessee*

Sometime soon

My dearest darling,

If you are reading this I will have passed. I am not sad, and I don't want you to be either. I am ready to go, and I know I am going to a better place where this body will no longer be in pain. I only hate to leave you and my children as they are the best things I ever did in this world. I thank God every day for the life he let me have with you and them. I have been blessed more than I deserve. Please my dear husband; promise me that you will find someone good and kind to raise my children. Do not be stubborn about this, as I know you can sometimes be. Life is for the living, and life must go on. You must go on. I need to know that someone good and kind is raising Sam, little John Wesley and Tom. They are good boys, and I know, with just a little guidance, will grow to be good men like their daddy. Will and Liz will both be alright as they have grown into wonderful young adults. Promise me you won't be too hard on the young men who come to call on Liz. You have to know that everyone is not up to your standard of what a man should be. My darling, I miss seeing your face and feeling your sweet touch so much! I have prayed that if it is God's will that I might see you one more time before I pass, but if it is not to be, know that I have been loved and I have loved you as much as is possible for someone to love.

With all my love forever,
Emme

GEORGE READ the letter when everyone had retired to their beds. He couldn't hold back the tears, and lay on his bed until he finally drifted off to sleep.

The next day, George asked to visit Emme's grave. Liz went with him and let him spend time by himself at the grave. When he came back to her, he didn't say anything; he just hugged Liz really tight.

At the livery stable where Will had formerly worked, George and Will went to get their wagon and horses. The man that ran the stable really liked Will and had let him keep the horses and wagon there in return for the work he did. Will was such a hard worker that the man started to pay Will also.

"I offered to let Will stay in the stable," the owner said, "but he didn't want his sister to live in a barn so he went with her to the factory. I would have taken both of them in at my home; but...well...we already got five orphans living at our place, and we couldn't take any more."

"I appreciate your giving him work, and keeping our horses and wagon for us," George said, "I'll pay you whatever you want now that I am here."

"No sir! You been fighting for us, and I ain't taking a dime of your money."

"Well, I appreciate your kindness," George said shaking the man's hand.

George and Will went to the dry goods store and bought things for the trip home. They had a few things; blankets, pots and pans that were in the wagon. George was thankful for the money that they had made gambling; betting on Bill jumping over horses, and George's out shooting everyone. George had enough money to pay for everything. They went to the butcher shop and bought enough salt pork and meat for the almost two hundred mile trip home. George believed it might take ten to fifteen days or more depending on the weather, the roads, and how the army was using them. The butcher was a short Italian man with a hook nose and a black beard. He asked how long their trip was; and then, started fixing them a small keg of salted meat and one of potatoes and vegetables. George suddenly had a thought and asked the man if he butchered his own animals.

"Sure, w'at kind of butcher you think I am? "he asked in his thick accent.

Do you...ah...have any animal penises?" George asked.

The man's face clouded up, " 'ey, I don't go' for no funny business!"

George explained that he wanted to send a message to someone who liked to mess with young girls. He thought sending a severed penis would be the right way to send the message. The butcher looked funny for a minute; and then, threw back his head and laughed.

"Wh's this vile creature? Where does he live? I will deliver the penis and message myself."

George explained the man was the owner of the factory a little ways out of town; and that he wanted to send a note with the penis warning that if Mr. Wise touched another girl, he would end up with the same treatment.

The butcher promised to deliver the message. He wouldn't take any money for the severed penis or the meat, only charging George a little for the vegetables. Leaning close to George he said, *"I might kno'ws someone, who kno'ws someone, who could take care of this man if you wish."*

George smiled, "No, a friend of mine says if you make your enemies think about you every night before they go to sleep...then you have already defeated them."

The butcher wrapped up some extra meat for them and said, *"You'se take'a this nice veal with you and cook it tonight for your family's supper. You'se have a good safe trip."*

When George and Will arrived back at the boarding house, Liz and the boys were standing on the steps with all their things in little white flour sacks. Standing beside them was Mary Sinyard, holding a small cardboard suit case. She just looked expectantly at George as he came walking up.

"Daddy, Mommy promised Mrs. Sinyard you would take her home to her family in Alabama," Liz said.

"Please, Daddy, can we keep her?" Little Tom said. That set them all to giggling.

"I don't see why not," George said, "after all, her name is Mary and all the women in my life are named Mary." Mrs. Sinyard smiled for the first time since George had met her.

They traveled as fast as the horses could walk; still, they only went about eight miles that first day. They got such a late start, before they knew it; it was time to make camp for the night.

George, Mary and Liz set about making a stew out of the veal the butcher had given them, while the boys played around the wagon; and Will staked out the horses. George built a fire and after supper they sat around it, and George told tales about life in the army camps. The kids laughed and smiled at the stories, especially the story of Bill who took everyone's money by diving over a horse. George just enjoyed being around his kids again. He even caught Mary Sinyard smiling a few times.

Finally, it was bed time. Liz, Mary and Tom all bedded down in the wagon while George, Will, and John Wesley spread out padding and made beds under the wagon. John Wesley made it close to an hour before he heard something in the woods, got scared and crawled up into the wagon with the others.

They made a little better time the second day, but had to stop several times to stand in lines at inspection points along the road. The Federals were not taking any chances on anyone smuggling weapons out of Nashville to the Confederates. The kids played and sang songs as they rode along, while Tom and John Wesley shot at things with stick guns. George and Mary rode on the wagon seat while Will, Liz, and the boys all were riding in the back of the wagon. When the sun was hot, Will would put up the wooden bands; and spread the canvas top over part of the wagon to make some shade.

The sixth night they were on the road, something unusual happened. When the kids were all bedded down, George was still up and drinking the last of his coffee. Liz was in the wagon with the younger boys and had been there for thirty minutes or so.

George noticed Mary getting out of the wagon, and assumed she was going to relieve herself before bedding down for the night. Instead she came and took George by the hand, and led him away from the wagon. George was getting better now at understanding her motions and gestures, but he didn't understand this. She led him about a hundred or so feet away from the wagon, to a blanket she had spread on the ground. She motioned for George to sit on the blanket. When he did, she pushed him back until he was lying down. She knelt down beside him and started undoing his belt and pants. George put his hands up to stop her, but she pushed them away and gave George a look that said 'STOP'.

She pulled his pants and underwear down, hiked her nightgown up and straddled his waist, settling on top of him. She wiggled around until she was positioned where she wanted. George started to reach up for her but she pushed his hands down, and violently shook her head. She rose up and down for a few moments; then, slumped forward until her hair was just touching George's face. She remained there for several seconds, breathing hard and crying softly; George could feel the tears falling on his shirt. In a moment, she rose and ran away back to the wagon; leaving a bewildered George to fasten his pants, pick up the blanket, and return to the wagon.

The next day, she avoided looking at George but he could see her blush every time he looked at her. From then on during the rest of the trip, every two or three nights, she would climb down from the wagon with a blanket in her arms and lead George away from the wagon. After the third time, she didn't stop George when he reached up for her.

They traveled without incident until they reached Decatur, Alabama. Everything above Decatur was firmly in Union control, and there were Union troops coming and going everywhere. There were several ferryboats operating to cross the river. They got in line and waited for their turn to cross. As they were waiting, Union soldiers inspected them, searching for weapons, powder or other contraband. The soldier in charge asked where they were going and what their business was. When George explained and showed his furlough papers, the soldier warned them.

"Things are pretty safe for about ten miles across the river because we have a lot of patrols out there. Beyond that, there are reports of the Home Guard and Partisan Rangers stopping and robbing people. If they find out you are Union, they will probably kill you and maybe your whole family," the Sergeant said.

George nodded, "We plan to be real careful and travel a lot at night. I also have some fake furlough papers from the Confederate army I plan to use," George said pulling out another set of furlough papers from his boot. The sergeant raised his eyebrows at that.

"And how do I know that those aren't the real papers, and the ones you showed me are the fake ones?"

George smiled, "Because I'm the Black Hawk, and I work for Black Jack Logan; I ride as a scout with the Black Fox."

The sergeant nodded, "Black Jack is one of the best we got. Any man who served with him is good enough for me.

When they had traveled a few miles south of the Tennessee River, George stopped and held a meeting. He told the kids their story, if they got stopped by anyone. They were to say they were traveling home from visiting their grandparents in Franklin, Tennessee. Daddy was home on leave because his wife died, and he had to get his kids because his wife's parent's health was failing. George also prepared them for the worst. He took Will aside to talk to him.

"Will, you get the double barrel loaded and a cap on the nipples. At the first sign of trouble you cock both barrels; you won't have time to cock in an emergency. Keep it hidden in the wagon under a blanket, but where you can reach it easily, on your right side. Son, if the time comes, you shoot to kill; because you are protecting your brothers and sister." Will nodded that he understood. "They will probably have at least one man at the front, and one or more at the rear of the wagon. You protect the rear and I'll take care of the front."

George took Mary away from the hearing of the young

ones. "Mary, take this smaller Colt," he said handing her a 'Pocket Colt' he had taken off a dead Confederate soldier. "It is only .36 calibers, but at close range it is just as deadly as the .44. Keep it under your lap blanket; and at the first sign of trouble, you cock the hammer. Keep your finger off the trigger when it is cocked. Mary," George said looking into her eyes. "Don't hesitate to use it, if the time comes. Do you understand?" She nodded her head. "You have to cock the hammer each time you shoot, and you have five shots, so make them count. If we are approached, there will be men on both sides of the wagon. If things go bad, you take care of those on your side."

George took Liz to the side and gave her his Bowie knife. "Liz I don't think you will need it, but you keep this by your side just in case," George told his daughter. "Don't let the little ones see it, because it might scare them."

George and his family loaded back up and went on their way. George put his Navy Colt 44 beside him under another lap blanket; the second Colt, he put at his feet. Of course, he had Ole Stumpy leaning beside him next to the wagon seat. George felt pretty good about their fire power, if they had to use them; but he didn't plan on risking the lives of his kids unless there was no other way. He would try to bluff his way out of most situations first.

They rode the rest of the afternoon with everyone in a somber mood. They camped that night way off the road in a thick group of trees and bushes. They ate a cold supper, and tried to remain as quiet as possible. George and Will took turns sleeping and standing guard. It was not a restful night. George thought they could get another day's travel before they had to start traveling at night to avoid the Home Guard.

The next day, they had traveled about ten miles when they were suddenly confronted by four riders coming at them from all sides. George reached down and cocked Ole Stumpy hoping the others had their guns cocked, too. There was a man who rode up to the front of the wagon and stopped the horses. Another was on Mary's side, one on his side and another one in the back. The men didn't come out with their guns drawn, but they looked threatening enough without them.

"Howdy, neighbor," the man next to George said.

"Howdy," George replied.

"Where you headed on this fine day?" the man asked.

"We are headed home to Double Springs," George said.

"Double Springs...lots of Tories around there. You wouldn't be one of them would you?" the man asked.

"Naw, I'm 3rd Alabama Cavalry. I've been up to Franklin to get my kids. My wife died and her parents were just too old to keep them any longer," George said going with their cover story. "I got my furlough papers right here in my boot. You want to see them?" George asked.

"Sure," said the man on George's side of the wagon. George pulled the papers out, and handed them to the man. He looked them over before handing them back to George.

"I knew a guy in the 3th once, big fella' named Jackson. You ever meet him?"

George recognized the trap right away. The officer in charge of scouts had warned Bill and George of this tactic. They ask if you know someone they made up; and if you say you know them, they will know you are lying.

"Can't say as I ever met the fella', but it is a big outfit, and a lot of men come and go. We spent half our time loaned out to the 5th Georgia and the 10th Tennessee," George said throwing out names of Confederate groups he had heard of. He thought the men were buying what he was saying, but then the one on Mary's side asked, "What about you, sweetie?

What have you been doing up in Franklin while your man was at war?"

George hesitated then said, "She don't talk. She's a mute; been that way since she was a kid."

"Well, she shore is a pretty thang. I bet I could give her something to shout about." The man laughed at his joke and the other men grinned. The man dismounted and approached Mary from the ground. "What about it, honey; want to see if old Fred can bring your speech back? I'll have you shoutin' and yellin' before I'm through," he said laughing and reaching for Mary while putting his hand on her leg above the knee.

"Not this time!" Mary whispered as she pulled the trigger on the Colt. The man looked down in surprise at the smoking hole in the blanket over Mary's lap, and down at the smoking hole in his chest.

In the next half second, George heard the roar of the shotgun from the back of the wagon. George pulled his Colt and shot the man on his side of the wagon under the left arm. As George swung the Colt toward the man in the front of the wagon, he could see the man had cleared leather and was aiming his pistol at George. The team of horses, surprised by the gun fire, lurched forward into the man's horse causing it to step sideways. George heard and felt the bullet whiz by his head. George shot at the man, but the man was able to wheel his horse and start riding away.

George couldn't tell if he hit him or not, but he couldn't let him get away or he might bring more Home Guard. George pulled Ole Stumpy from beside the seat. It wasn't too hard a shot. The man was riding straight away from them. George aimed a few inches over the man's head and squeezed the trigger. The man jerked upward in the saddle; and then slowly rolled over to his right, and off the horse. His foot hung for just a second in the stirrup, he bounced once on the ground, the foot pulled loose and he rolled over on the ground a couple of times and was still.

When George turned his attention back to the men around the wagon, he turned around to look at the one behind him. The man was lying on the ground; the left side of his head missing where Will's blast had hit him. The one beside George was lying on the ground, almost on his head in an impossible position that said he was dead. George stood up to look at the one on Mary's side of the wagon, and saw that he was trying to crawl away.

Mary saw him too, stood up, and holding the pistol in both hands shouted, "Die! You Bastard! Die!" She then unloaded the Colt, putting four more shots into the man, then stood there cocking and firing the pistol on empty chambers.

George, Will, Liz and the children were shocked, at Mary's behavior and her speech! George reached over and took the pistol from her hand saying, "It's alright. I think you got him." Mary burst into tears and sat down. Tom started crying, and she turned around to pick him up.

George now sprang into action. "Will, get their guns and put them into the wagon. Liz, help him drag them off the road." George jumped off the wagon and ran down the road to check the man lying in the road there. Approaching slowly, George nudged the man with his foot; but he could see a big hole in the man's back where Ole Stumpy did her work and another place bleeding through his shirt at his side where he guessed his first shot went. George pulled the man's body off the road and into the bushes. He broke off some bushes and used them to sweep dirt over the blood in the road.

Going back to the wagon, he helped Will and Liz drag the others off the road and sweep dirt over their blood making the scene look as if nothing had happened. "Will, unsaddle their horses, and let them loose. An unsaddled and unbridled horse wondering around could have just got loose, but one with a saddle will draw attention." While Will and Liz were doing that, George went did the same to the horse of the man he killed.

When they had cleaned up the scene, George hid the guns behind the seat in the upper end of the wagon, covered them with the blankets they were hauling and had the kids sit on them.

"Will, reload just in case there are more around." George did the same and handed the pistol back to Mary.

George opted to travel all the rest of the day and night to put as much distance as possible from the scene, in case someone heard the shooting and came to investigate. No one said much as they rode along. Luckily it was a moonlit night, and they could see the road pretty well. After a few hours, the children were all asleep. Mary laid Tom down with Liz and was just sitting beside George, when he heard her crying quietly.

"It's okay," George said quietly.

Mary looked at him in the pale light. "I'm definitely going to hell now," she sobbed.

"Look, it was not your fault. They were bad men and would have hurt you and Liz and probably killed me and the boys," George said. "It was either them or us."

"It's not just the man I killed today. I... killed... my... baby, too," Mary said in a voice so low George was not sure he heard her right.

"What?"

"I.... killed.... my.... baby, and now.... I killed.... a man. The Bible says thou shall not kill, and I killed twice so I'm going to hell."

"I...don't understand," George said.

"Joe Franklin and I were sitting at the house with my boys

eating supper, when our neighbor came riding up and told us that he had over heard some men talking about who was on the list to be arrested and forced into the Rebel army and Joe's name was on the list. We knew he had to leave right away as they would be riding in our direction. Joe didn't want to leave us, but I made him go.

"When they came, I told them Joe had left the day before. They didn't believe me, so they tore the house and barn apart looking for him. They came back into the house and ate all the stew we had left, and then made me cook some more food for them.

"As I was cooking, they brought out a bottle and started drinking. I could feel them watching me, and they started making comments about how I looked and stuff like that. I knew I was in trouble. The boys were asleep now, and the men were getting drunker and drunker. They tried to force me to drink the whiskey; when I wouldn't, they held me down and poured it down my throat. I fought and fought, but they just held me down. Finally, one started to pull my clothes off," Mary said starting to whimper at the memory.

"They...took me, all...of...them...over...and...over. She sobbed. I don't remember everything, but I remember enough. I still have nightmares about that night. I must have passed out. When I woke, they were gone, and it was morning. My little boys were crawling around the cabin. I mean...they could have crawled into the fireplace and got burned up! I cleaned up and feed my babies. I went to my parent's house. I never told them what happened to me. I knew my dad would go looking for them and just get killed. I just told them that Joe Franklin had to run off or the Home Guard would have gotten him, and I was scared to stay there by myself." Mary took a deep breath and continued.

"When I found out I was pregnant, I didn't want to have a

baby from those...those animals! I knew it wasn't Joe's baby because he got kicked by a mule after our last one was born and ...well, he couldn't make any more babies. I wasn't going to bring a baby into the world like that. I told my parents that I had to go see Joe; that I had gotten a note from him, and I would be gone a couple of days. I went to Looney's to talk to Mrs. Looney because...well, people say she knows someone to go to, to stop a pregnancy. I didn't know what had happened to her and the tavern until I got there."

"I was shocked when I saw the tavern. No one was there, but Johnny Two Feathers. He told me what happened to Senie. He said I was lucky that they didn't kill me and my boys. I told him what happened to me; he just listened and sat there for a while. He said he would take me to someone, if I was sure that was what I wanted." Mary looked at George, "Do you think I did wrong?"

George paused before answering. "I...don't know. I don't know what I would have done. I can't say what you did was wrong, because I ain't a woman."

Mary continued, "Johnny Two Feathers took me off the road, a long ways into the woods and I was really afraid I would never find my way out of there. Finally, we came to a little cabin that was built into the side of a bluff. There was this old Indian woman...I think she was a medicine woman. She said her name was Nanny Long Eyes. I told her what I wanted and she said she could help, if I was sure.

Johnny left us; she told him to come back in two days. We went into the woods and she found a bunch of berries and roots and stuff. I know she used some holly berries and other berries that I thought were poison. She mixed it all up, ground it, and put it on the fire to cook for awhile. She again asked me if I was sure, and then she gave me a bowl of the mixture to drink. It tasted terrible and I gagged trying to drink it. I don't remember much after that. I remember waking up and drinking some more from the bowl. I felt very ill, and I remember throwing up a lot. I thought I was going to die. When I finally woke up a day later, she said the baby was gone. I stayed half the next day; then Johnny came back for me."

"So now you know," Mary sobbed. "I'm a terrible person... I killed my baby...and I killed a man so...I'm sure...sob... I'll going to hell. God is...is...sob... punishing me. My husband got killed,...sob... my boys got the measles, and...sob... I got the measles. I prayed to die after my boys died; but God made me live and...sob... took my boys," Mary continued to cry softly.

George put his arm around her. "Mary I don't think God is punishing you. Things just happen sometimes. My Emme said God sent you to help take care of our kids. She believed that and so do I." Mary gave him an incredulous look.

"Did Emme believe that?"

"Yes, she said so in a letter to me. Her heart was breaking, seeing you suffer so much," George said.

"I...don't...know...what to think. I swore I wouldn't speak again until God forgave me for what I did...then I broke that promise, and I killed someone," Mary choked out.

"It's okay. I'm sure God will forgive you for all this," George said. She was silent for a while, just thinking. In a few minutes, George felt her lean over against him as she went to sleep.

When first light came, George found a place to pull the wagon off the road. He wanted to be off the road in case the Home Guards came looking for the others and found the bodies. Will stood guard while George slept. Will reported that no one came down the road except a couple of wagons with supplies and two farmers on mules. Still, George thought they should wait until night to continue.

The children were all trying to talk to Mary now that she was talking. They all asked why she wouldn't talk before but she just said God didn't want her to talk, but now he told her it was alright. The kids asked her a million questions about her family and her husband and children. Mary very patiently answered them, even though George could see it hurt her to have to answer some of their questions.

They were very close to the farm of Mary's family which was near a small crossroads called Addison. After dark, they set out and reached it in about two hours. Her parents were overjoyed to see her again. She had written them about the death of her husband and children; they were sad about her loss, but happy she was home safely.

Mary gave all the kids big hugs and kisses. Little Tom cried and clung to her legs. "Please Mary, come and live with us," Tom begged. "We need a new mommy."

"Oh, Tommy, I can't come just now. I have to stay here with my Mommy and Daddy they need me, too. I'll come see you soon, I promise." She came to George and gave him a long hug. She had tears in her eyes as she said, "George, I don't know how to thank you for...for...everything."

George smiled at her, "I am the one who needs to thank you for helping my Emme when she needed you the most, and for helping with my kids."

CHAPTER SEVENTEEN

George and the kids went on to their home. They arrived about nine that night; but just to make sure no one was watching and waiting for them, George insisted that they spend another night in the wagon and watch the house. They spent the night in the woods behind the house while George and Will watched the house trying to figure out if there was anyone around. They saw nothing to make them think anyone was watching, still George wasn't going to take any chances with his family.

George waited and watched a couple of hours the next day. About ten in the morning, a rider came up to the house and dismounted. He walked into the open door of the house, and then went to the barn. George thought he recognized the rider so he sneaked up to the barn. As the man was looking around, George called out, "Freeze! Get your hands up!"

The man just about jumped out of his skin, but he put his hands up and said, "Don't shoot! I ain't armed."

George said, "There ain't no hogs around here to steal."

The man turned to the sound of George's voice, and seeing George said, "Damn it, George, you about gave me a heart attack! You know dang well I didn't steal no hog, and I'm getting tired of people saying I did."

George laughed. The man, Jacob Miller, went to the same Methodist Church George and Emme attended. Once a hog wandered over, dug under the fence into Jacob's hog lot, and started to eat with Jacob's hogs. A new neighbor who had just moved in and didn't know Jacob, came over looking for his hog, found it in with Jacob's hogs and accused Jacob of stealing it. Ever since then, everyone had given Jacob a hard time about being a hog stealer. Some even started calling him, Hog Miller.

George walked up and shook Jacob's hand. "It's sure nice to see a friendly face for a change," George said.

"I feel the same way. Where's Emme and the family?"

George clamped his lips tight and said, "Emme passed away a while back."

"Oh, George, I'm so sorry. I didn't know. She was one of the best women I ever met. What happened? Was it female trouble?"

George nodded.

"I'll have to tell the wife; she will be so upset," Jacob said. "What about the kids?"

"They are hiding over in the woods behind the house. I didn't want them to get caught up in something...if the Home Guard was about."

Jacob shook his head. "I don't think you need to worry about the Home Guard any more. They are on the run and scared. Things have turned on them...people they did wrong are all looking for them now. Two weeks ago, seven families of the Guards loaded up on wagons and pulled out; said they were headed to Missouri."

"Old Stokes Roberts and his bunch of outlaws have been picked off one by one. Someone is hunting them down and killing them. Eight of them been found dead...some tortured. Old Stokes was found nailed to a tree, upside down. His brother and one of his buddies were found hanging upside down over a fire, burned to death...couldn't hardly recognize them."

"Were any of them scalped?" George asked.

Jacob nodded, "Yeah, scalped and their scalps stuck in their mouths. How did you know?"

George smiled, "Sounds like Bill Looney is getting revenge for what they did to Senie and his tavern."

"Just this morning, they found four more dead out on the main road, about fifteen miles from here. Someone blew one of their heads nearly off and shot one of them a half dozen times," Jacob said.

George just nodded.

"I wouldn't worry a bit about them if I were you," Jacob said again.

After Jacob left, George called the family home. The house had been ransacked, but was mostly intact. Everything was just super dirty and dusty so everyone set about cleaning and straightening everything up.

While they were cleaning, Rascal their dog came whining up to the house. He was skinny as a rail and you could see his backbone and every rib; but he was alive, much to the joy of the younger boys.

"I didn't think we'd ever see him again," Will said. "We tried to get him in the wagon; but he took off after the livestock we had let loose, and we never saw him again. I thought he might follow us...you know...track us, but I guess he thought his job was to keep up with the cows and chickens."

They worked hard all day; only pausing to eat some salt pork and potatoes they had leftover from the trip. That night George fed Rascal a big piece of meat and tied him to the front porch. He felt sure Rascal would let them know if anyone came within a mile of the place. For the first time in months, George got a good night's sleep in his own bed.

He couldn't bear to sleep in Emme's bed so Tom and finally John Wesley joined him in his bed. Liz came wondering over and Will heard them, and he came too. George got up and put all the beds together in a little circle, and the family spent the night within an arms length of each other.

George and Will spent the next few days working on repairing the roof of the barn and house. Sam and John Wesley were playing around the grown up fields, when they discovered a dozen chickens living in the weeds. They chased and chased them, but just drove them all over the place. George got some corn meal from the supplies they brought and spread a little close to the chicken's roost and pretty soon the chickens were following a trail of corn meal to the repaired chicken house.

A week after they arrived home, Hog Miller showed up with one of their old milk cows, two half grown calves and two small hogs.

"I didn't want to be accused of stealing again." Hog said. "We found the cow wondering around a couple of years ago. We saw tracks of a few more but we never did find them. She had another calf but...I'm sorry... but we ate that one and we ate the mother of these pigs. I'll be glad to pay you for them when I can. We...the wife and kids were just so hungry..." Hog said hanging his head a little and avoiding looking George in the eye.

"You'll do no such thing." George said. "I'm sure you did what you had to do to feed your family, and I'm sure I would have done the same thing. Thank you for bringing her back to us...and the calves and pigs...you could have just kept them and we would have never known." George said looking Hog in the eyes.

Hog shrugged his shoulders, "Yeah I guess, but I would have known." He said as he walked to his horse and rode off.

Liz was cooking and taking over the role of woman of the house. She even began bossing everyone around, insisting that they take baths. They settled into a nice routine. The only thing missing from their old life was Emme.

Some weeks later, George and Will were cutting bushes and trying to get the fields ready for plowing. George was planning to start plowing the next week, if they could get a little more cleared. Suddenly, they heard gunfire from down the road and they all scrambled to get their weapons and take up the positions George had laid out for them, if trouble ever came.

In about fifteen minutes, a rider raced up the road toward the house, firing his pistol into the air and yelling as he rode. When he was close by, he started yelling, "It's over! It's over! Lee surrendered to Grant at Appomattox!" The rider was a man George vaguely knew. "It's finally over! George, it's finally over!" Then he turned his horse and rode away.

George stood there for a few minutes, not saying anything. "Dad?" Will said, "What happens now?" George just shook his head.

"I don't know son...I don't know." They went back to cutting brush.

Two weeks later, they had just put in a hard week plowing and were bone tired. It was Saturday morning; Liz spent a while drawing water and filling two wash pots that she had set on a fire. She had gave the order and everyone was taking baths. When George was finished shaving and bathing, he came in to find his Sunday suit of clothes clean, washed and laid out on the bed.

"I guess you're right...we need to get back to going to church," George said to her.

"Those ain't for church," Liz said. George looked at her puzzled.

"What are they for then?"

Liz looked to where the boys were all taking turns in the wash tubs, to make sure they were out of hearing distance.

"Daddy, it's time you paid a visit to Mrs. Pruitt," Liz said.

"Liz...I ain't...ah...ready to see Mrs. Pruitt or any other woman. Your mother has only been gone..."

"Ain't no use to argue with me," Liz said cutting him off and giving him a look. "Momma made me promise...just before she died...she called me in and explained some things to me...she said I was old enough to understand." Liz gave her Dad a look.

"I know all about Hannah and Mrs. Pruitt; and Daddy, I know why Mrs. Sinyard was slipping out of the wagon so many nights."

George looked wounded. "I..." he started to say something, but it just died in his throat.

"Momma made me promise that I would not let you pine away for her. She said if you didn't get out of the blues, you would die. Daddy, we...all of us...need you. So you go and see Mrs. Pruitt...I don't know what will come of it...or if Mr. Pruitt is coming back from the war...I just know Momma would want you to go and see what becomes of it," Liz said standing with her hands on her hips.

George just looked at her for several seconds. "Liz you are growing up way too fast. I'm sorry you had to take on such a burden."

"It ain't no burden...its family. Now breakfast is about ready. Go and hurry those boys up, and don't let them track up the floor with their wet feet."

George had Will saddle up Dolly while he put on his Sunday clothes. Liz had packed him a bag with some jerky and salt pork in it. She came out to give it to him. While the boys were saying good bye, she leaned in close and whispered, "We will be alright for a couple of days. You stay as long as you need to." George told the boys he needed to check on Mrs. Pruitt.

CHAPTER EIGHTEEN

George rode away and headed toward the Pruitt Plantation. When George cleared the stretch of woods at the beginning of the plantation road, he could see the big house up ahead. The fields were all covered in weeds and brush, much like his farm had been. Even from a distance, he could see the paint on the two-story house was peeling. When George was nearer the house, he could see five or so slaves and a woman in a faded dress, working in the field directly beside the house. They were hoeing the ground behind a single slave who was plowing with a mule.

As George neared, they stopped to look up at him. The slave plowing stopped, moved toward a wagon nearby and pulled out a rifle. The woman held her hand up shading her eyes and looking at him. In a moment, she dropped her hand, pulled her dress up with both hand and started running toward him. George knew it was Mary Pruitt. They were about a hundred yards apart so George pushed Dolly into a trot in Mary's direction.

When he drew near, he jumped down and took a couple of steps toward Mary who was running full force. She flew into his arms and gave him a big hug while bursting into deep sobs. "Oh, my Lord! I didn't know if I would ever see you again!" She sobbed out, while kissing George's cheek and neck and running her fingers around his shoulders. Then, she drew him down into a long kiss.

"Mary...I...ah...Mary...Emme died and I...had to go and get my children...I meant to write you...but was afraid Jim might get the letters and beat you or hurt you."

"It doesn't matter...I knew about Emme being really sick. George, she and I wrote letters...she told me...she asked me... to take care of you and the children if anything happened to her. I told her about...us...she said she knew in her heart, and she wanted it...wanted you to be happy," Mary choked out between sobs. George was amazed that his wife and his mistress would write to each other about him.

"Jim?" George asked looking around.

"I still haven't heard from him since that night...Olaf Reese's son, Mason, lost his leg at Petersburg and he said, he saw Jim covered in bloody bandages in the hospital tent. He didn't know if he was mortally wounded or if he survived," Mary said. "We haven't heard a word since the end of the war."

The slaves had been watching them, and now some of them came closer. George turned to shake hands with Matoomba.

"It... is good... to see you... my friend," Matoomba said in much improved English.

"It is good to see you too."

A very pregnant Wana was standing nearby; she came over to give George a hug. "Mr. George, it is good to have you back again."

George smiled at her. He pointed to her swollen belly, and she blushed and gave a little smile. "This is going to be our second," she said as Matoomba pulled her close to his side.

"Well, congratulations," George said. He shook hands with the other men, Cee and the women slaves, some of whom he remembered. They all started walking toward the house which was just a little ways off.

As they neared the house, Hannah appeared on the porch, with a baby in her arms and another one about two year's old holding to one leg. The baby in her arms was very black; the one at her leg was very light skinned. When she saw George, she cried out, "*Oh my Lord my Lord! Mr. George, I's so glad to see you.*" She bent down and pulled the light skinned little boy away from her leg and the dress tail he was hiding behind. He had a head of curly hair which was slightly red in color.

"*Comes on now, don't be shy. Comes and meets your Daddy,*" she said. "*This is Little George and this one is Michael,*" she said indicating the other little one. One of the male slaves climbed the steps and stood beside her. "*This here is my man, Slick,*" she said indicating the man who now stood with his arm around her waist.

George looked puzzled at first; when he realized what she was saying, he smiled. "They are very beautiful children, I know you are proud of them," he said nodding to the man beside Hannah. Just then, Tee appeared on the porch holding another young boy on her hip. She handed the boy to Mary who smiled at George.

"George, this is Christian...your son," Mary said with a twinkle of love in her eye. George looked shocked, and then a smile spread across his face.

"Come here, let me hold you," he said to the little boy. He wiggled and tried to get down. He appeared to be about two and he didn't know nor like George at the moment.

"I'm sure he will warm up to you in a little while," Mary said.

"Oh! My gosh! This is not what I expected at all," George said looking around at all those standing there.

"I's tried to tell these women to stay away from you. I could see you was trouble right from the start," Tee said chuckling.

"Where is Moses?" George asked looking into the house.

Mary looked at George and shook her head.

"He done gone to be with the Lord about six months ago," Tee said. *"Lordy, how I misses that man."*

"I'm sorry...I didn't know," George said.

"Ain't no need to be sorry...he be in a better place than we in, and I's gonna see him soon enough," Tee said. *"Now ya'll come on in and I'll make ya'll something to drink."*

They spent the next several hours talking. George told them how Matoomba and Bill rescued him, and about Bill and his service in the Union army as scouts. He told about Bill jumping over a horse and how it made them some money but had almost gotten them in trouble.

Mary talked about how the slaves all left, a few at a time, when they heard they were free; and how some came back, when they couldn't find work or a place to live. Matoomba and another slave talked about the reason they stayed; and how there was a feeling of fear about going out on their own. Finally, George talked about what he and Bill had seen after the Battle of Atlanta, and the Union troops looting and killing people. George talked about what a good man General Black Jack Logan was.

Before they knew it, Tee was bringing supper and everyone ate at the big table. Mary said those that remained on the plantation were now family, and she promised to pay them; if and when, they could grow a little crop. Until then, they worked for food and a place to live. Matoomba and a couple of others fed them by hunting, and Tee cooked fruit and vegetables from the cellar.

After supper, the slaves all drifted off to their cabins leaving George and Mary alone. Mary rose and held out her hand to George and led him up the stairs to her bedroom. Christian slept beside them in his crib.

In the morning, George rode around the plantation and looked everything over. The swamp was now growing back up and holding water again. The fields were all overgrown and in need of work. The slaves were working to try to plant about five acres of cotton with seed they had left from last year's small crop.

George spent another night. He and Mary discussed what they would do if Jim returned. Mary said she would file to divorce him, even though they both knew it would be very hard to do. George worried about what Jim Pruitt would do, when he found out Mary had a child by another man. Mary said she hoped he didn't return, but that they would deal with it, when and if, it happened. She wanted George to bring his children over to live with her, but George refused to do that because he was worried about what might happen if Jim returned. George said he would just travel between the two places. He had a crop to plant, and he could help Mary plant her crop also.

When George returned home, he told the boys he had checked on Mrs. Pruitt and everything was good. She wished she could see them, and maybe she could come to visit or they could go visit her. They all jumped up and down wanting to know when they could go, because they had so much fun the last time. Liz looked at him carefully, trying to see if his looks were giving away anything that happened with Mary Pruitt.

George and Will worked hard trying to get the plowing done and the land ready. George was worried that he was running out of money and didn't know if he would have enough to buy cotton and corn seed. The money he got paid from the Union and the money he and Bill made off the bets in the army camp was just about gone.

Another month passed. George traveled back and forth between the two places. He would spend a night or two with Mary; then come home to the kids He was beginning to think that maybe Jim Pruitt had been killed and wasn't coming back. He also knew that the railroads were not operating between the south and Virginia where Jim was last seen, and it just might be taking a long time for him to make his way back home.

One day, just as they were settling down to supper at his place, one of the Pruitt slaves come riding up on a mule. Rascal was tearing the ground up and barking when he was a good half mile away.

"Mr. George! Mr. George! Tee says you better come quick. Mr. Pruitt is home, and he is tearing the place up. He done slapped and beat Mrs. Mary and he shot Matoomba in the shoulder. He's threatening to kill little Christian."

George grabbed Ole Stumpy and his Colts while Will ran to saddle Dolly.

"Dad, I can come and help too," Will said.

George shook his head, "You stay here and take care of everyone. If anything happens to me, they will need you." With that, he rode away as fast as Dolly could carry him. It was a good two hour ride from Pruitt's to George's farm and two hours back, so the slave couldn't keep up on the mule and soon fell behind.

Dolly was covered in sweat by the time they arrived at the plantation. It was well after dark, and there wasn't much light at all. George pulled Dolly up well short of the house, and taking Ole Stumpy, walked as quietly as possible to the side of the house.

Matoomba was lying against the side of the house in a pool of blood. Wana was trying to stop the bleeding from a hole in his shoulder with a bloody rag. George held his finger to his lips to signal them to be quiet; he pulled off his belt, and wrapped it around the rag on his shoulder and pulled it tight to stop the flow of blood. He stood on a wooden bucket to peer into the house. Seeing nothing in the living room, he moved to the kitchen window.

There he saw Mary sitting in the corner holding Christian. She had a swollen eye and a busted lip which was bleeding down her face and onto her dress. Tee was lying face down near them, and George couldn't tell if she was alive or not. Jim Pruitt was sitting at the table with a glass and a half empty bottle of whiskey. He looked years older. He had a full beard that likely hadn't been shaved for the four years of the war. He had on his Confederate uniform pants with the stripe down the side and a long sleeved shirt that was tattered and worn. On the table lay his Colt side arm and his sword.

He was swaying and looking very drunk. George wondered for a minute if he should just wait until he passed out, but Pruitt suddenly lunged to his feet and started cursing at Mary and the boy.

George went to the kitchen door and leaned Ole Stumpy against the house; George pulled his pistol and stepped into the room. Jim Pruitt saw him, and a look of surprise passed over his face.

"I guess you have come for your whore and your bastard son," Pruitt said.

"That and I've come for you," George said. "You are the reason my wife and kids had to flee; Emme might still be alive if she had been allowed to live at home."

Pruitt just looked at George. "I guess a man can make himself believe that, if he wants; but remember, if you hadn't been messing around with my wife, you could have stayed here, and I would never have drafted you. If you are going to kill me, then go ahead and do it! Let your whore and son see you shoot an unarmed man." Pruitt said sitting back down at the table and reaching for the glass of whiskey.

George knew he couldn't just shoot him, as bad as he wanted to. "Get your gun! Go ahead, and we'll settle this like men, fair and square."

"Not likely," Pruitt said. "I'm a little drunk and might not shoot straight. I'll tell you what. Why don't you put your gun down, and we'll settle it with bare hands; that is, unless you are afraid of a gimpy Confederate soldier?"

George didn't trust the man one bit, but he slowly lowered his gun. "Step away from the table, and I'll put my gun away," George said.

Pruitt smiled, feeling that he had at least bought himself a chance to live. He stood up unsteadily, and walked a few steps across the room. George put his pistol into its holster and unbuckled the belt. He laid it on the floor; as he did, Pruitt made a lunge for his gun on the table. George dove straight for him, grabbing his hand just as it wrapped around the butt of the Colt.

The two men wrestled for control of the pistol. George slammed Pruitt's hand down on the table again and again until the pistol went flying across the room. George punched Pruitt in the face as he grabbed at George's face, trying to poke his fingers into George's eyes. George twisted his head away from the hand, but Pruitt gouged four long scratches across George's face.

George punched him again, and threw the man across the

room. Pruitt recovered and charged George, grabbing at his throat. George twisted around, and the men fell to the floor where they punched and grabbed each other. Pruitt was choking him; George couldn't breathe, and he couldn't break the man's grip. George punched and punched, but with no results. Finally, in desperation, George cupped his hand and slapped it over the other man's ear. It was a tactic that Bill Looney had shown him. The slap forces air into the ear and puts pressure on the eardrum, it can even rupture it. Pruitt screamed and loosened his grip on George's throat for a second. George got his hand and arm inside Pruitt's hands; broke his grip on his throat and pushed him off. Pruitt rolled backwards and scrabbled to his feet. George regained his feet and the two men started exchanging punches. They both grabbed with one hand and threw punches with the other. They twisted and turned back and forth across the room sending chairs and tables flying. George could feel the man's grip weakening as he pounded him repeatedly in the head and face.

Finally, Pruitt flew backwards into the table where his sword lay. Feeling he was weakening and seeing the sword, he grabbed it, and turned on George. Both men looked at each other, sensing the importance of the moment.

Pruitt wiped his bloody face with one hand and said, "I'm going to slice you into little pieces!" He drew back the sword, but never swung it. Suddenly, the room was filled with the loud discharge of a gunshot. The first shot hit Pruitt in the left shoulder and spun him around so he was facing the source of the shot. He looked surprised to see Mary on her knees holding Christian in one arm and the big Colt in her other hand. She struggled to cock the hammer on the pistol again. With one eye swollen shut, she seemed to have a hard time aiming the heavy gun. The second shot hit him in the right hip and knocked him to the floor, where he laid wriggling and moaning in pain.

George took the gun from Mary's hands. She burst into tears and covered her face with the hand that had been holding the pistol. George walked over to where Pruitt lay. George leaned over close to Pruitt's face and said, "This is for both Mary's." Pruitt's eyes grew large as George pressed the big pistol to Pruitt's chest just over his heart and pulled the trigger; the man's body bucked up, and then fell back to the floor. Pruitt let out a long gasp and was silent. His eyes glazed over and his body went slack.

George went to Mary, whose face was badly swollen and helped her and the baby to their feet. Mary grabbed him in an embrace and cried on his shoulder. Christian, who had been crying and watching everything, suddenly stopped crying. George sat them down in a chair, and went to check on Tee.

Tee was bleeding from a large gash on her head where Pruitt had pistol whipped her. George sat her up, and found a cloth to hold on her head until she came around enough to do it herself. Next, he went outside to get Matoomba. His wound was the worse and most dangerous.

George checked the wound and found the bullet had passed all the way through and out the back. That was a good sign, because it meant it didn't hit any bones. George had learned some things on the battlefield and he applied pressure to both sides of the wound. Soon the blood flow seemed to slow to just an ooze. Matoomba was still not out of danger, but George felt better about his condition. It was a long night as George, Hannah, Wana and the others tended to the wounded. By morning, it looked like Matoomba would live.

As dawn was breaking, George got Slick; and together, they pulled Pruitt's body out of the house and onto a wagon. They had discussed it during the night; and decided that things might get complicated, if they let anyone know that Pruitt had been killed.

Mary and George would have to explain who killed him. Mary would have to explain why she had a baby when her husband had been away for four years. There were also the three bullet holes in the body, and the powder burns where George pressed the gun to his chest. They decided that it would be best if Mr. Pruitt never returned from the war. If people had seen him on his way there, they would just say he never arrived. It was pretty clear that he had made many enemies from his job forcing people into the Confederate army. Any number of people could have wanted him dead, and bushwhacked him on his way home.

They carried Pruitt's body deep into the woods. Matoomba told them of a place where a mother bear was raising two cubs. She was living in a den under a clump of roots from a downed tree. She was probably very hungry with two cubs sucking on her, so they dumped Pruitt as near to the den as they dared to get. Pruitt's body would disappear in a day or so.

George went back to the house to find the slaves cleaning up the blood. He explained that Mrs. Pruitt might get in a lot of trouble and have a lot of explaining to do if people found out she had shot Mr. Pruitt. "Even though she saved my life by shooting him, and I am the one that killed him...it might be hard to explain everything...Mrs. Pruitt having a baby by another man...all that," George explained.

"*Don't you worry none, Mr. George, ain't nobody here sorry to see him gone, and ain't nobody gonna say nuthin'. He just never came back after the war...ain't that right?*" Slick said, looking around at all the slaves. They all nodded their heads.

Mary was a wreck. She was crying and sobbing every few

minutes. Like Mary Sinyard, she was sure she was going to hell or jail or both. George spent a lot of time making the same arguments all over again. Finally, he convinced her that she needed to take Christian and spend some time with him at his house.

The children were thrilled to see her and little Christian. Little Tom wanted to play with him all the time. Liz wanted to mother him, and the older boys wanted to teach him everything they knew. In just a day, George could see Mary's mood changing. She couldn't help but laugh at the kids and all the silly things they did to impress her and Christian.

Liz especially seemed to have a bond with her. She loved having another woman around again. George caught them talking in whispers several times. They always seemed to stop talking whenever he arrived.

At bed time that first night, there was an awkward moment when everyone was getting ready for bed. Mary waited to see where she would sleep. Liz solved it by saying, "Mary, you and Christian can sleep in Momma's bed. She would want that."

Mary smiled. She and Christian settled down on the bed. It had freshly washed sheets, but Mary could still smell Emme on them or on the quilt. After they were asleep, a thunderstorm blew in with a lot of heavy rain, thunder and lightning. Something woke Mary up she looked around and saw little Tommy standing beside the bed.

"Are you scared?" she asked. Little Tommy nodded his head. "Okay, crawl in," Mary said. Tommy crawled in the bed on one side with Christian on the other. That is where George found them the next morning, and he couldn't help but smile.

The week passed much too quickly for everyone; soon it was time for Mary and Christian to return home. No one wanted to see them go. Earlier in the week, they had all been sitting around after supper. George was watching the kids play. Sam and John Wesley were playing with pretend guns; shooting at each other while playing hide and seek. Will was cleaning Ole Stumpy and the musket. Tommy and Christian were on the floor playing with the wooden horses George had bought when he got the blue dress for Emme's birthday. Suddenly, Tommy stopped playing and looked at Mary who was brushing Liz's hair. Staring at Mary he asked, "Are you going to be our new Mommy?"

Mary smiled at him, leaned over and said, "I don't know, maybe. I guess we will have to wait and see," she looked at George, and they exchanged a look. Liz caught it, and she smiled, too.

George took Mary and Christian home the next day. When they arrived, the house had been scrubbed clean of all signs of the blood that had been spilled there. A rug covered the hole in the floor where the bullet went through Jim Pruitt's body.

They settled into a routine, spending three or four days a week at each place. When the war had been over about three months, Mary got a visit from a man at the bank. It seemed the bank and been taken over by a big outfit from up north. They had bought the bank and all the notes that the bank held. Mary got a notice that she had to pay a $4,000 note on the plantation by the end of the month. Mary didn't even know there was a note on the plantation. She asked George if he would accompany her to the bank to check on this matter. When they arrived in Double Springs, they went to see the sheriff first. He was a friend of George's and had been unable to serve in the army because of a badly broken leg which caused him to limp.

When they shook hands, and George explained what was happening, the sheriff said, "I'm sorry. This has been going on for a while now...ever since the end of the war. These carpet-baggers have been taking people's land and farms because they can. There ain't nothing I can do about it. They got the law on their side. I just try to keep everyone from killing each other."

Together, they went to the bank where they were greeted by a short, fat man who was constantly wiping his forehead with his handkerchief. When they were seated in the office, the man whose name was Weismann, brought out a book and showed Mary where Jim had signed a note for $4,000 in March just before the war started. Neither Mary nor George could figure out why Jim would do that, when they were making more money with the cotton crop than they ever had. The plantation was producing more bales of cotton and the price per bale was more than ever. George began to wonder how this was possible. When he asked about this, Mr. Weismann said that Jim had signed the note in Virginia where he was serving.

"Mr. Weismann, just take the $4,000 from our plantation account," Mary said.

Mr. Weismann looked very nervous. "Ah...that is just it, Mrs. Pruitt...your money is all Confederate money; it is all worthless now. Your property taxes haven't been paid in four years, and they are also due. You see, your husband transferred all his money over to Confederate currency shortly after the war started. If he hadn't done so...if he had left it in Federal 'greenbacks,' it would still be good."

Mary was speechless. "What if I don't have $4,000?" Mary asked.

"Mrs. Pruitt, I'm afraid the bank will have to repossess your land," Mr. Weismann said.

Tears started to flow down Mary's face. "I'll sell some of the land and raise the money that way," Mary said.

"Mrs. Pruitt, you can't sell land with a loan on it. Even if you could...there is no market for land right now. There is land all over the South for sale, and no buyers," Mr. Weismann said.

"I'm sorry, Mrs. Pruitt, but the bank has to have its money by the end of the month."

George could feel his face getting red and his temper rising. "Mr. Weismann, where are you from?" George asked.

Mr. Weismann looked troubled. "Well, I'm from New Jersey. What does that matter?"

"Mr. Weismann, down here in the South, we believe in helping our neighbors and giving a neighbor more time would be something a neighbor would do," George said.

Mr. Weismann was getting flustered. He looked at the armed guards and the sheriff who were standing just outside the door, to let them know that things were tense, and they might have to come in. "It is not the bank's policy to give more time to people who owe money...especially to those who tried to destroy the country."

"Mr. Weismann," George said through clinched teeth, "Mrs. Pruitt didn't fight in the war. She has a young child, and you are talking about throwing them out because of something her husband did. He has not returned from the war and may never come back. Now, the Christian thing to do would be to give her some more time... a chance to raise a crop," George said.

"I can't do that. My job is to collect the money for the bank or to repossess the land. I'm sorry, but that is just the way business is done."

George bit his tongue. He wanted to tell this carpetbagger to go back up North. Hell, he wanted to shoot him right between the eyes, but he knew it wouldn't do any good. If Mr. Weismann left, the bank would just send someone else.

"Let me see if I understand what you are saying. If someone didn't convert their money over to Confederate money; then, it is still in the bank, and still has its value?"

"Yes sir! Only those who fought for the Confederacy and converted their money have lost it."

George smiled, "Then I'd like to withdraw my $800. I never converted my money, and I didn't fight for the Confederacy."

Mr. Weismann just looked at George. "How do I know that? Ah... what was your name again?"

"Kilgo, George Washington Kilgo. Here are my furlough papers from the Union army; now, I want my money. I'll take it in the new *greenbacks* or gold, either one will be fine," George said staring down the fat man.

"I'll have to check with my teller and see if he can find your account," Mr. Weismann said. He signaled for a teller to come in, and instructed him to look into George's request. The man came back in a minute and said that he couldn't find any record of George having any money in the bank.

"Well, that is strange," George said, "because I got my receipt right here." George said pulling out a piece of paper. Mr. Weismann reached for the paper, but George pulled it back.

"Sheriff Graves, could you step in here for a minute?" George asked. He handed the slip of paper to the sheriff who looked it over and smiled.

"Looks like a genuine receipt to me...signed by Mr. Hawkins, the past president of the bank. I guess you better get the man his money," the sheriff said.

Mr. Weismann turned red faced and told the teller to get George's money. When the teller returned, Mr. Weismann counted it out for George and said, "Are you sure you want to take it out? There are a lot of thieves out there so having this much cash is dangerous. The bank would be glad to keep it safe for you."

George grinned at Mr. Weismann, and leaned over very close to the man's face. "My name is George Washington Kilgo. I rode with Bill Looney... ask someone about him and I served with Black Jack Logan during the war. I have killed more men than I want to admit. If you got someone in mind... that wants to take this money from me...send them. I'll look forward to meeting them and sending them to hell."

Mr. Weismann looked shocked, and leaned backward to get away from George.

George, and a tearful Mary, rose and left the bank. Just as they started out the door, George turned back and spoke again, "Mr. Weismann, I understand you have repossessed and moved into the Whitman house, big white house on the Post Road, near the edge of town. That's a real nice house. I bet you sleep in that big bedroom up on the second floor, the one with the big windows, don't you?"

Mr. Weismann nodded, "Are you threatening me, sir?"

"Oh no, sir!" George said. "We don't make threats down here in the South; but sometimes, we make promises."

They left Mr. Weismann standing with his mouth open. "Did you hear that, Sheriff? He threatened me!"

"I didn't hear a threat...just heard the man compliment you on the house you live in," Sheriff Graves said grinning.

On the way back to the plantation, George stopped the wagon and turned to Mary. "Well, I guess we have settled the question of where we will live. Mary, I would ask you to marry me, but we both know we can't do that until the issue of your husband is settled, and he is declared dead. I will just ask this. If you will, please, come and live with me and my children. You know that I love you, and so do the children."

"Mary's eyes filled with tears, and she hugged George,

"You know I love you, too. I love being with the children. I want Christian to grow up with his brothers and sister. I just hate to disappoint the slaves...I mean the freed slaves; they are counting on me. Where will they go? What will they do? I can't give up Tee! She is like my mother!" Mary broke down crying again.

Mary was almost inconsolable. She couldn't believe she was losing her home and the plantation. She apologized to the former slaves who were working for her. She told them what was going to happen, and she couldn't offer them a place to live after the first of the next month.

George and Matoomba spent the next weeks moving the contents of the plantation house, to George's house and barn. George's house couldn't hold all the things, so they put them in the barn and covered them with cloth. Matoomba, Wana and their two kids would live in the barn along with Tee, until George and Matoomba could build them a cabin on land near George's house. George used some of his $800 to loan Matoomba the money to buy ten acres next to George's farm. It was land that had belonged to a man killed in the war, and the county had reclaimed it.

Land in the South was dirt cheap. Matoomba only paid $15.00 per acre for 10 acres. At a time when most blacks were going back to work on the same plantations where they were slaves but now working for wages, Matoomba was a land owner.

Hannah and Slick went to work for Mr. Keller on his plantation, working for wages and living in one or his cabins. So did the other former slaves who had been working for Mary.

As soon as Matoomba's cabin was built, George and Matoomba went to work on an additional bedroom for George's house. One day when they were working on the addition, after a long day planting, a single rider came riding up to the farm.

George recognized the rider from quite a ways off, even though he hadn't seen him in a while. When he came closer and started to walk the horse, Matoomba also recognized Bill Looney. "How are things going on the farm?" Bill asked.

"About like you would think. Cotton prices are so low you can't afford to sell what you raise," George said. Bill nodded.

"Yeah, that is what I thought. Kinda makes me glad that I never could grow anything," Bill said.

"How have you been?" George asked. Are you still working on that list of Home Guards?"

Bill nodded. "It's getting harder and harder to find them anymore. Seems like they all lit out...headed west, I hear. I guess they don't like being the hunted as much as they liked the hunting."

"How many...if you don't mind me asking?"

"About sixteen I guess...I mean, that were on the list. Some more that just had the misfortune to be with them when I arrived."

"Ain't you getting tired of all the killing?" George asked. "I mean...after all the slaughter we saw... I would think...you know...it just seems like life is worth more now that the war is over."

Bill nodded, "I know what you mean. Just the other day, I met this man on the road...he tipped his hat as he rode by, and I nodded. About fifteen feet past, I recognized him as Martin Stout who used to come into the tavern; one of the men on the list. For about two seconds, I thought about letting him go. Then, I called out his name, and when he turned around; I shot him through the heart. All I could see was Senie lying on the floor of the tavern, and all those men."

George and Matoomba just stared at Bill.

"That brings me to why I rode all the way out here...I ran into Sheriff Graves the other day out on the Post Road. I asked him if he had a warrant for my arrest yet, and he just laughed and said, *"Bill, you know as well as me that no grand jury in Winston County is going to return a true bill against you or any other man who kills a Home Guard."* I'm pretty sure he is right, but they might return one for a Confederate soldier who disappeared. You know there are a lot of Rebs coming back; and mostly, everyone but me seems to be willing to let the past go." Bill stopped and took a breath.

"Sheriff Graves said there was a Pinkerton Detective in Double Springs asking a lot of questions about Jim Pruitt. It seems that Big Jim Senior hired this detective to find out what became of his boy. Colonel Pruitt was released from the Southern army in Virginia and as far as anyone knows, was headed this way. He just disappeared."

"I know, and the Sheriff knows, there are a lot of people around here that would like to see Jim Pruitt dead. After all, he forced a lot of people into the Rebel army...some of them got killed, and some of their families would like to see Pruitt dead. Some families got run off by the Home Guard just like yours. There is no shortage of people who would have killed him if they had been given the chance. The problem is one of those people is *you*. It won't be long until that detective finds out about you and Mary living together, and about that little boy; about Jim trying to force you into the Rebel army, and Emme and your kids having to leave. If he couldn't get a true bill around here, he might decide to take you back to Montgomery to stand trial there, where folks might not be so sympathetic," Bill smiled.

"That is why I told the Sheriff I killed him. I said I found Jim and a couple of former Home Guards camping down by the Sipsey, and I killed them in a shoot out. I told him I threw their bodies in the river. I told him I heard the others talking, and I knew their names were on the list, but I didn't know the other man was Jim Pruitt until it was all over. I told him he could tell that to the Pinkerton man," Bill said then he stopped talking and just looked at George and Matoomba.

"Why did you tell him that?" George asked. "Won't that just put the Pinkertons on you? They could take you back to Montgomery just as quick as they could me."

Bill smiled, "I have killed so many now that one more will not make much difference to the Lord. I am getting credit for killing people all the way over in Mississippi and Louisiana now. Hell, the other day I heard I killed someone in Missouri. Since my reputation is already so far out west, I have decided to actually go west, to Texas or maybe Oklahoma. I am thinking about visiting some kin on the reservation in Oklahoma. Eddie is going to bring Senie back from the mountains, and we are going to head out."

"I don't know what to say," George said.

"You don't have to say anything. I want to give you and Mary a chance. I don't know who made Jim Pruitt disappear, and I don't want to know. It is enough that I know he hurt a lot of people around here, and he didn't deserve to live. You just tell that detective that Jim never made it back here. Tell him Bill Looney told you that he killed him and threw him in the Sipsey River," Bill said grinning.

"By the way, I also saw Joe Tucker in town; he had his daughter with him, the one that married that Sinyard boy that got killed in the war. I believe you know the one I mean; I heard you helped bring her back home. She is a pretty little thing. She was nursing a baby, just thought you ought to know," Bill laughed.

Bill shook hands with George and Matoomba. "If you ever

make it to Oklahoma, look me up." Bill rode off, and George never saw him again.

The Pinkerton detective came and asked his questions. He seemed very suspicious of the relationship of George and Mary Pruitt. Mary was very up front and told him that she and George had a relationship during the time when he was overseer, and they had a child together.

George also confirmed that Jim Pruitt had tried to force him into the Confederate army. George went so far as saying he would probably have killed Pruitt, if he had the chance; but Bill Looney told him he took care of that for him. George retold the story Bill Looney had told him. The Pinkerton man took a lot of notes; but in the end, he left with nothing that would discount the story that Bill Looney had killed Jim Pruitt.

George and Mary settled on his farm and enjoyed a rich life together. A few months after the Pinkerton visit, little Christian contracted pneumonia and died before his third birthday. Mary was devastated. George and the children tried their best to make her feel better but the only thing that helped her overcome her grief; was her becoming pregnant again.

Baby Jo Anna was as cute as she could be, and because she was only the second girl, in a family of boys; she was spoiled rotten. A year later, Lavonia 'Vonnie' Louise was born.

One day, George and Will were splitting wood out by the house, when George looked out at the family all sitting or playing in the yard. Will noticed his dad had stopped splitting, and looked up to see what had caught his dad's attention.

"Will," George said, "I think I am just about the luckiest man in the world." Will followed his dad's eyes to the scene before them and said, "I think we are both pretty lucky." George nodded.

EPILOGUE

Mary Jaggers Pruitt Kilgo contracted typhoid fever and died in August 1876.

At the age of 53 years, George Kilgo met and married 19 year old, Lou Synthia Jane Thompson on Christmas day in 1876. They had three children: Sarah Florence born in 1877, Georgia Ann born in 1879, and Charles Mitchell born in 1883 who is the author's grandfather and whose stories of his father, The Black Hawk, are the inspiration for this book.

George Washington Kilgo, The Black Hawk, was originally listed as a deserter from the Union army; but in November of 1885, the charges of desertion were removed from his record and his honorable discharge was backdated to June of 1864. It is believed that General Logan was instrumental in this action. The Black Hawk died on February 20 1910 at the remarkable age of eighty-seven. He is buried beside Mary Jaggers Pruitt Kilgo in Shady Grove Cemetery at Logan, Alabama. Lou Synthia Jane Thompson Kilgo is also buried in Shady Grove Cemetery. Mary Emiline Entrekin Kilgo is buried somewhere in Nashville, Tennessee.

Bill, The Black Fox, seemed to disappear after going west.

Many rumors circulated about what might have happened to him. One rumor has him tracked down and killed in Mississippi by a man from Winston County named Hyde. Others believe he may have changed his name in order to escape his reputation and those who wished him dead. Bill and Senie had four children: Henry, Mary, Anderson and Sarah.

John Alexander Logan, 'Black Jack', was elected to state offices in Illinois before the war and was elected to the US House of Representatives as a Democrat just as the war broke out. He fought in First Bull Run as a volunteer. He later resigned from Congress to join the army. As a Colonel, he fought in Grant's army in the west. He proved to be a good officer, and was promoted several times for his leadership in battle, finally to Major General. He was involved in several major battles including Vicksburg, The Battle of Atlanta and at one time commanded the Army of Tennessee. When the war was over, he went back into politics. He was elected to the House of Representatives, this time as a Republican, and was later elected to the US Senate. He ran for Vice President in 1884 on the ticket with James Blaine. 'Black Jack' was well liked by his men, and had a large following of political supporters. He died in 1886, and his body lay-in-state in the US Capitol. Statues were erected of him in his home state, and many things were named for him not only in Illinois but in other states as well. George Washington Kilgo's sister, Betsy Ann Kilgo Freeman, is credited with naming the community of Logan, Alabama, in his honor when she and her family settled there after the war.

Ole Stumpy, a valuable heirloom, remains in the Kilgo family.

– THE END –

THANK YOU

Dear Reader,

Thank you so much for taking the time to read my book. Your time is the most precious thing you own and I am thankful that you spent a little of it to share my adventure and effort in writing this book. I hope you consider it time well spent. I hope you enjoyed learning more about this period of time in Alabama History and the men and women who lived it.

You can contact me at dbrock6569@att.net or on Facebook.

– Darrell Brock

ABOUT THE AUTHOR

Darrell Brock is a retired educator who lives in North Alabama with his wife Charlotte, two dogs, a cat and a pet crow. A life-long baseball fan he started playing little league at age six and continued playing through high school and college. As an adult he played independent league baseball, fast-pitch softball and slow pitch softball for twenty-five years. He was hooked on reading when he read his first Clair Bee-Chip Hilton sports book as a youngster. He coached high school baseball, basketball, football and tennis over a twenty-five year coaching career and served as a high school principal for eighteen years. Writing this novel is another check off his bucket list.

Made in the USA
Columbia, SC
11 February 2020